...can remember. Her first play, written when she was seven, was performed at her school. In 2019, inspired by a positive experience and encouraging feedback from the Introduction to Writing Crime Fiction course run by UEA, she carved out space in her diary and wrote a story she had always wanted to. *Secret Places* is the first in her series featuring DI Greg Geldard.

The space between the play and the book has been filled by a busy career mainly in agriculture. She has been a senior civil servant in the Ministry of Agriculture/ Defra (her farmer husband was described as 'sleeping with the enemy') and has bred both sheep and alpacas commercially. Since then Heather has pursued her passion for animal welfare and served on a number of Boards as Chairman or Director. She is currently Chair of Lantra UK, a Trustee of Norfolk Citizens Advice and a volunteer in the Witness Service. She lives in Norfolk with her husband, two springer spaniels and four hens. www.heatherpeckauthor.com

SECRET PLACES

Heather Peck

First published in 2021 by SilverWood Books
This edition published in 2022 by Ormesby Publishing

Copyright © Heather Peck 2021
Author photograph by John Thompson 2021

The right of Heather Peck to be identified as the author of this work has
been asserted in accordance with the Copyright, Designs
and Patents Act 1988 Sections 77 and 78.

All rights reserved. No part of this publication may be reproduced,
stored in a retrieval system, or transmitted in any form or by any means,
electronic, mechanical, photocopying, recording or otherwise,
without prior permission of the copyright holder.

This is a work of fiction. Names, characters, places and incidents either
are products of the author's imagination or are used fictitiously.
Any resemblance to actual events or locales or persons,
living or dead, is entirely coincidental.

ISBN 978-1-915769-04-6 (paperback)
ISBN 978-1-915769-05-3 (ebook)

Page design and typesetting by SilverWood Books

Acknowledgements

My thanks go to Geoff Dodgson and Alison Tayler for their invaluable feedback on the first draft of this novel, to Sam Steggles of Fielding Cottage for his advice on goats, and my husband Adrian for his unfailing support and encouragement.

If anyone wants to learn more about the secret auxiliary units established during World War 2, I strongly recommend a visit to Parham Airfield Museum, Suffolk.

Prelude

Yorkshire, August 1940

The sealed van clanked wearily round the lanes to the outskirts of the village, then turned up the track to the rough grazing the villagers called 'The Coombes'. At that time of night there were few people about. The local poacher, Sam Doble, slid silently through the dark copse by the road and lights were on in one of the barns as the farmer tended a late calving. If anyone noticed the van at all, it was probably to wonder how someone had managed to get their hands on petrol. No one commented. Less than a year into the war, everyone knew better than to poke their nebs where they weren't wanted.

Its four occupants clambered out at the top of the track and were met by the Rector, exercising his war-time rather than his pastoral role. A quick word with the leader of the team, and the men unloaded their equipment and set to, digging into the side of the ancient chalk quarry wall.

At the end of all the work a new, standard design observation base had been sunk into the hillside. Its curved metal walls and roof were covered in soil until nothing showed; other than the disturbed soil, the hatch at the top of the hill that gave access to the shaft down, and the end of the concrete piping lower down the hill that provided the concealed emergency exit.

The van and its crew disappeared into the night, and were replaced by the Rector's hand-picked team. They were a mixed bunch, drawn from the only remaining men in the village who were neither ancient nor disabled. Sam Doble was recruited both for his marksmanship and his ability to slide stealthily through the night. Nearly as good was Andrew Jenkins, the neighbouring estate's junior gamekeeper. Only the most extreme need could have brought members of these two families together. Of the other four men, three were yeoman farmers and the fourth a retired miner with a useful skill in handling explosives.

Swiftly the men transferred their stores into the OB. The wet cell batteries and the limited ammunition were no problem. Sam took a particular interest in the gallon of rum and was sternly reminded by the Rector that it was for emergency use only. Sam and Andrew were despatched to string the aerial for the radio along the thorn hedge that marked the edge of the field, while the others debated the storage of the phosphorus hand grenades. There was a unanimous view that no one wanted to share living space with them and they were moved, with extreme caution, to the village and a pit under the corner of the Rector's garden shed.

OB 478 and its team of auxiliaries were ready for invasion.

1

Yorkshire, June 2015

The day was sunny, light rippling on the ceiling as it reflected from the River Ouse running past the apartment. Music played in the background and Detective Inspector Greg Geldard was not happy. He scowled in the mirror as he shaved, and nearly cut himself as he practised his happy face. He tried again, but it still wasn't very convincing and he sighed as he turned away, wiping the remaining soap off with his towel. His wife Isabelle was singing as she rushed around the bedroom, collecting clothes together and packing them in the special light case she used for air travel. Her carry-on bag was, as usual, crammed with music. She turned as he came into the room.

'Oh Greg,' she said, 'it is only four weeks. I'll ring every night.'

'Yes, I know. Take no notice of me. I hope you have a super time and a really successful tour. The time will fly and when you get home we'll have a special night out in Grape Lane.'

'That's something to look forward to. My favourite restaurant.' She kissed him lightly as she passed through to her music room. 'Must make sure I've everything I need.'

A horn tooted outside and Greg went to the balcony. 'It's your car. Bye darling. Have a great time and see you in four weeks.'

He carried the case down to the waiting car and waved her off, the unconvincing smile still on his face, then went back up to the flat to collect his wallet and case for work. Four weeks until she got back from what would doubtless be another highly successful tour for The Byrds in the Midwest of the USA. Four weeks of ready meals in front of the TV and missing her every moment of every day, even when at work. He clattered down the stairs to the basement car park and set off for the police station in Malton.

'Not a routine week, please God,' he thought as he drove through the early York traffic. 'I need some distraction.'

Across the Vale of York, Tristan Smith was minding her business and her goats. Coombe Farm clung to a slope carved from chalk by the ice and water of millennia. Rich neighbours in the valley bottom enjoyed deep soils and gentle gradients. Up on the wind-scoured plateau of the wolds were more wide fields with thick crops. Here on the escarpment between, life was different.

Coombe Farm was perched halfway up a hillside over-looking the Vale of York. Depending on your point of view, this meant either spectacular views, or bone-freezing winds. Both were equally prevalent regardless of the season. As successive owners had discovered, many of the fields had a gradient that discouraged any form of land-use by large and expensive machinery. It was just about possible to make hay or silage over most of the farm, but only if the baling operative was both skilled and cautious. Tristan had witnessed the results of a self-confident novice at the controls. The first big round bale had spun off the wrapping machine and barrelled into the adjacent hedge. The second had made a stately but inexorable progress down the field, through the hedge, over the road and into the bottom of the neighbouring dale, whence it was never extracted.

The other drawback to spectacular views was that they were two-sided. Not only could Coombe Farm see much of the Vale of York, but also, as Tristan was ruefully aware, every farmer in the Vale could see every mistake and accident at Coombe Farm. Tip a tractor over, and you would be asked when you were fitting wheels to the roof. Should an animal die in a public place – and they never died unobtrusively under cover – every livestock farmer for miles around noted both the demise and the swiftness of the tidy-up. Miss a strip when spraying off weeds, and the bright red stripe of poppies was visible for fifty miles. Coombe Farm was an agricultural goldfish bowl.

Tristan's less than traditional approach to farming had therefore been a source of infinite fascination to her neighbours. Many sceptical comments at village events had made this all too clear. She had gritted her teeth at the frequent facetious remarks and smiled, albeit tiredly, at the many old jokes about maiden lady smallholders and their strange preoccupations. It was only in recent years that she had begun to feel a little hard-earned respect. As one of her neighbours had said,

'Tha stock's in good fettle missus, tha work 'ard and tha's paying tha way. There's a few round 'ere as can't say that. All credit missus.' And he'd raised his greasy cap. It seemed she was forgiven her choice of species (goats and alpacas as well as the more usual sheep) and her end products (cheese and rugs) in the light of her success and hard work. She had glowed with the praise.

The fact that many of her livestock had names and were at least halfway to being pets had earned less scorn from her neighbours. Too many hard-bitten Yorkshire shepherds have been embarrassed by the antics of an ex-pet lamb to cast scorn on anyone else. The previous year, one local had been horrified to see his grown pet lamb Terry included in a group of sheep rounded up for a sheepdog trial. Sure enough, once released at the top of the field Terry had ignored her fellow sheep and the hapless dog and galloped down to put her nose in her mortified owner's pocket. That particular farmer, cover blown forever, had to take refuge in the tea tent to avoid Terry's persistent efforts at ingratiation.

Tristan stood up and pressed her hand to the small of her back. In her fifties, and built for strength rather than elegance, Tristan was finding some of the work increasingly hard; especially anything connected with bending. Unfortunately, as she often reflected, most jobs on a livestock farm involve bending, especially milking goats. Today, apart from Heidi 4, the newest introduction to the herd, the milking had gone smoothly. The latest Heidi was, however, showing clear signs of her maternal ancestry; a mind of her own being the dominant characteristic. All the Heidis had been bossy and opinionated. Today, the muddy trotter-print on Tristan's knee was H 4's protest when the feed ran out. The last of the fifty milking ladies trotted out to the paddock to begin the days hard browsing, except for Noemi 3, who paused for a scratch and carrot.

Tristan pushed her wind-tousled brown hair off her brow, noting that a trim was now over-due if she wanted to continue to see out, and turned into the house for second breakfast. Like a hobbit, she found that farmers were best fuelled on multiple breakfasts, especially when doing the early milking.

She was all set for a morning in the dairy when she was interrupted by the phone. It was not a number she recognised, not even the location code; and she was on the verge of not answering, fearing a spammer. On this occasion she gave them the benefit of the doubt and contrary to her fears there was no computer-induced delay nor trans-Atlantic accent but a real person based in Suffolk.

'This is Parham Airfield Museum,' said the voice. 'Sorry to disturb you, but my name is Roger Field and I've been doing some research into the secret World War II stay-behind bases that were set up to resist invasion. Most of the documentation is still restricted, but according to some of the maps, there was one on your land. I wonder if you would be willing for me to pay you a visit and have a look around? It will be just me and one assistant, not a crowd. And we just want to explore the area and perhaps take some photos.'

Only then did the voice pause for breath. It sounded, reflected Tristan, as though he had practised getting his message out quickly before cut off with 'not today thank you.'

'I've no objection in principle,' she said cautiously, 'but I have to say I don't think there is one on my land. I've never seen one anyway. What should I have been looking for?'

'It may not be obvious,' replied Roger. 'They were intended to be hidden after all. It would be underground, and all you'd see from the top might be perhaps a hatch for access, or the end of a tunnel. Or maybe some old ceramic insulators in a hedge—'

'Oh, I've seen some of them,' interrupted Tristan, 'I thought they were from an ancient electric fence.'

'No!' exclaimed Roger, quite excited. 'If they are what I think they are, they were used to trail a long cable aerial for the radio. Along a hedge line was much less conspicuous than straight up into the air. If you have an email address I can send you a photo.'

As he spoke, Tristan was having what looked set to qualify as an awful thought. 'You're welcome to come and have a look, but I think I need to warn you. What you're describing sounds very like what we and the previous owners used as a fallen-stock disposal pit. It's pretty full of dead sheep and goats, although we haven't put anything down there recently.'

'No problem,' said Roger. 'This *is* exciting. Can we come tomorrow?'

Tristan's assistant Chris seemed surprisingly chilled about the news of a secret army base on the Coombes. 'Of course,' he said, 'I knew there was something down there. My granfer remembers his dad talking about being part of the team, but he never said much. Even years 'n years after the war, he still thought it was secret. The only time it came up was when they found those grenades under the Vicar's garden shed.'

'Grenades!' Tristan was amazed. 'When was that?'

'Oh, I suppose that was before your time,' replied Chris. 'I were only a nipper myself, but it was reported in the papers. The Vicar found a case of grenades he din't like the look of when his garden shed fell down in a gale. They spotted something while they were clearing the rubble and had to send for bomb disposal and everything. The papers reported they were phosphorus hand grenades and it could've been really nasty if they'd gone off. Come to think of it, they didn't come as a surprise to everyone,' he went on. 'Old man Doble knew something about them too. I s'pose if they recruited the team locally, there might be a few folk still about who knew something.'

'Old man Doble, was he any relation to Sharon?'

'Her granfer,' replied Chris, 'and a right old rogue he were too. He were the village poacher and suspected of small thefts round the village. If there were any mischief going off, you could bet old man Doble was at the bottom of it. He were a lovable old rogue though.'

'Not very like his granddaughter then,' commented Tristan. 'If there's any problem in this village you can bet Sharon's gossip is somewhere at the root. I have never known anyone with such an evil mind. It wouldn't be so bad if she made it all up, but there tends to be at least a fragment of truth, which means people believe the whole lot.'

'She didn't get on too well with your predecessors neither,' said Chris. 'She really had the knife out for poor

Rachel, and she were the first to suggest that Matthew'd run off wi someone else when he disappeared. She had all sorts of theories about what Rachel had done to drive him away.'

'And now we're gossiping as well,' commented Tristan. 'Perhaps we'd better get on with some work while we're waiting for the archaeologists. I need to sort out yesterday's cheese and package the last batch for the market. Could you check round the sheep please? I haven't done that yet today. They should be okay now they've been dipped but they might need moving to new grazing soon. The eggs haven't been collected either.'

Coombe Farm had what you might call a mixed economy. Most of the income came from the fifty invaluable goats, by way of a soft cheese that was becoming very well known locally and was much favoured by restaurants seeking a 'Yorkshire gourmet' aspect for their cheeseboard. The twenty-odd Jacob sheep and four guard alpacas contributed their wool and fibre to the other main enterprise – the hand-woven rugs. Between the cheese, the rugs and the general livestock jobs, Tristan had not had time to turn round until she recruited the young, enthusiastic and inexhaustible Chris to her team. Even now he was jogging steadily over to the sheep paddock and Tristan marvelled at the spare energy that could be used for *voluntary* running about.

It was late morning when the team from Parham Museum arrived. As promised there were just the two. Roger (excited, lean, greying and, so Tristan estimated, in his sixties) got out of the pickup first and was followed by his young, distinctly hairy assistant, who came over to be introduced.

To Tristan, he had the distinct air of an environmental enthusiast, which, she supposed with an inward sigh, only exposed her prejudices.

'This is Tim,' said Roger, 'who's going to be going down into the observation base.'

'I hope he knows about the corpses,' commented Tristan.

Tim, a gangling teenager with wild woolly hair and a wild woolly jumper, added wild eyes to his general ensemble. 'It shouldn't be too bad,' said Tristan, 'it's years since anything went down there. The rats and bacteria will have cleared it all up long since.'

Tim looked anything but reassured. 'Rats!' he exclaimed. You didn't say anything about rats, Roger.'

'You'll be fine,' said Roger, 'just remember to tie the baler twine round your knees and they won't be able to get up your trouser legs.'

The pickup bounced over the grazing land to the far corner of the field and they got out. Tim, baler twine firmly tied around his legs below his knees, pulled the ladder from the back of the pickup and they all went over to the hedge.

'Here you are,' said Roger, as he pointed at the old ceramic insulators now half buried in the elderly, overgrown hawthorn, 'they're the insulators for the aerial.'

'They're the ones I thought were part of an old electric fence,' said Tristan.

'No, definitely the aerial fixings I think you'll find. Look, all along this old hedge trailing from here right the way to the top of the hill. This would have been the line for the aerial.'

Tim had been kicking around among the longer grass by the trees. Tristan pointed to the sheet of plywood held down by breeze blocks that covered the shaft to the old buried Nissen hut. 'That's where the bodies went,' she said. Roger and Tim went to inspect the shaft.

'Originally there would have been a hinged hatch or trapdoor on the top of this shaft, probably with turf or other material fixed to the top so it couldn't be seen when it was closed. And look, look at the sides of the shaft. You can see the old metal rungs they would've used to go up and down. Some are missing however, and those that are there don't look very safe. I think it's best we use the ladder, Tim.'

Tim heaved the ladder over and lowered it down the shaft. Checking the security of his baler twine, he scrambled down. Roger hesitated at the top, but curiosity overwhelmed his concern about the rats and he soon followed. Their voices echoing in the chamber below sounded quite excited.

Roger came to the bottom of the shaft to call up to Tristan. 'We'll be here a while. Most of the fittings have gone. There would originally have been wet cell batteries and some other supplies, but I expect they were removed at the end of the war if not before. But you can still see where the bunkbeds were. The rats aren't too bad!' he added with a grin. 'Mostly what's down here are sheep fleeces.'

'In that case,' replied Tristan, 'Chris and I will get back to work. Come back to the house when you're ready for a cup of coffee.'

Tristan went back to the dairy and Chris to look around the flock. The grazing was getting a bit tight where they were and he moved them over to the next paddock. As ever, all it took was an open gate and a shout of 'Come up! Come up!' The four guard alpacas came through at the same time. Fernando, the grey one, paused to see if Chris had anything in his pockets and was disappointed. On his way back to the house Chris collected the eggs then went into the milking parlour to finish the clean-up.

It was close to lunchtime when Roger and Tim came back to the house. Tristan emerged smiling to ask if they were ready for coffee and was surprised. She had expected excitement and enthusiasm. There was certainly plenty of excitement on their faces but a layer of shock too. Roger's face was white, Tim's was green. Neither of them seemed willing to meet her eyes.

'Coffee? she asked. 'And I have some home-made biscuits too. Or if you're feeling peckish now, how do you fancy some bread and home-made goat's cheese?'

'Tristan,' said Roger 'I'm afraid we've some bad news. We found something down in the observation base. A body.'

'I told you there were lots of those,' said Tristan.

'No. I'm afraid we found a skeleton. A human skeleton.'

They all four sat in the kitchen while they waited for the police to arrive. Tristan discovered, to her surprise, that she was shaking.

'What sort of a state was it in?' she asked carefully.

Tim was still green and very quiet. He sat at the table, holding the edge with his finger tips, and his knuckles were white. After a moment's silence, Roger answered.

'Tim found it. He said he tripped over the skull. It was all bare bones,' he added hurriedly. 'We found it when we were looking under the old fleeces to get down to the original floor. As far as I could see it was almost complete, but we didn't mess about too much. We thought we'd better leave it to the police.'

'Could it have been there since the war?' asked Tristan hopefully.

'Well possibly—' said Roger, but Tim interrupted.

'I don't think so,' he said. 'There were fleeces underneath the bones. Surely that points to the skeleton having arrived there sometime since the base was used as a disposal pit.'

2

Coombe Farm and
Malton Police Station, Ryedale

Tristan was surprised and horrified at how long a time elapsed between the 999 call and anything happening. She realised that a skeleton might not generate the same urgency as a bleeding body and a smoking gun, but even so, a two-hour gap seemed excessive. She felt her tensions rising every time she thought of the body, hidden beneath her feet for years, and every time she considered where the police might look for their prime suspect. Moreover, the difficulties of making polite conversation between the team that had discovered the skeleton and the person presumably suspected of having created it became considerable. In the end, the party of four tended to divide into two, the archaeologists at one end of the kitchen table, Chris and Tristan at the other. Had Tristan been thinking a little more logically, she would have realised that her willingness – nay enthusiasm – for them exploring the observation base was some evidence that its unexpected occupant was as much a surprise to her as them. The archaeologists might have realised too, but the discovery of human bones had derailed rational thought.

Eventually, and after what seemed a very long wait, they were blessed with the arrival of one junior uniformed constable. Tristan was reminded that increasing age was commonly defined by finding police officers youthful. This one made her feel ancient. Aged around twenty-five, Peter Armstrong was tall, slim, dark-haired and likeable. As he explained, he had been working this particular North Yorkshire beat for around three years. What he didn't add was that his last visit had been to a distressing road traffic accident involving a teenager on a motorbike and a tractor. He was somewhat relieved that all he had to face this time was bones and he moved swiftly to secure the scene by draping several metres of police tape around the hatchway. He then had recourse to his radio for reinforcements. He pondered, but swiftly dismissed, the idea of contacting his Detective Inspector direct. While always keen to collect brownie points, he was well aware that DI Geldard had been distinctly crabby that morning and a call to his sergeant, in line with the rule book, seemed prudent.

'Sarge, human skeleton found on Coombe Farm, Langfirth. I've secured the scene and detained those present. The finders say it looks like foul play.'

'Stay where you are and I'll be with you in twelve. I'll alert the DI as well. Well done so far Peter.'

What Sergeant Horsfall knew, and Peter did not, was that DI Geldard's morning grumps had their origin in his wife's absence. Isabelle Geldard sang mediaeval polyphony in a group of professional singers with a soaring reputation and modest financial success. 'The Byrds', as they were known, were currently touring the Midwest of the USA, where their oeuvre of sixteenth-century English church music was particularly well received. Greg Geldard was always short-tempered while she was away. The call to a mystery skeleton was, therefore, a welcome distraction as well as something of a relief from rural petty theft, an outbreak of sheep rustling in the Dales, and a missing quad bike taken from a big arable farm in the Vale of York.

Gary Horsfall and Greg Geldard could not have been more different, but the contrast in their backgrounds and approaches had immediately attracted. They had both instantly recognised the potential of complementary attitudes and rarely had two opposites settled down in harness together with such ease. Gary Horsfall was Yorkshire born and bred; blunt both of speech and build, clear-headed and suitably cynical after twenty years on the force. Greg Geldard, by contrast, was an off-comed-un in more ways than one. He had joined the Met fresh from a degree in psychology and transferred up to Ryedale on promotion from sergeant. Gary's initial impression of a posh academic had been rapidly dispelled by a violent rugby match and a night's hard drinking, while Greg knew how to recognise good sense and local knowledge when he saw it. It was with total confidence, therefore, that Greg took the briefing from Gary, on its basis initiated the major investigation protocol and called together his core team.

The third and fourth members of the core team were

younger constables, both embarking on their first murder investigation. Peter Armstrong, already on the scene, was another graduate entrant; slightly too keen to demonstrate his educational advantages in Greg's opinion, and just beginning to get his corners rubbed off. Fiona McRae was a highly reliable import from Scotland with a good reputation as family liaison, but keen to broaden her experience.

To the residents both permanent and temporary of Coombe Farm, the lack of action seemed to last a geologic age. The young constable remained uncommunicative. He did not share the fruits of his frequent radio conversations and it seemed to Tristan that skeletal remains were ranking a poor second to whatever else was happening in Ryedale on a pleasant June day. The eventual arrival of one sergeant and the local GP was a distinct anti-climax and requiring the latter to certify a skeleton dead fell comfortably over the boundary into the surreal, if not the bizarre. However, procedures are what they are and Dr Rayner duly did the necessary, complaining bitterly about the environment in which he found himself.

That was the calm before the storm. Hot on the heels of Sergeant Horsfall and the doctor were the rest of the team. The scenes of crime officers were not any happier with the ossiferous environment and it was with some glee that they pointed out the need to recover all the remains from the observation base. The plentiful supply of bones, fleece and hair promised long hours of sifting in order to see if any clues could be recovered that might provide evidence both of identity and cause of death. The latter, to Dr Rayner, seemed pretty obvious even though he was not a pathologist. The hole in the skull did not appear to be post-mortem.

Once DI Geldard arrived, he pretty much took over the house. With scant politeness he commandeered the dining room and both Roger and Tim were interviewed about their reasons for being present and what they had found, before being released to return to Parham Museum. Roger hesitated over saying goodbye to Tristan, but after a difficult pause contented himself with a non-committal wave. After another look at Tim and his still viridescent complexion, he took over the pickup keys for the drive back to Suffolk. Tristan and Chris were left in the kitchen drinking endless cups of coffee, in Tristan's case with her shaking hands firmly wrapped around the mug. A female police officer sat with them more, it felt, to listen to anything they said than to provide comfort or reassurance.

Detective Constable Fiona McRae, making tea, was quietly fuming on the side-lines. Unlike most of her colleagues she was not born and bred in North Yorkshire but on the east coast of Scotland. Tall, she had fair hair tinged with red and, despite the reputation of redheads, was the mildest-mannered officer in the bunch. Although she didn't realise it, this was why she was often picked out for family liaison. Her interpretation was that she was not so much picked out as picked on, as a female officer, and she resented it accordingly.

In the dining room DI Geldard was reviewing the statements from the two archaeologists when Dr Rayner returned.

'I reported my findings on the obvious human remains, but there's a bigger issue. I don't know if the SOCOs have shown you their pictures of what's down there. There's quite a pile of bones, hair and fleece, and more skulls than an ancient Roman ossuary. The skulls are pretty easy to identify. Even I can tell a sheep skull when I see one. But I am not sufficiently expert to swear that all the other bones are animal; and SOCO haven't finished looking yet.'

'You mean there might be more human bones?'

'I simply don't know. I think probably not, but probably isn't enough is it. What I'm saying is that I don't think the obvious human skeleton is all that needs attention from the forensic anthropologists. And I think they'll want to see everything in situ, not just get a skipload of bones delivered to Bradford.'

Geldard sighed. 'Well that's the budget for the year gone. I'd better have a word with upstairs. They'll need to authorise this one. I'll get onto that in a moment. Let's just check what we have here.

'Judging from Doctor Rayner's expert opinion' – he nodded in the direction of the departing doctor – 'it looks as though we have either a very nasty accident and a concealed body or a murder. As one of the archaeologists pointed out,' Geldard checked his notes, 'the one named Tim; the fact that the bones are above the level of the lowest layer of animal corpses would suggest that John (or Jane) Doe arrived in the observation base sometime after it became used as a disposal pit. If that's the case this isn't a wartime incident. We'll need the forensic specialists to advise on whether rat activity could have pulled fleece and hair beneath the skeleton but to have done that without disturbing any of the bones seems unlikely. And although some of the smaller bones from the hands and feet appear to have gone, the major parts of the skeleton are in place. Taking that, together with the hole in the skull, the presumption must be murder until we have evidence to the contrary.

'Gary, what do you know about our friend Tristan Smith? How long has she been here, is there a Mr Smith and if there is, where is he?'

'I don't know much,' replied Gary. 'To the best of my recollection she moved in here when the previous owner sold up. That would be about eight years ago now. I'll check the dates with the Land Registry.'

'Let's have Ms Smith and Chris Jenkins over to the station,' said Geldard, 'and we can interview them formally. Gary, you take Fiona and start a house-to-house in the village. I'm interested in anything you can find out about the current occupants of Coombe Farm and the last lot. Some local gossip might be useful. Peter can go back to base, check the Land Registry, dental records, missing persons and so on. I'll sort out the forensic anthropologists with the bosses and have a preliminary chat with Tristan Smith.'

Geldard went back to the dining room and its owner, noting as he did so the oak table, oak carved chairs and oak dresser. Not to his taste, which ran more on Scandinavian clean lines, but at least it did show some degree of choice, not just the random accumulation of generations. The rug he did like, a textured weave of natural fleeces that he thought would go rather well in his own flat. It was a pity he couldn't bring Isabelle out to see it, and he recalled with a jolt that that was the first time he had thought about his absent wife for some hours. The distraction was working.

'Ms Smith, quite a day you've been having,' he remarked

as he sat down with the owner at her own dining table. 'I can understand you've had a bit of a shock, so if it's okay with you, we'll just get some preliminaries out of the way now, then continue our conversation at Malton police station. Let's begin with the farm. Explain Coombe Farm to me. How long have you been here?'

'Since I bought the house, buildings and some of the land from Rachel Wade in 2008.'

'Only some of the land? Did she keep any?'

'No. I don't think so. Coombe Farm was originally much bigger, but the better land on the lower slopes was snapped up by my neighbours – largely the Asquiths. I got seventy acres of mainly hill land around the house and buildings.'

'And is that big enough to make a living? Forgive me, but I am no farming expert and it seems quite small.'

'It is by today's standards, but it is just enough to make a living if you are creative in what you produce.'

They were interrupted by a knock on the door and a disembodied head, belonging to one of the SOCOs.

'Sorry to interrupt, but there's someone on the phone wants to talk urgently about the forensic anthropologists.'

When Geldard, official authorisation reluctantly in place, did eventually speak to Forensic Anthropology, Bradford, they were irritatingly cheerful.

'Thought you'd be in touch soon,' said the voice. 'We'll send George and Mildred.'

'Oh joy,' muttered Geldard, he hoped inaudibly, and put the phone down.

*

George and Mildred had been christened George and Mollie by their respective, loving parents; but the serendipitous combination of the names and their personalities made the nicknames inevitable. George was short, slight and wizened for his age (fifty-two). His voice was nasal and his temperament complaining. Mollie/Mildred, although fifteen years younger, could have been his twin in attitude and general belief that the world was organised to inflict the maximum of unearned inconvenience. Her hair was a vivid auburn, because she felt she was worth it, which did not complement her sallow complexion to any degree whatsoever. They were efficient, knowledgeable and wholly irritating.

They arrived at Coombe Farm with commendable speed later that day and everything went downhill from there. They complained about having to transfer their kit to the police Land Rover, the bouncy journey across the paddock and the presence of the rightful occupants, the goats. Noemi and Giulia brought the whole herd over to investigate any likely-looking buckets, and Mollie screamed, occasioning still further caprine curiosity.

Geldard, there to supervise, and Tristan, to answer any questions about animal disposal, exchanged glances before their attention was abruptly returned to a kerfuffle around the Land Rover.

'Dear God, they're trouble and they haven't even got out of the Land Rover yet,' he muttered, striding over to see what the problem was. Gary and Peter, standing guard over unloaded kit, seemed to be in the throes of unprofessional giggles and Tristan had a sinking feeling that she could guess what was causing all the screams of rage. She was confirmed in her assumption by the presence of a perky little upturned tail protruding from the passenger door of the vehicle.

'It's okay, it's just Giulia's kid,' she said, with a faint hope that her explanation would be deemed both acceptable and reasonable.

'Julia's what?'

'No, not Julia, Giulia's kid.'

As they came level with the altercation, all became clear. A goatling had taken advantage of the open door to enter the car. She was currently engaged in a tug of war with Mildred over Mildred's mud-coloured cardigan, which she, the goatling, appeared to be winning. As they watched, another inch or two of hand-knitted wool went down her throat, and Mildred shrieked again; understandably, as she was still wearing part of it. The human/caprine standoff was terminated by swift action from George who, wielding a sizeable pair of shears, severed the few inches held by the kid from the main part of the cardigan still worn by Mildred. Mildred shrieked again, this time with rage. Both Geldard and Tristan beat a hasty retreat, leaving Giulia the only clear winner and Mildred raining down vituperation and exasperation on George's unmoved head. Briefly detective and suspect were united in a shared sense of disbelief. Then Tristan turned away and Geldard girded his loins for the fray.

To their credit, George and Mildred were remarkably insouciant about going underground and un-fazed by the pile of remains that greeted them at the bottom of the shaft. However, they waxed eloquent about the lighting (inadequate), the disturbance caused by the Parham historians (criminal) and the lunch (nutritional quality of). By the time George had whined his way back to the top of the shaft Gary, for one, would have cheerfully pushed him back down again.

'Well?' he said.

George looked at him down his nose. 'Well what?'

'Have we any more bodies?'

'Scores,' said Mollie morosely, 'but not human.'

Gary and Peter, who had both, for a fleeting second, envisaged mass murder, began to breathe again.

'Not human so far,' corrected George. 'The disturbance is quite disgraceful, but so far as we can see at this moment in time the bones and associated mummified material are from smaller livestock species. Mostly sheep. The most recent and less decomposed remains include a couple of goats.'

'Pity there aren't one or two more,' said Mollie viciously, still aggrieved about her cardie.

George continued to sail on over interruptions, 'but of course we'll need to check our current findings at the lab. So, if you could proceed with removing the remains with immediate effect we can complete our work. Regarding the human remains you do have, they are of course of a male, roughly middle aged when deceased. For anything else you'll have to await our report. In the current climate that might take a little time unless you have authorised priority working.'

'I'm sure the inspector will get back to you,' said Gary firmly, keen to send the gruesome twosome on their way as rapidly as possible and to organise the tricky task of recovering a tonne or two of animal remains from an underground chamber.

3

Interviews

Detective Constable Fiona McRae was bored. She had spent what felt like hours sitting with Tristan Smith and Chris Jenkins, and neither of them had said anything very interesting. When Sergeant Horsfall came in and said they were due for some house-to-house it was actually a relief. She looked sideways at her colleague as they got into the squad car. Both bald and wide, he more than filled the passenger seat, his head scraping the roof. Grunts accompanied his move into the car, and more grunts as he struggled with the seat belt.

'Right,' he said, 'let's be moving then. Haven't got time to waste. The wife's expecting dinner out tonight and she'll not be best pleased if she's hanging around while we clear up here.'

'On it, Sarge,' said Fiona and put the car in gear.

They followed the hill from Coombe Farm to the village of Langfirth below and the small collection of cottages and farmhouses. The lane became a quiet tunnel between trees as it got nearer the village, a small beck burbling in the bottom of the dale to their left. At this time of the year, the lower branches of the trees were festooned with scraps of hay, pulled from passing trailers as they negotiated the narrow byway.

The farm on the hill the other side of the village was large and apparently prosperous, with spacious barns housing cattle and well maintained grain-stores. It had eschewed the normal farmyard ambience of machinery graveyard and, even to Fiona's eyes, the fields and fencing looked tidy. Between the hill on which Coombe Farm sat and the large Manor Farm opposite nestled the village centre. The east side of the high street was dominated by a large stone house set in imposing grounds. Once the Rectory, its life as a churchman's residence had ended when the village church was demolished half a century earlier. The remains of the churchyard could still be seen on the edge of the village alongside the old motte and bailey castle. The C of E had conducted a, possibly high-handed, takeover of the almost defunct Methodist chapel, and such services as were now available were conducted by a visiting curate from Helpington. The west side of the high street contained a row of stone cottages, some outbuildings, and what looked like two old farmhouses. It seemed that these had been swallowed up by the larger farms on the edges of the village. A village pub, somewhat unenterprisingly titled the Stone Inn, sat on the tight bend out of the village towards the large farm, where it constituted a regular challenge for harvest machinery seeking to pass through the village in the summer.

'We could try the pub first,' said Gary firmly. 'Usually the best place to find people at this time of day.'

'No need,' said Fiona, the relish showing in her self-righteous expression. 'We can start with the woman over there,' and she pointed her chin towards the nearest cottage.

It was, inevitably, Sharon's obesity that they noticed first. The woman outside the cottage was short, just under five foot tall and nearly as wide. Her arms had deep folds of fat at wrists and elbows and the fingers resting on her knees were splayed, as though too wide to fit comfortably within the confines of her bones. Her greasy hair was dark and tied back in a careless ponytail at the nape of her neck. Although there were chairs to either side of the one that she generously overlapped, she did not invite the officers to sit down.

'Lots of activity up the hill,' she said. 'Never seen so many police cars here, not since the fight at the Stone anyway, and that were a good few years ago. What's amiss up there?'

Fiona pulled one of the chairs a little distance away and sat without being invited. Gary put his foot up on the rockery and rested his elbow on his knee. Neither of them answered the question.

'We wanted to ask you a little about your neighbours,' said Gary. 'What can you tell us about Ms Smith?'

'*Miss* Smith!' said Sharon with emphasis. 'No man involved up there, unless you count that lad Chris Jenkins. *Miss* Smith has never had a man as far as I know. Probably one of them.' And she winked knowingly. Fiona would have recoiled, partly from the implications of the wink and partly from the body odour that was making itself felt as the sun warmed Sharon up, but the back of her kitchen chair was too rigid to permit much movement.

'And you are?' she asked.

'Sharon Dyble,' said Sharon. 'Born a Doble and married a Dyble. Lived here all me life and know everyone.' Somehow, the implication was made that what she knew was disreputable, and both officers recognised that here they had the village gossip; possibly an information goldmine, possibly a minefield! Only time would tell.

'And so, Mrs Dyble,' said Fiona, getting her notebook out, 'how long has Miss Smith lived at Coombe Farm?'

'Must be about six or seven year,' replied Sharon. 'When she bought from the Wades, it were part of a much bigger farm. Wades had land all the way down to the village and round the back to Manor Farm,' she pointed to the dairy farm on the hill. 'But when Rachel Wade gave up, she sold the better land to the Asquiths at Manor Farm and all that were left were the farmhouse and outbuildings, plus the paddocks on the hill. No one else wanted those!' She sniffed. 'I think Rachel Wade thought it would go to someone from the horsy set. But then that snotty cow Tristan Smith turns up and sets up her goat and sheep farm. Named for a man and looks like one too,' she said irrelevantly.

'You don't like Miss Smith much then,' remarked Fiona, making notes, and Gary, wise in the way of village gossips, chipped in before they got a long account of who had said what to or about whom during the big row at the village fete/ church bazaar/strawberry tea/winter craft fair, at least two, five, ten or even twenty years ago.

'The Wades sold the farm to Miss Smith around six years ago,' he repeated. 'Why did the Wades sell up?

'Well, strictly speaking,' said Sharon, 'it were Rachel Wade what did the selling. The farm had been bought for them by her granfer, what had made lots of brass during the war. War profiteer, some might say! Any road up, though Matthew Wade had the connections, it were old man Treadwell that had the brass, and he had no intention of letting it out of Treadwell fingers. So when he bought the farm as their wedding present, it were in Rachel Wade's name and it stayed that way. Not that you'd ever have thought it to hear that Matthew talk. He reckoned, just 'cause he had his name in one of them books about the aristocracy,' she said the word with exaggerated care, 'he were the village squire and he carried on like one too. Always buying drinks all round at the pub, and inviting us plebs to garden parties on his lawn to raise money for this 'n that.'

'Didn't he have something to say about the farm being sold from under his feet?' enquired Fiona.

'Oh he'd long gone,' replied Sharon, fishing under her chair for the mug of tea she'd stashed there. 'He'd buggered off more than a year previous. Another woman they all said, and it didn't surprise anyone. That Rachel Wade was a mean, cold fish. Never 'ad a word to say to any folk and looked like she lived on vinegar and lemon. A skinny, miserable-looking thing. Although,' she said, sipping her tepid builder's tea, '*I* always thought that it might have been another man.' She paused for effect, but was disappointed by the lack of reaction from her listeners. By that time, Fiona would have swallowed a wasp sooner than give Sharon any satisfaction whatsoever.

Information from other villagers was reasonably consistent with Sharon's version of events. Jenny-the-Pub described a generous man with a loner wife. The local curate, caught as he cycled through the village from one church to the next, gave a similar although more charitable description. He also described Matthew as generous, but thought that Rachel had some mental health issues. His comment was that Rachel seemed to 'drift off' when people were talking to her. As Gary remarked, even the local church seemed to have been infected by political correctness.

'I bet he would have described her as moody, miserable and rude only a few years ago,' he remarked. Fiona, somewhat distracted by a notice on the Village Hall inviting everyone to a talk on his 'prostrate' cancer by a local borough councillor, failed to react.

'If ever I saw a definition of too much information,' she muttered disbelievingly, before turning her attention back to the job in hand.

Only at Manor Farm were the descriptions more nuanced. Certainly Mr Asquith senior had little time for his erstwhile neighbour.

'Lazy sod,' he said. 'They say that a farmer with neither cattle nor potatoes is a lazy beggar and he definitely was. Always ready to knock off for a drink and a chat. It was his poor little wife that did most of the hard work. And she had a day job as well!'

'I think that's a bit harsh Dad,' remarked his son. 'I always thought he was lonely at home and went out to look for some company. Rachel Wade never joined in much with anything.'

'And did you ever ask yourself why?' asked his father. 'She was a bright enough lass when I first knew her. Her grandfather Treadwell was well-known round here and he thought the world of his granddaughter. That's why he bought her the farm. I always thought he knew something about that Matthew Wade that the rest of us didn't. Why else was the farm in her name not theirs?'

'Tight with his brass Dad,' asked his son with a grin, 'like the rest of his generation?'

'I'll give you tight,' replied his father, flicking him on the ear with the edge of his newspaper. 'Just careful I'd say. I don't think he trusted Matthew, and knowing old Treadwell I'd guess he probably had good reason. There was something not right there.'

His daughter-in-law, Mary, had been sitting so quietly at the kitchen table they'd almost forgotten she was there.

'I always thought he bullied her. If you got her on her own for any length of time she would start to relax, but the moment Matthew entered a room she went stiff again. And if you looked at their wedding photographs, she'd lost a lot of weight since then. I was always suspicious too, about the long-sleeved blouses she wore even in a heatwave. You can hide a lot of bruises under long sleeves.'

'You never said anything,' her husband said sceptically.

'What would've been the point?' she asked. 'Would you have believed me? To you Matthew Wade was a good chap who stood his round in the pub and played golf. Men like that don't abuse their wives do they?'

'And what about the current owner? Tristan Smith? What do you know about her?'

'Just that she's a hard worker and apparently making a success out of not very much. All credit to her,' remarked the older Mr Asquith. 'It's not easy making a living out of farming even when you inherit land and a going concern, as these two,' he nodded to his family, 'will find out. But to start from scratch on a few acres no one else wants – that takes graft and ideas. I take me hat off to her.'

'That's not what you said when she arrived,' remarked his son.

'Ah, well, happen not. Goats seemed a pretty odd choice and as for alpacas!' He shook his head. 'But she makes a right good cheese, she's got a good eye for stock and she works all the hours God sends and then some. She deserves to succeed.'

'What about her personal life?' asked Fiona.

'No concern of mine young woman,' he snapped, and Fiona blushed, much to her own irritation. Before Gary could intervene, Mary chipped in, 'it's a murder inquiry Dad, they have to ask these questions.' And to the police she said, 'Tristan spends too much time working to have much time for socialising, so we don't see a lot of her except at sales and markets. She does have a friend to stay from time to time and he calls in at the pub. But I haven't seen him for a while. His name is something like Ben, or Tim.'

The police station in Malton was an old Victorian villa. As such it had its charms, as Geldard had noted when he first arrived a couple of years ago, but modern efficiency wasn't one of them. Although the rooms must once have been spacious areas for entertaining, as communal work areas they were distinctly cramped. Normally this didn't matter too much as the recent cuts in staffing had at least had the perverse benefit of reducing pressure on space. But setting up a major incident room was not easy. Geldard wondered whether the travel time saved in using the nearest available police station compensated for the inconveniences, but the decision had now been made. The chief superintendent for Ryedale, Maurice Jones, had made it plain that he expected the investigation to be operated out of Malton. Geldard looked around the space that he had been allotted. The tables in the station meeting room had been moved out of their boardroom layout and pushed against the walls. Workstations had been set up all round the room and some clerical staff as well as a couple of community support officers were starting the work of checking available databases. One had already been on to the Land Registry, confirming the date at which Tristan had taken over Coombe Farm, and in the process turning up the interesting information that Matthew Wade's name had never been on the deeds of the farm. No one so far had turned up anything about Tristan Smith. Not even a parking ticket. Geldard found himself in two minds about her. On the one hand, he found it hardly credible she had never explored the wartime base hidden on her land, and surely if she had, she would have found the body. On the other, he found himself reluctantly liking her. She seemed straightforward, honest and hardworking. He liked the way she looked him in the eye. He sighed and shook his head. An open mind was what he needed at this point.

*

Al Paulet returned from the dusty depths of the station basement.

'One report of a missing Matthew Wade, Guv,' he said. That's all. I'll get on to the dentists now.' Geldard heard the first of many calls as Ed started working his way around all the dentists in the area to see if any had records of Matthew Wade's teeth that might exclude him from consideration as the skeleton.

'Fred, can you check our records for the time when Matthew had disappeared and Rachel Wade had sold the farm. See if you can find anything relevant. You know what we're looking for; a disappearance, anything odd.'

After a stuffy, and distinctly mouldy, search through the archives, Fred returned, sneezing.

'One thing odd, Sir,' he said. Fred Swithibank, ex civil servant, had never embraced the 'Guv' usage of his peers. 'A far as I can see, Rachel never declared her husband missing nor, as far as I can tell, did she make any enquiries about his departure. Following the paper trail,' he shuffled the mouldy records with a fine disdain for the dust that flew off, 'I have found some records of a visit to the farm during the summer of 2007. It would seem that some friends of Matthew's reported his absence at the time, and a team did go to see Rachel Wade at Coombe Farm. According to their notes, they saw evidence that Matthew was alive and well and living, or at least spending, in north London and the surrounding area.'

'What evidence?'

'Bank statements and credit card statements. It seems Matthew and Rachel Wade had a joint bank account and he continued spending on that account until Rachel withdrew most of the remaining cash in the summer of 2007.'

'And no reaction from Matthew when he suddenly found his money gone?'

'Nothing recorded. There is a suggestion he had other bank accounts to which Rachel had no access, and the joint account had no money going into it other than revenue from the farm and her salary. I imagine she felt that as she was the one doing all the work and earning all the money she had every right to withdraw the cash when the balance started to shrink significantly.'

'Where was he spending and on what?'

'Mostly north London and then the suburbs north of London. There isn't a lot of detail in the notes. Mainly dates and sums, but it would seem that there were a number of relatively small expenditures in the King's Cross area and up towards north London. Then a couple of bigger expenditures including one at John Lewis at Brent Cross, and that was the point at which Rachel pulled the plug.'

'If I was being super cynical,' remarked Geldard, 'I would say that's the classic pattern of use of a stolen credit card. A few small uses to test the water and then some big ones, often for items such as laptops, before the owner of the card stops it. It would be interesting to know what happened after Rachel pulled the cash from the bank account. Chase the banks for records of that time both for that joint account and for any personal accounts that Matthew had separately.'

'You think the skeleton may be Matthew then?'

'It has to be possible. We need to rule him out. But we also need to chase up the unusual Ms Smith and her contacts. We have nothing so far that rules her out either.'

*

Down at the interview suite, there was a hold-up while they waited for Chris Jenkins' father to join him. The local gamekeeper had not been an easy man to find, as mobile phones don't work well in some parts of the Yorkshire Wolds. By the time they eventually began the interview, Chris was beginning to look a little stressed.

'I need to be getting back to milk the goats,' he protested. 'You can't just leave them you know. It's cruel!'

At five foot ten and wiry in build, he looked like a lad who had yet to come into his full strength, thought Geldard.

'Let's get on then,' he said. 'Soonest started soonest finished!'

Once they had all introduced themselves for the benefit of the tape, he began by asking Chris what he was doing on Coombe Farm.

'I work there,' said Chris. 'I'm going to Agriculture College next year. In the meantime this is work experience. Tristan's bin brilliant. She's paid for me to do some really great courses and my CV looks a lot better now than it did a year ago.'

His father grunted and Chris looked at him.

'I know you'd like me to take up keepering, Dad,' he said 'and I like the life well enough, but farming's what I really want to do as well you know. And Tristan's proved that it *is* possible to get started even on a small patch of land. If all else fails, I can try contract farming.'

'So what do you do at Coombe Farm?' asked Geldard again, recognising the start of a well-rehearsed family debate.

'Pretty much anything,' said Chris. 'Anything to do with

the livestock that is. I help milk the goats, I'm learning to shear sheep, and I do just about anything at lambing and kidding time. I collect eggs, top pastures when they need it and help the contractors when we're making hay and silage. Thanks to Tristan I've got my tractor certificates now and I know how to use the milking parlour. The only thing I don't do is anything to do with the weaving.'

'Has anyone else worked there that you know of?'

'Not while I've been there. A friend of Tristan's comes up sometimes to help out. You know, at busy times like hay or silage making. Otherwise it's just her and me.'

'His name?'

'Ben. Ben Asheton.'

'When did you see him last?

'Last summer, for silage making.'

Geldard made a note to ask whether a body would skeletonise in less than a year and went on, 'and have you used the waste disposal pit?'

'No,' said Chris. 'All dead stock has to go to the knackerman for disposal these days. Tristan is a stickler for the rules. I think she used to use it when she first came to the farm, but as you'd know, the law changed and we can't do it any more.'

'But you did know it was there?'

'Sort of. I mean, I knew where the top hatch was and where a tunnel came out lower down the hill, and I knew what it had been used for, because Tristan mentioned it when she was explaining the deadstock disposal rules. But that was all.'

'Did you never see anything that looked suspicious?'

'Never looked,' admitted Chris. 'I had no wish to look down a hole full of dead things. I didn't know what I might see—'

'Dried-up fleeces, you great soft lummox,' interrupted his father. 'What would you expect to see after years and years?'

Geldard frowned at the interruption and went back to Chris. 'And did you ever go down the hole?'

'Never, said Chris. 'Never fancied it and never saw no reason to neether. It were just a hole—'

'Not been listening to your granddad!' then interrupted his father again.

'Granddad?' asked Chris. 'What's it got to do with him?'

'The old man was one of the original auxiliaries when he were nobbut a nipper,' said his father. 'He don't talk about it much, but he could have told you what that hole was for and how it came to be built. Not that that has a lot to do with why we're here today. As lad has milking to do, can we go now?' he demanded.

'Tristan Isolde Smith—' began Geldard at the next interview.

'Interesting name,' interrupted Tristan.

'Come again,' said Geldard.

'You were going to say, "interesting name",' said Tristan. 'It's what everyone says. Shall I get the explanation over and done with now?'

'Be my guest,' said Geldard.

'My parents were a bit new-age,' said Tristan 'and were also determined to brighten up Smith with something a bit more interesting. They were sure they were having a boy, thanks to some mucking about with spinning knives and peacock feathers, and had settled on Tristan. When they saw that they'd got me, they thought Tristan and Isolde were a good combination. Now that's out of the way, I imagine you want to get on. Would it save some time if I pointed out that had I put a body down that hole I would hardly have invited the archaeologists to take a look?'

'According to your lad Chris,' said Geldard, with a strong feeling that he needed to get a grip on this interview, 'you did put some bodies down that hole when you first arrived at Coombe Farm. Was one of them human?'

'Don't be ridiculous,' responded Tristan. 'They were sheep and goats and the odd hen.'

What made you decide to use the observation base as a waste disposal pit?'

'First of all, I had no idea it was an observation base. That was complete news to me. In fact, when the chaps from Parham got in touch I was quite excited. The reason I put bodies down the hole was because my predecessors had. I assumed that they must have dug the pit. The land agent told me the farm had a waste disposal pit and showed me an ancient ADAS booklet that described the construction of one. I looked down the hole, saw lots of old fleeces, and thought "how useful". I stopped using it when the law changed.'

'ADAS?' asked Geldard.

'ADAS used to be the Agricultural Development Advisory Service. It was a government-funded advisory body, even part of the Min of Ag originally I think. Anyway, they used to produce advice on just about everything and one leaflet described a waste disposal pit. The land agent gave me the impression that the Wades must have built it. Either way

I found it very useful at lambing time in particular. Having to pay to have dead stock taken away is a real pain.'

'Did you ever go down the shaft?' asked Geldard.

'Never,' replied Tristan. 'Would you?'

'And who else lives at Coombe Farm with you?'

'No one,' said Tristan. 'I did once have vague ideas of a B&B but the farm keeps me too busy for that. I've always lived alone. I lived alone in Norfolk where I worked on a livestock farm before I came here. I bought Coombe Farm, or at least as much of it as I could afford, around seven years ago. I had a small inheritance from my grandparents that paid for the land and enough stock to get started. The rest I've built up from scratch.'

'What about Chris Jenkins?'

'Chris? Chris is worth his weight in gold!' said Tristan. 'He's desperate to get into farming and I can understand that. It's not easy unless you are lucky enough to be born the son or daughter of a farmer. Like me, he is going to have to work his way in creatively. The only way is lots of skill, hard work, bright ideas, and a measure of good luck. He's willing to put in the hard work and he's building his skills. I think he'll have a great future. At the moment it's a win-win for him and me. I can help him get the skills and experience and he works really hard for me. He's a great lad. What I'll do when he goes to college I don't know!'

'What can you tell me about your predecessors?' asked Geldard.

'Very little,' replied Tristan. 'I only met Rachel Wade once, the first time I looked round the farm. After that I only dealt with the agent.'

'Did you meet Matthew Wade?'

'No. And according to all the village gossip, by which I mean all the gossip emanating from Sharon Dyble, he had made tracks a year or two before. If you listen to the rest of the village he left with a lady friend. Sharon will have it that Rachel Wade was so cold he turned homosexual and left with a boyfriend, but I trust Sharon as far as I could throw her, and not being a Russian Olympic shot-putter that wouldn't be far.'

'Did Matthew sign the transfer documents when you bought the farm?'

'No need,' replied Tristan, 'the farm was only in Rachel's name. There were no difficulties at all about the paperwork.'

'Who's Ben Asheton?' asked Geldard changing tack with deliberate suddenness.

'Ben?' asked Tristan, surprised by the sudden change of subject. 'Ben is an old friend.'

'And where is he now?' asked Geldard.

'At home in Norfolk I should think,' said Tristan. 'He doesn't live with me,' she said, light dawning, 'he never has. And to the best of my knowledge he's not missing. He lives and works in Norfolk. He has a wife, a home, and a very busy job as a first responder. Who on earth has suggested that skeleton might be Ben? Don't tell me! Sharon Dyble! It has all the hallmarks of her vivid imagination and malicious tongue.

'If you're listening to Sharon, you're going to have a busy few months. By the time she's finished, you'll have the entire population of the village on your suspect list. And personally, I'd say that the only time that would be justified would be if Sharon was the victim.

'I suggest you check with Norfolk on the current whereabouts of Ben. It shouldn't be too difficult. He's been a policeman himself.'

The team were pulling together reports and reviewing the notes of interviews in the relative peace of the Ops room, when there was a sudden commotion in the outer office. Mr Jenkins senior was back, accompanied by an elderly, frail, but very vociferous old gent in a wheelchair.

The receptionist came through to Geldard. 'There's a Mr Jenkins demanding to see you,' she said.

'I have seen him,' said Geldard, 'in fact I've seen two Mr Jenkinses. Which one has come back? Has Chris something to add to his statement?'

'No not Chris Jenkins,' said the receptionist, who if truth were told had been rather taken by the young man, 'nor even his father although he is here too. This one seems to be his grandfather.'

The very senior Mr Jenkins was a little huffed it had taken so long for Geldard to see him.

'I thought you were asking for help,' he said, 'then when someone comes to help, you practically have to fight your way in. Do you want my information or not? I haven't all day you know!'

'What do you have to tell me Mr Jenkins?' asked Geldard politely, wondering what other pressing business was awaiting the nonagenarian. 'Do you have some information about the bones found at Coombe Farm?'

'Aye, I do that! At least, not the bones as such,' replied Mr Jenkins 'more about the observation post. But first, can

I be sure that what I have to tell you isn't going to get me into any trouble?'

'Well how can I answer that when I don't know what you're going to tell me,' said Geldard reasonably. 'But I can tell you that not telling me something I ought to know is not a great idea. This is a murder inquiry you know.'

'Is it then? Well now. I thought maybe I shouldn't come,' said Mr Jenkins, 'but I thought you ought to know. I were part of the observation post team run by the old Rector. I were only fifteen at the time and covering for me old dad as gamekeeper and farmworker, but the Rector was desperate for men who were good shots and good woodsmen, and he didn't have too many to choose from. Auxiliaries we was called. We was supposed to be saboteurs and agents if the Germans came. The observation post was equipped with a radio and all sorts of supplies. Most of the ammo was taken away when the post was decommissioned in 1942, except for the phosphorus hand grenades we had hidden under the old Rector's garden shed, as we didn't fancy sharing an underground space with them. They were found ten or so years ago when the new owner of the rectory decided to move the shed. You might have seen it in the evening papers.'

'This is all very interesting, Mr Jenkins,' said Geldard, 'but what does it have to do with the skeleton?'

'I'm coming to that,' said the old man. 'Also in the observation post were several gallons of rum and a couple of wet cell batteries. Old Sam Dyble took the rum in the early forties. What went back to the War Office might've looked the right colour, but you wouldn't have wanted to drink it. Old rogue he were,' he said reflectively.

'The wet cell batteries went the same way. After that as far as I know no one went into that post until we had a final look round in the 1990s when Rachel Wade's granfer, old Treadwell, bought the farm. Old Sam and I thought it might be worth a last look just to make sure nothing had been left behind that might be worth something. Given how long it had been since anyone went in there, neither of us wanted to go alone. Just in case of a roof fall you understand! So we went together. I can tell you for sure that there were no bodies in there then, neither animal nor human. It was the Wades who had the bright idea of using it as a disposal pit. When they bought the farm, the observation post was empty.'

'How many other people knew about the observation post?' asked Geldard.

'Just the auxiliaries,' said Jenkins, 'and I suppose there'd be some records at the War Office. But we all signed the Official Secrets Act tha knows. Even now, it's still secret, as far as I know. That's why I asked you if I might get into trouble.'

'Who were the auxiliaries?' asked Geldard.

'Me, Sam Dyble, a miner called Ashton; Treadwell, Asquith and James, all lads off local farms, and the old Rector of course. He was in charge. Far as I know, I'm the only one still alive. Old Sam Dyble went last year and Asquith's old granddad the year before.'

4

Yorkshire – Reviewing Progress

Geldard was well aware that if there was one thing that his team found odd, it was his choice of coffee bar. Most of them, given half a chance, retreated to the nearest greasy spoon. The one serving the cattle market was particularly favoured. Geldard, on the other hand, preferred the quiet ambience of the Talbot on the main square. If asked, he maintained that the extra you paid for the coffee was compensated by the quiet corners and the comfort of the lounge. Early that evening therefore, he had his way. The core team of Geldard, Gary, Fiona, Peter and Ian-from-crime-scene retreated from the crowded station and gathered in the Talbot. They found a quiet corner where they wouldn't be overheard, and the waiter brought over the coffee. Geldard poured, a habit born out of his home life with his busy wife. He had no idea how much Fiona appreciated the gesture.

'Preliminary reports through from Bradford state that

the skeleton belonged to a middle-aged man over six foot in height and probably medium in build. The skeleton is not ancient, by which they mean it was walking around less than fifty years ago. In the circumstances found in the disposal pit the body would have skeletonised rapidly. On the other hand, given the evidence of animal bones and hide remnants underneath, it is unlikely to have been there since the end of the war. The tentative conclusion therefore is that the body was probably placed in the pit sometime during the ownership of Coombe Farm by the Wades or Miss Smith.'

'Which is confirmed by the evidence of old Mr Jenkins, if we can believe it,' chipped in Fiona.

'Oh, I think it's credible,' replied Geldard. 'Especially as it fits with the explanation from the Parham lot.'

'So far we haven't found anything else down there other than animal remnants,' went on Ian-from-crime-scene, 'no clothes, no jewellery, no watch, nothing that might give a clue as to the identity of the body. We don't yet have a report on the dentistry.'

'Missing Persons,' said Geldard, 'you were checking that, Peter.'

'Excluding women then,' said Peter, 'and limiting the search to the last thirty years, we have around forty-eight missing persons who would match the rough description we have. On the other hand, we have one person who seems to have gone missing but was never put on the list. Matthew Wade.'

'So, taking together the evidence from the Jenkinses and the forensics, such as they are, we can't rule out Matthew Wade. The other possibility is someone connected with

Tristan Smith. She lives alone and admits to making active use of the pit in her early time on the farm. She would have had plenty of opportunity to dispose of a body. On the other hand, we haven't yet identified any missing person connected with her. The friend Ben Asheton is a possibility, but we're checking that with Norfolk Police.'

'And, she was happy to have the team from Parham go down into the pit,' said Fiona. 'Surely she'd have told them no, if she knew there was a skeleton down there.'

'She might not have felt able to. They seem a pretty persistent lot and they might've kept pushing. Or just turned up anyway, in which case being difficult about access would have looked suspicious when they found the bones.'

'Finally, there's the possibility that someone, entirely unconnected with either the Wades or Tristan Smith, dumped a body in the pit. The key question then is, how widely was the existence of the pit known?'

'The auxiliaries themselves obviously, but they seem to have been pretty close-mouthed about the existence of the OB and most of them are dead or geriatric,' commented Fiona.

'Also, anyone who worked on Coombe Farm and knew about the disposal pit,' said Peter, not to be outdone. 'But that seems to be a pretty short list too. The Wades managed on their own and Tristan Smith only has Chris Jenkins.'

'We shouldn't close our minds to the possibility,' said Geldard, 'but the stronger lines of enquiry remain Tristan Smith and Rachel Wade. So, where is Rachel Wade? We know she worked at the hospital for a year or so after selling the farm, but so far no idea where she went after that. Peter, any luck with the family?'

'I've found a brother, courtesy of information Sarge turned up in the village. One Edgar Treadwell. I've spoken to him on the phone but he doesn't know exactly where Rachel is now. Last location he had was somewhere in Norfolk. No precise address.'

'Right. We'd better put him on the list for a visit. See what else we can find out.'

It proved surprisingly difficult to get any dental records for Matthew Wade. None of the dentists in Malton were able to help. Widening the search to York proved no more fruitful. It seemed unlikely that someone of Matthew's age and class would have neglected his teeth to the point of never seeing a dentist, and even the village gossips had made no mention of black fangs or halitosis. However, short of a nationwide appeal, that particular avenue seemed unlikely to get anywhere. As the team continued their trawl through old records, Norfolk Police returned the call.

'Ben Asheton,' said the voice with a pronounced Norfolk burr, 'yes, there is a Ben Asheton currently working as a first responder in Norfolk. He was previously employed by us but retired around five years ago to take up his new role. According to some of his old mates here, he had a rather interesting career path. He was a district nurse before he joined the police. I have a contact number if you'd like it, or you could try East of England ambulance service. Not in any trouble is he?'

'Not at all, at least not on our radar at the moment,' said Peter. 'In fact, we were more concerned he might be the victim, but it's not looking very likely now. At least, not unless you've got him on your missing persons list.'

'Exact opposite,' replied the Norfolk voice. 'He turned up last week at one of our regular darts matches and helped wipe the floor with our team. So unless he's gone missing in the last few days he can't be your man.'

'Definitely not our man then,' said Peter. 'The corpse we're investigating has been a skeleton probably for around a decade. We've managed to keep it fairly quiet so far, but given the nature of the village gossips up here it's likely to be in the papers soon and the boss will probably want to pre-empt that with a press conference. In fact, he may have no choice, as we've had no luck with any local dentist and an appeal for some help might be one way forward.'

Peter was spot-on. Even as he spoke, DI Geldard was in conference with the communications team about a press conference.

'I have been tipped off,' said Susan Temple, currently PR guru in the North Yorks Police, 'that something will be in the local press tomorrow. After that it won't be long before the big boys are here. The combination of World War II secret depot and unidentified skeleton is going to be irresistible. I am only surprised it's taken them this long. In fact, if it hadn't been for Sharon Dyble, they'd probably have been here days ago.'

'Gary said Sharon would be the one shooting her mouth off!' commented Geldard, surprised.

'So she was,' said Susan, 'but she's not exactly persona grata with the *Evening News*. They've been caught out before for reporting her malicious gossip, and their lawyers now run a mile at the mere mention of her name. I don't think the local reporters are willing to go anywhere near her. Greatly to her frustration, it has taken her more than a day to get anybody to listen. Heaven knows what she's actually told them, but shorn of the less publishable details it appears to revolve around a conspiracy involving half the village, sexual deviancy, fraud and mass murder. She even managed to work in the discovery of weapons of mass destruction under the Rectory garden shed. Something to do with phosphorus hand grenades.'

'Ironically,' said Geldard 'that bit is reasonably true. They did find some hand grenades in the garden ten or so years ago and it was reported at the time. And they were left over from World War II. In fact, not for publication but according to one of our witnesses, they seem to be just about the only supplies from the hidden base that were not nicked by Sharon's grandfather. There appear to have been some very dubious shenanigans connected to some rum supplies and you really don't want to know what he is reputed to have replaced the rum with. However, it strengthens the argument for a press conference this afternoon.'

'Covering what?' asked Susan.

'Mainly, a very brief rehearsal of the few facts we have and an appeal for information about Matthew and Rachel Wade, with particular reference to anybody who thinks they may know the whereabouts of either of them.'

'Haven't you found the wife?'

'Not yet. You would have thought that was the easy bit wouldn't you, but so far we have nothing from electoral rolls, utility suppliers or any other of the obvious databases. We're waiting to see if bank details might help, but so far nothing. She may, of course, have gone abroad, but that's pure speculation. We have found a brother and we'll be seeing him tomorrow but it seems he doesn't have an address for her either.

'We checked out Tristan Smith's other contacts and those seem to be fine. The one possible victim is alive and well and living with his wife in Norfolk. And so far, we have no reason to see him as perpetrator either. He's an ex-district nurse and ex-policeman and apart from trashing his old colleagues at darts, appears to have no vices at all. We won't be writing him off yet, but he's not a strong possibility.'

The press conference, as it happened, was relatively low-key. Although all the local press was present most of the nationals were represented only by local stringers. By the time DI Geldard had gone through the basic facts about the discovery of the skeleton, its location, and their requirements for information about the previous owners of Coombe Farm, press interest appeared to be fairly evenly divided between the possible identification of the skeleton, the gruesome nature of its immediate vicinity, and the fascinating secret wartime connection.

Locals and stringers alike, they all disappeared in a hurry to dictate their articles and look up further background.

'We'd better warn Tristan Smith to expect visitors,' said Geldard. 'Gary, get Peter out there to keep an eye on things. He can ring in for more help if it's necessary, but we can't afford too much effort on crowd management. Mainly we need to keep them out of the observation base.'

*

For Tristan Smith, the invasion was horror piled on horror. She and Chris had barely covered the normal farming chores between them after the interruption of the discovery and the subsequent interviews. She was behind in the dairy and she was behind on the weaving commissions, but the welfare of the livestock took priority over everything else. What felt like an army of vehicles pulling into her farmyard and getting in the way of tractor movements was just the last straw. Chris hurriedly parked a tractor across the gateway to the buildings and the fields beyond, but was too late to stop them entering the main drive. Microphones were pushed in Tristan's face, notebooks waved, and what felt like a thousand voices shouted fatuous questions along the lines of 'how do you feel?' She narrowly resisted the temptation to ask them how the fuck they thought she felt, and beat a hasty retreat into the house.

She watched Chris barricade himself in the dairy and start to hose out the morning's muck. Some well-directed jets of mucky water deterred the more ambitious journalists from peering in through Yorkshire boarding and gave Tristan her first smile of the day, as she drew the curtains and headed for the phone.

'Get them off my land!' she demanded of the police. 'This is harassment, trespass, and just about any one of multiple offences I can list if I put my mind to it. I don't have to put up with this. They're stressing my livestock and they're stressing the hell out of me. One constable is not sufficient to keep this lot off my land. And he's not a fat lot of help just standing on top of the hatch lid.'

Geldard's attempts at peace-making were not particularly successful and he sighed as he put the phone down. 'Gary,' he said, 'you'd better get yourself up there as well and take a look at the situation. See if you can deflect them away from Tristan Smith. I'm sure Sharon Dyble would be happy to provide some interviews, but don't quote me on that.'

Back at Coombe Farm, Tristan had had further recourse to the phone.

'Hi Paula,' she said, 'sorry to disturb you but can I have a word with Ben? If you haven't seen anything in the press yet you soon will. It'll probably be on the news tonight. They found a skeleton on my farm and I'm up to my ears in offensive reporters. Worse, I seem to be a prime suspect. I wondered if Ben could give me some advice.'

Ben, when approached, didn't waste any time. He had some leave coming, and although it was far from convenient as his despatcher made clear, he negotiated at least a week off with the possibility of a further week if needed. Paula was tied up at school until the end of the working week but offered to come at the weekend to help out in the dairy or even with the weaving. Ben made tracks for the north.

When he arrived at Coombe Farm, the reporters had been augmented by a TV van and additional microphones. Most of them appeared to be employed in getting background shots of the farm, goats, and the Jacob sheep. Ben was delighted to see one intrepid reporter, on venturing into the paddock, receive the coup de grace from the latest Heidi. Had she only realised, a handful of carrot would have ensured her safety, but being goat-ignorant all she did was irritate Heidi and had to sacrifice her furry microphone cover as fodder in order to escape in one piece.

He had some difficulty getting through the crowds. The

sudden arrival on the scene of a tall lean stranger with film-star good looks attracted a lot of attention from cameras both still and moving. By the time Ben got into the house, he was almost as irritated with reporters as was Heidi. But with less ability to butt.

'How are you?' he asked Tristan, as she threw herself into his arms for a consoling hug.

'This is so kind of you, Ben,' she said, 'but I couldn't think of anybody else so well qualified to advise me. I've spoken to a local solicitor, but he was as much use as a wet lettuce. For a while I seemed to be prime suspect, I've no idea whether I still am. As far as I can tell, they seem to think the bones belonged to one of my predecessors on the farm. Or at least that they had something to do with the bones arriving there in the first place. My number one problem at the moment is the reporters. After that, I would love to know what happened to Rachel Wade, what happened to Matthew, and how the devil this is going to be resolved so that my life can return to normal.'

'Do you know if they've done a search for similar incidents on Holmes?' asked Ben.

'Not a clue,' said Tristan 'they don't share their thinking with me. According to Sharon Dyble either I or Rachel or Matthew or all of us are serial killers that have been splattering bones over most of North Yorkshire, but luckily I don't think the police are listening to Sharon. On the other hand, the press probably are, which might account for some of the excitement.'

'I might see if I can call in some favours,' said Ben. 'Some of my old mates in Norfolk might be willing to take a look on Holmes if they can't get an answer out of their colleagues up here. At the very least, I might be able to find out how far they've got in investigating what happened to Matthew when he stopped being seen around the village. And whether they have any other victims in mind.'

5

Yorkshire, 2007 –
The Abandoned Wife Rachel

The few days 'after Matthew' passed me by as though my glasses were permanently covered in silt. Then, and subsequently, I find I have measured time in that way, like AD and BC, only my dateline was dictated by life with Matthew and life after. So, after Matthew I fed and watered, lambed, tagged and castrated as though on autopilot. With hindsight this was partly shock, and partly lack of sleep. Managing lambing on my own was the hardest thing I'd ever done. It was lucky that these were the weeks I'd already arranged to take off work. After about forty-eight hours, the workload started to slacken a bit. We'd always lambed in two sections, taking the rams out for a fortnight between the first batch and the second, which were mostly ewe lambs. I was now entering this blissful interregnum, and after one night of at least six hours' sleep I started to think again. I knew that it would be a while before Matthew was missed from the village, but for my own piece of mind I needed to establish a cover story for him; to lay a trail to his continuing existence elsewhere. Against all advice to the contrary, Matthew had always written his passwords and code numbers in a little black book. It didn't take me too long to find it, tucked into the bookcase by his desk between the *Oxford Book of Quotations* and what I had always secretly referred to as 'Burkes of the Realm'. The following morning, I loaded up all the troughs and silage rings to capacity and drove to York in Matthew's car. Mine I left ostentatiously in front of the house, clearly visible from the road, and drew my bedroom curtains. I hoped that if anyone came round and found the sheds empty of all but sheep, they would assume that I was in bed, catching up on my sleep.

At York station I used one of the machines to buy a ticket to London with Matthew's card. There was a train leaving within a few minutes, which I caught by the skin of my teeth. At King's Cross I used the card again to draw cash from a hole in the wall. I did take a careful look round and I couldn't see any CCTV associated with the machine. I checked the time of the return trains and walked out of the station. There were plenty of coffee bars, snack bars, a McDonald's and chip shops on the opposite side of the road. I picked one of the scruffier but busy greasy spoons and, looking around the clientele, I ordered what pretty much everybody else seemed to be having. Sausage, egg and chips with a cup of tea and some bread and butter on the side appeared to be the norm, and went down very nicely thank you, after two days of solo lambing and not much time to cook. Keeping a careful eye on the time, I sat and read the freebie newspaper I had picked up outside the station, then paid for my meal in cash.

Looking at my watch again, I rushed out of the cafe as though late for my train, in my hurry leaving my wallet on the floor near where I had been sitting. No one shouted after me. No one raced out of the cafe waving my forgotten wallet. I got on the return train to York and began to smile. In my pocket were my cards and cash and the return ticket I had bought with cash in King's Cross. In the wallet in the cafe were Matthew's debit card, an old business card of his, with his bank passcode written on the back, and just over £35 in cash. All I could do now was wait. I spent the two hours back to York fast asleep; in fact, I nearly missed my stop and ended up in Durham. Luckily the announcement eventually penetrated my haze. The last thing I did before leaving the train was to remove the SIM card from Matthew's phone and flush it down the loo before we arrived at the station. I was back with the sheep by mid-afternoon. I approached the farm by the back road at the top of the hill, and passed no one.

I spent the rest of the week tidying up and catching up with jobs. It was still hard work, but nowhere near as hard as those two days of solo lambing; and at least I could eat, drink and watch whatever telly I liked, without fear of criticism. Between work I binge-watched *Babylon 5*.

At the beginning of the following week the bank statement arrived. I opened the envelope with shaking hands and my vision blurred.

'Yes,' I shouted and punched the air. 'Yes!' It was lucky I was alone, as explanations would have been difficult, but if any of Matthew's contacts asked, I now had evidence that he was in London. There on the bank statement were the entries for the ticket bought in York and the cash at King's Cross. Then a few more. A small sum out of a cash dispenser in Finsbury Park. A couple of days later, expenditure in a takeaway and another item at an off licence, both in Muswell Hill. The last item was a larger sum spent at John Lewis in Brent Cross. It would seem that whoever had the card was getting bolder. I tapped the statement on my chin as I thought. While it was good to have evidence of Matthew's movements around north London, I didn't want him to bankrupt me. I decided to give it at least another week before I drew cash from the bank account, especially as that would involve a visit to the bank in York. But there was another precaution I could take. I picked the phone up and spoke to the Personnel team at the hospital. It didn't take long to change the bank details for my salary payments. As they knew me well, they agreed to action the change immediately, and I could sign the form when I was next in.

That was my next problem. Lambing was due to resume in a few days' time and I was due back at work. It was obvious I couldn't cope on my own for much longer, but neither could I afford hired help for more than a few days. The only solution I could see was to swallow my pride and appeal to the family.

Given how much they had been ignored over the years of my marriage to Matthew, their response was generous and heart-warming. Somewhat to my surprise I burst into tears on the phone as I explained that I had been deserted by my husband of ten years. I was deluged with offers of help ranging from an aunt to come and stay with me, to offers of holidays with a range of relatives scattered around the UK. I explained about the sheep and managed to politely decline the aunt, but was much relieved when my elder brother was delegated to come and assist. Although recently early-retired from his role as a solicitor, he was still fit and more than able to assist with the jobs around the farm, not least because he'd always helped Grandfather Treadwell. It was arranged that he would join me in a couple of days. That was good, because it gave me time to catch up with another little task that I had been putting off. Most of Matthew's clothes were still sitting in his wardrobe and tallboy and I couldn't bear to have to look at them for much longer. I went up to the bedroom, pulled open the wardrobe door and some of the drawers. There was a lot of clothes and shoes. What the devil could I do with them? I could take them to a charity shop, but I didn't have time to go far now the ewes were lambing again, and they might be found and recognised in a local shop. Also, the last thing I wanted was to see them walking around on someone else in the neighbourhood. That would be more than disconcerting.

I also needed to do something about a suitcase. I looked at our small collection of cases and that gave me an idea. The set we had was only a part set. We had got it cheap in a sale because the biggest case was missing. The only time we had used them was for our honeymoon. Suppose I didn't use a case at all? If anyone asked, Matthew had taken the big case with him. I went through the room pulling out all the most expensive and smartest clothes he possessed. All the things I thought he would have picked if he had time to plan leaving me. I added three of his best pairs of shoes and some cufflinks from the safe under the stairs. Then I looked at the pile. It was quite formidable.

In the end, bit by bit I burned everything that would burn in the boiler and raked through the ashes for the incombustible items. That was mainly buttons and zips. Those went in the rubbish the next day and disappeared to the corporation tip. I pushed the cufflinks down a rabbit hole. A gift for archaeologists of the future.

Edgar and I actually settled in quite well together. After the first day, when he was looking at his soiled trousers and jumper with distaste, I offered him the loan of Matthew's overalls.

'He left everything like that behind,' I said, showing him the part empty cupboards and drawers. 'He only took his city stuff.' Edgar grunted and accepted the overalls. As the days passed and he discovered that his post-solicitor retirement clothes were inadequate for hard work on a farm, he also helped himself to some jumpers and shirts.

We shared a taste for homely cooking and red wine and while I was not a bridge enthusiast, it took him only a matter of weeks before he found like-minded players in the village and set up a club. Seeing him sitting around in the evening in one of Matthew's sweaters did feel a little odd, but that apart it was an oddly relaxing time for me.

Towards the end of the ewe-lamb lambing, I made a final trip to the disposal pit with the dead bodies. The smell was no worse than usual.

The next task was the trip to the bank. By then 'Matthew'

had been spending all over north London and out as far as Brent Cross. Around £4,000 had gone. It was time to call a halt. At the NatWest branch in York I cancelled all the direct debits that paid bills and drew out 80 per cent of what was left in the account (which by then amounted to less than £1,000). While there I bumped into one of the old hags from the village. It was clear from her sympathetic and knowing tap on my arm that she knew about Matthew's running off. Without going into details I muttered something about sorting out the joint bank account. While she was busy in NatWest I went down the street to Lloyds, who still had my personal account in my maiden name. I set up some new direct debits and went home. In my mind my actions were justified by Matthew's desertion. I hadn't chopped him off at the knees, having left some money in the account. But I saw no reason why a deserted wife should have to continue to support her errant husband.

It was exactly three weeks after Matthew's departure that I took a call from the golf club.

'This is the second time that Matthew has missed his regular round of golf with us,' said the voice. 'We rang his mobile a couple of times but he hasn't answered. We thought we'd better check he was all right.'

'As far as I know he is absolutely fine.' I was irritated by the enquiry and that made my voice rather tart. 'He skipped off a couple of weeks ago and I haven't seen him since.'

'Oh sorry,' said the voice. 'Sorry to have bothered you. Do you have a forwarding address? No, sorry that's a rather stupid question I expect.'

'As far as I know he's in London,' I said and slammed the phone down.

A couple of weeks later there was another, similar call. By this time Edgar was with me and he picked the phone up. He was much blunter than I had been.

'The little shit buggered off in the middle of lambing. She's a sight better off without him.' From the squawking coming from the receiver the voice was still talking when he rang off. A day or two later, the police made contact. Rather than ringing they actually called round; two of them in a marked police car. They came to the door and politely removed their helmets.

'May we come in Mrs Wade?'

I took them into the kitchen and put the kettle on.

'Coffee?' I asked. Edgar came in from the hay barn just as I was pouring. I served coffees all round and got a plate of biscuits out. The two officers looked round the kitchen, apparently noting what they saw; the fact that there were dishes for two on the draining rack, and two pairs of damp overalls drying on the Aga.

The older of the two, a man I took to be approaching his retirement with more hair on his chin than on his head, took the lead.

'I'm Constable Taylor and this is Constable Wright. Could we speak to Mr Wade?'

'I'm sorry.' I sat down and took a biscuit. 'My husband is not here.'

'And you are?' said the policeman to Edgar.

'Edgar Treadwell, her brother.'

'This is a bit unconventional Mrs Wade, Mr Treadwell,' said Constable Taylor, 'but we've had Mr Wade reported to us as missing.'

'Well he's not here,' I said. 'Hasn't been for a couple of weeks. And I have no idea where he is, but while that does make him an absent husband I'm not sure it makes him a missing person. As far as I know he's in London, at least that's what the bank accounts appear to indicate.'

'Have you had any contact from him?'

'Not directly, but the bank certainly has.' I reached behind me to the pile of paperwork awaiting attention, most of it bills. Shuffling through, I came to the one I wanted.

'This is our latest bank statement. You'll see that he appears to have been spending money in London.'

The two policemen studied the bank statement, making some notes as they did so, then looked at each other.

'We're very sorry to have bothered you Mrs Wade,' they said. 'Thank you for the coffee.' And they left. I heaved a sigh of relief and went back to work.

Edgar stayed with me all the way through the summer of silage making and straw gathering. By the autumn sheep sales, it was clear that the current arrangements were not a long-term solution. The farm simply couldn't make money in any commercial sense, and given that I had a career separate from the farm, the logical thing to do was to cash in and leave. Edgar and the rest of the family were starting to gang up on me with helpful suggestions. I thanked my lucky stars, now, that I had never given way to Matthew's pressures to put his name on the deeds. At the time it had been very difficult to resist, but now, whatever the other difficulties and worries, that was one problem I didn't have.

Most of the sheep were sold in a dispersal sale in the autumn, leaving just a few cull ewes and store lambs for the winter market. Edgar and I hosted a delightful Christmas for the family at Coombe Farm. Then I put it in the hands of the land agents in Malton and York in the spring. As my actions had been watched with considerable interest by my farming neighbours, it wasn't long before they snapped up the better land. I thought the house and home paddocks would probably go to someone from the hunt, but there was more interest from prospective smallholders. I forbore to point out that we had been unable to make a living even with more land and made encouraging noises. I drew the land agent's attention to the extremely useful disposal pit at the far corner of the first paddock, now mercifully smell-free. I even gave him a copy of the old ADAS leaflet that described the construction of such a pit, so that he could show it to prospective buyers. Coombe Farm was sold by May and I left without a tear.

I began my new life in a small flat not far from the hospital in York. I took up singing again, this time with the Chapter-house Choir at the Minster. But I soon began to get itchy feet. After all, I no longer had to stay in York or even Yorkshire. I had a substantial balance in my account from the farm sale and was free to go wherever I wished. I found I was not willing to cast myself loose on the world with no job, but I was willing to try somewhere new. I started searching the NHS websites for a new role in a different hospital and eventually found just what I was looking for. A new, slightly bigger job in a new rural location. After all the years of decisions being taken for me, or more accurately being taken away from me, it seemed I was now free to make some of my own.

6

Edgar

The call to the family exploded like a star shell, scattering speculation and discussion over a substantial area of northern England. The general conclusion was that Matthew was a cheating shit that no one had ever liked. Admittedly, Aunt Audrey's version was that he was 'not a nice man' and 'always looked shifty' but the judgement was the same. Phone calls criss-crossed the northern counties with suggestions for help, some more practical than others but all well-meant, including the frail Aunt Audrey's offer to go and stay to 'keep dear Rachel company.' As that would both have created more work and driven Rachel even further round the bend than Matthew had already succeeded in doing, she was tactfully deterred from implementing her offer.

The family consensus, reached with remarkable rapidity, was that the recently retired elder brother (ie me) should move in with Rachel for a spell, and other family members would help out as needed, whether with hard work, loans or just moral support. There was a lot of the latter and Coombe Farm was deluged with cards, letters and messages. The postman got quite short-tempered.

As the aforementioned holder of the short straw, I packed my bags for an extended stay with mostly casual and hard-wearing clothes. We had grown up with frequent visits to Grandad Treadwell's farm, so we were used to the farming life with few illusions about its glamour. I was well aware, given the time of year, that the next few weeks were going to be a hard slog, especially for a man who had spent most of the past few years behind a desk. While I made sure the rest of the family knew what a sacrifice I was making, in truth I was glad of the change. I was already finding retirement a drag, and it felt good to be needed.

I arrived at Coombe Farm two days after Rachel's call. She met me in the yard with a big hug, and then I stood back to look at her. She was surprisingly upbeat, and while clearly exhausted, she was not as distressed as I feared. She showed me to my room, thanked me for coming, then disappeared out to the lambing shed again, where a ewe lamb was struggling with a big single. I hauled my cases out of the back of my too-citified BMW and rushed to change into working gear. I found Rachel in a pen in the barn, struggling to manipulate the coming lamb while also hanging on to the uncomprehending and outraged ewe lamb. The poor animal appeared to have a head at each end, as its part-born offspring had its head out, but nothing else. I left the gynaecological bit to Rachel as she had the smaller hands, but I could at least restrain the unwilling mother-to-be. Between us, we managed to extract the lamb in one piece and still breathing. After a while its reluctant mother decided that motherhood was, after all, inescapable, and started to lick it dry. Rachel and I perched on a stack of straw bales and I surveyed my already filthy jeans somewhat ruefully.

'There are some overalls of Matthew's that should fit,' she said, as she pushed her hair out of her eyes with the back of her wrist. Her hands were covered in blood and some fluids probably best not listed.

'Thanks. So, Rachel, what about Matthew? Where's he gone? What's the story?'

'I don't know. One day he's here, the next he's gone. No message, no warning and I've heard nothing from him since. He pushed me to mortgage the farm and I refused. Apart from that, he was quite normal.'

'Or at least, normal for Matthew,' I said. 'Was he in trouble? Financial trouble I mean? Could he have been fleeing a debt collector?'

'Well he always spent more than he should, but I don't know of a specific problem. He may have had debts I don't know about, but I haven't found anything in his papers and no one has landed on me with demands for repayment.'

'Was he having an affair?'

'Not that I know of, Edgar, but it's possible, you know.'

She looked impossibly weary and I held off on further questions, but determined to spend every spare moment I had going through all the paperwork.

The next couple of weeks flew by. Between lambing the remaining ewes, walking around the rest of the flock to make sure they were all the right way up, and scrutinising paperwork at night, I had little time to focus on anything other than Rachel's problem. She gave me bank statements showing that Matthew had carried on using their joint account after his departure, and I approved the actions she had taken to put a stop to him spending her money. The one thing that puzzled me was that Matthew's car was still in the yard. Why hadn't he taken it with him? Admittedly it was elderly and not worth much, but even so. And how had he got to London without it? Rachel pointed out that one of the payments on the account was at York railway station and for a sum that would have bought a London ticket.

'He must have had a lift to the station. Or a taxi. Perhaps his fancy woman drove him there.'

'But he only bought one ticket to London,' I pointed out. 'Would he have left her to buy her own? Getting out of the way of some dodgy lender looks more and more likely.'

'I don't know, Edgar. Look, I'm tired of Matthew, tired of thinking about him, and in fact just tired. I'm going to bed.'

Just before she left the room, the phone rang and I answered it. It was the golf club, of all things, wanting to know why Matthew hadn't turned up to some game or other.

'The little shit's abandoned his wife in the middle of lambing,' I snapped. And put the phone down.

The police turned up a few days later and I told them the same thing. Rachel showed them the bank statements, and off they trotted. We were left in peace to slog on through silage making, hay making and taking lambs to market. Rachel went back to work, and I kept things on track, with her help in the evenings and at weekends. It was hard work, but I found I was enjoying myself. I began to meet more people in the village and our embryo bridge club, begun at the end of lambing, went from strength to strength. Rachel began to seem more like her old self.

One night however, we sat down after supper with the farm accounts and I raised the subject that had been bothering me for weeks.

'Rachel, I don't understand how the farm makes a living.'

'It doesn't,' she said.

I looked at her in some surprise. 'So all this hard work is for nothing?'

'Nothing financial. Matthew felt it gave him status and the lifestyle he was entitled to. But it's been bleeding money for years.'

'You know it can't go on, don't you? You're killing yourself with work and the longer you hang on the worse it will get.'

'I know. I just haven't had the energy to face it. But I know you're right, Edgar. Will you help me make a plan?'

'Of course I will. In fact, I've been thinking about it already. I don't think you should just dump everything onto the market. That will just push prices down. If you can bear to hang on here a few months, I think we should sell most of the stock at a dispersal sale in the autumn, then any remaining cull ewes and fat lambs over the winter, and put the farm on the market in the New Year. As there aren't any mortgages or big debts, that should leave you with a nice sum to start over somewhere; in York perhaps. There aren't any debts I don't know about are there?'

'No. None in my name anyway. I don't know about Matthew, and I have wondered if that's why he left. To escape from a debt collector?'

'Very lucky you did what Grandfather told you and kept the deeds in your name only.'

'You knew about that!'

'We all did. And it was the best piece of advice he ever gave you. It makes things a lot easier now. By the way, you have changed your will haven't you?'

'Changed my will?' She looked startled.

'Of course. If you haven't I can help you with that. You should realise that if anything happened to you, it would all go to Matthew, and I don't imagine you would want that.'

'No. No I don't. I'll do as you say, Edgar. Thank you. And I've just had a great idea. We'll plan the sales as you suggest and then have one last family Christmas here at the farm. You've all been so great. It will be my thanks to you and everyone else.'

So that's what we did. And it *was* a great Christmas, goose *and* turkey and all the trimmings. The farmhouse dining room was full to bursting with more laughter and goodwill than at any time in its past; fuelled partly, I must admit, by Matthew's excellent taste in wine. My one nervousness, that the spectre might return to ruin the feast, was not fulfilled. Early in 2008 I went back to my bachelor pad in Whitby and Rachel started her new life in York.

7

Ben

If Ben had a hotline to HQ in York, he couldn't have been more accurate in his assessment of their current pre-occupations. Holmes, the Home Office computer, so far had thrown up very little in the way of lookalike crimes. The records of some years ago were more interesting. Although Rachel had not reported her husband missing, some of his friends in the golf club had asked a few questions. A check on his credit cards demonstrated that he had used them a couple of times in railway stations in York and in London and subsequently in a number of busy shopping centres in north London. Nothing had shown up on any CCTV cameras and no alarm was raised. As he had taken his clothes with him, albeit not his car, it was assumed that he had quietly disappeared to make a new life for himself. With no concerns raised by the abandoned wife, who continued her normal quiet life, the investigation had been dropped.

Ben did some hard thinking as he helped Tristan to milk the goats. He always enjoyed handling the goats, appreciating their different personalities and the mostly cooperative approach they took to their partnership with the human contingent. Admittedly some of them took more concentration than others. The Heidi line for example was notorious with everyone who had ever helped Tristan, but Noemi and Giulia also had their little peculiarities. Noemi, for example, was even now pushing her nose into Ben's pocket looking for a carrot. Giulia, on the other hand, wouldn't give you the time of day for a carrot but would do tricks for a wedge of apple.

'Tristan,' he said, 'I think we're best leaving it to the police to follow up what happened to Matthew Wade through databases and the like. They've access to information that I can't get at any more, even via friends. But I do think we should do some questioning around the village. Small villages are always very well informed about their inhabitants. I think I'll start with Sharon.'

'Well good luck to you with that. Personally I wouldn't go near Sharon if she had the last dose of anti-Ebola vaccine in the world, but I expect she'll get on with you like a house on fire.'

Ben's eyes crinkled in a grin. 'You think she'll fall to my inescapable male charm?'

'Without a doubt.'

Sharon wasn't difficult to find. The WI coffee morning was in full flow when Ben reached the village hall and Sharon was presiding over the cakes. Most of the more delectable offerings had been snapped up but there were still some cupcakes. Sharon offered them to Ben with a gesture that recalled irresistibly the famous *Calendar Girls* line about requiring considerably bigger buns. Taking a chocolate cupcake and a coffee, Ben asked, 'I wonder if you could spare me a moment, Sharon?'

He indicated a currently unoccupied table in the corner of the room. Sharon glanced around to make sure WI colleagues had noted how she was being singled out by the most handsome (albeit the only) man in the room, and waddled over with her own builder's tea and a large wedge of coffee cake, retrieved from where she had hidden it beneath the table.

'Staying with Tristan?' she asked.

'Just for a week,' said Ben and, well aware of some of the gossip, he added, 'my wife is joining me at the weekend. I know you all in the village will help, but we thought Tristan needed a bit more support.'

'Well of course we'll help,' said Sharon mendaciously, 'always ready to help a neighbour.'

'What I wanted to ask you,' said Ben, 'is about your old neighbours, the Wades. I know you've lived here all your life and always have your finger on the pulse, so I thought you'd be the best person to ask. After all, I always say it takes a woman with acute powers of observation to get the real picture of what's going on around her.' He wondered if this flattery with a trowel was overdoing it, but it appeared not.

'Well I probably saw more than most. I can't say I ever warmed to Rachel Wade, but I don't think Matthew was easy. Always down the village pub on his own or going to shows and golf clubs. My man would say as how he never did a hand's turn, but then he hasn't got much patience with the aristocracy. Not that Matthew was anything special,' she added, 'although hearing him carry on you'd think his parents were lords and ladies at the least. Not even particularly well found, although you'd never have thought it to watch him throw his brass about.'

'What do you think happened to Matthew?'

'I always thought he ran off with someone,' said Sharon.

'You said he ran off with a man,' weighed in a well-built lady on the next table, whose occupants had all been ear-wigging busily.

'I never,' denied Sharon hotly. 'Well I might've said something like that,' she added hurriedly, noting the sceptical looks from the next table and pre-empting the probability of contradiction, 'but what I meant was, that it seemed he'd gone off with someone and given the funny habits of those what've been to public school it could have been a man or a woman.'

'Did any of you see him with anyone else?' asked Ben, widening the interrogation to include all the neighbouring tables since this was clearly a public conversation.

Several ladies in hats turned their chairs to create a conversational ring. Ben was reminded of a coven, or the old harridans in *Last of the Summer Wine*, half expecting one of them to make a grab for his chocolate cupcake.

'There was that blonde shortly before he took off,' said one.

'No that was her from the golf club,' interjected another, 'and she's still around.'

'I don't think he'd have been stupid enough to have brought his fancy piece to the village!' said a buxom lady with wild hair escaping a felt hat. 'More like someone he met at a show or someone else from the golf club.'

'But it was the golf club that reported him missing!' said a fourth.

'So what?'

'So if he'd gone off with one of them,' argued the lady with the hat, 'why would they have reported him missing?'

'How do you know they did?' asked Sharon, irritated that someone else appeared to have gossip that had not come to her ears.

'Because that Gary Horsfall's wife's sister takes tea with my cousin Muriel's youngest and she said that Gary had said the reason he was late for their dinner that night was because he was looking up the old records and found an enquiry from the golf club.'

'Was that Anne Waters?' asked someone else.

'That's right,' said hat lady, 'Anne Smith as was.'

Avoiding the dynastic complexities and sifting through to the information, Ben said, 'No one actually saw Matthew Wade with another partner. It was just assumed he'd run off.'

'Well why else would he have gone?' chorused the ladies; and hat lady, proving to be a mine of information, added, 'Rachel Wade had to clean out their bank account. Wherever he'd gone, he carried on spending. When she found that she was struggling to pay bills she had to shift money out of that account and into another before he spent the lot. That was weeks after he left.'

'How do you know that?' asked Ben.

'Because I saw Rachel in the bank and overheard the conversation she had with the counter chap. It was pretty much the only time she left the farm in those few weeks but she'd had to go in to sort out the mess that Matthew was making.'

*

Back at Coombe Farm, Ben found Tristan in the bedroom she had dedicated to her weaving.

'I'm so behind,' she said, 'at least four commissions waiting. From the point of view of my budget that's good news, but I hate having stuff hanging over me.' She picked up some hanks of dark Jacob fleece and wove them into the rug. Ben stepped back, the better to see the whole creation.

'I do love those rugs,' he said. 'I must commission one for Paula. One of those would look great in front of the fire in our sitting room. I particularly like the ones where you mix in some of the alpaca colours. There's a real shine to the alpaca fleece.'

'I bless the day I saw this technique demonstrated at the Great Yorkshire Show,' she said. 'It's a really good side-line for me, given that the fleece from the Jacobs isn't worth a lot as raw fleece. I wouldn't have the patience to spin as well but this approach, just using carded wool in handfuls, really suits my personality.' She grinned up at Ben.

'Random, haphazard, and minimum effort,' she said. 'It's quite therapeutic too.'

'You underrate the artistry that goes into these.' Ben was flipping through a small pile of completed rugs on the table at the side. 'But I didn't come up here to talk rugs but to report back from the village. Have you ever been to one of those WI coffee mornings?'

'Not very often,' said Tristan. 'I contribute some cheese to their fundraising stalls from time to time but I find the coven a little scary.'

'Funny, that's the description that occurred to me too.

However, they were quite informative. Or at least, the information they had was interesting and the information they didn't have even more so.'

'Now don't be cryptic!'

'It's interesting that while everyone assumes Matthew Wade left with a new partner, no one actually ever saw him with one. That could be said to point to the skeleton being his. However, other information points in the opposite direction. It would seem that he was still accessing his bank account for some weeks after he left the farm. And if a certain lady with a felt hat remembers correctly, it would also seem that Rachel Wade hardly left the farm during those weeks. So while a nasty suspicious mind might think that she had travelled the country using his debit card, it would seem that she was here all the time.'

'Maureen Little. Sorry, irrelevant I know, but the lady in the felt hat is Maureen Little. She has some sort of connection with the police. At least, she always seems to be up on their gossip. So, where does that leave us with Matthew?'

'Either he left with a new friend no one knew anything about, or left for some other reason, perhaps to avoid some dodgy loan shark, or he never left at all.'

'So,' she said, picking up a different shade of wool, 'I suppose any of those could be true. And none of those rule out the skeleton being Matthew and the murderer being Rachel. Or, he could have returned to the farm some months later without being seen by the village, and still have ended up in the disposal pit. Or the skeleton could belong to a complete stranger to us all, and this circus could go on for months!'

*

Greg Geldard was, at that very moment, addressing those questions. The press conference had produced the desired effect. At least, although they had been bothered by the usual array of nutters, more politely known as concerned members of the public, they had also had a report from a dentist with a practice just outside Cambridge. It appeared that Matthew had retained the habit of visiting his old dentist rather than engaging with a new one in York or Malton. Whether that was because it also gave him an excuse for visiting his university haunts was another question. Either way, the information the Histon dentist had provided was good evidence that the skeleton was indeed Matthew Wade.

Greg sighed, and hitched up his natty trousering over his knees to avoid damaging the crease. The recipient of much ribbing in his junior days, he was well aware that his more rustic colleagues thought his attire unsuitable for a predominantly rural beat. However, notwithstanding the often ruined shoes and the unfortunate effect that borrowed Wellingtons tended to have on his trouser legs, he had never broken himself of the habits caught from his accountant father.

'Fiona, tell us again what you found from the bank records.'

Fiona shuffled the paperwork and cleared her throat.

'Several entries over a period of just under three months from Matthew's last recorded sighting at Coombe Farm. It seems that they had a visit from the local vet in early March, called out to a ewe that had prolapsed. Matthew was definitely present on that occasion. The vet is still in practice in Malton. Both the time and date of the visit were recorded, together with details of the work done and subsequently the fact they were late paying the bill. After that, it would appear that the debit card was used to pay for a rail ticket in York, at a cashpoint at King's Cross, and subsequently in a number of locations mainly in north London and a few in Potters Bar. At that point it would seem that Rachel Wade became worried that Matthew was removing substantial amounts of cash from their joint account. She would appear to have cancelled all the direct debits and removed most of the balance. Her salary payments were also diverted from that account. It would seem that more attempts were made to use the debit card but with no cash in the account the payments were refused. After that we haven't been able to find any record of Matthew Wade at all.'

'So it's possible he disappeared for a while,' commented Gary 'but then came back to the farm and ended up in the disposal pit.'

'Possible,' said Peter, 'but on the other hand it would seem that there was someone else living at the farm besides Rachel Wade.'

'A fancy man? Perhaps she was the one with the enterprising lifestyle.'

'Probably not,' said Peter, 'it seems it was her brother.'

'So not impossible,' said Gary, with memories of some unorthodox family arrangements in remote Yorkshire villages. 'But not probable,' he conceded. 'Where's the brother now?'

'Edgar Treadwell, retired solicitor, delegated by the family to give Rachel a helping hand when Matthew disappeared off the scene. He apparently stayed at Coombe Farm until late 2007, shortly before the farm was sold. According to the village, the Treadwell family celebrated Christmas en masse at the farm and had a whale of a time. I got that from the village pub, who said that the whole party went down for Christmas Eve drinks, and were obviously having a really jolly time. The landlady said she had never seen Rachel so animated. Like another person, she said. But going back to Edgar, the village Bridge Club, of which he was a founder member, will have it that he used to wax eloquent on the subject of his shitty brother-in-law and the way he had abandoned his sister, disappearing without a trace before the end of lambing and never reappearing. The fact that it was before the end of lambing appears to have been the absolute pits, far worse than the simple fact of his disappearing at all. The reason the brother had moved in was to give Rachel a hand at a very busy time of year. He seems to have lived there for some months, judging by his attendance at Bridge Club meetings and local tournaments.'

'And today? Where are we going to meet him?'

'His practice was in Whitby and it seems he still lives there. As you know, I spoke to him briefly on the phone the other day when he claimed to have lost touch with Rachel after she moved to Norfolk. According to the electoral roll he still lives alone in a flat in Whitby.'

When Peter and Geldard pulled up outside the property in St Hilda's Terrace, they both whistled. The flat was in a grand, end-of-terrace Georgian house in the centre of Whitby. Geldard was even more impressed when they had walked through the formal walled garden and the grand communal hall. Edgar's flat on the first floor must once have been the main reception rooms, and as such benefitted from gracious proportions, high ceilings and stunning views. The room to which Edgar welcomed them was lit with a brilliant light from the tall windows. It was clearly both study and sitting room. At one end was an imposing desk from the same era as the house, with a leather captain's chair behind it and two very comfortable-looking leather wing chairs in front. At the other end were three sofas arranged around what seemed to be an Adam fireplace, and occasional tables conveniently placed for a glass of wine or cup of coffee at one's elbow. A cafetiere and mugs were waiting on the desk, together with a plate of biscuits.

'Since you kindly gave me warning of your visit, I've made us some coffee.'

Edgar took his seat behind the desk and waved his visitors to the two in front.

'How can I help?' He busied himself pouring the coffee and offered them milk and sugar. Geldard took the opportunity to scrutinise their host. He saw an elderly man, spare of frame and smartly dressed in chinos, blue striped shirt and dark blue waistcoat. His remaining hair was brushed back, his blue eyes still sharp with wit.

'We are trying to establish the whereabouts of your sister Rachel,' said Geldard. Deep in his chair, Peter unobtrusively took out his notebook and prepared to make notes.

'You may have seen from the news that a skeleton was discovered at Coombe Farm. I am sorry to have to tell you that it has been identified as being that of your brother-in-law, Matthew Wade.'

Edgar took another sip of his coffee before putting his mug down, with precision, exactly in the centre of a mat.

'I am, of course, sorry that the skeleton is Matthew, but the news of his death is not a sorrow for me.' He looked up. 'Matthew Wade was an unmitigated shit who treated my sister abominably.'

'Where is Rachel now?'

'I have no idea. I have not heard from Rachel since,' he paused and pulled open a desk drawer. He shuffled through some correspondence then said, 'January 2012. At that time, she had moved from her job in York and was buying a boat in Norfolk. I have not heard from her since.'

'Was there a row?'

'Not at all. You probably know that I went and stayed with Rachel shortly after Matthew's disappearance. That would have been towards the end, or perhaps the middle of April 2007. Matthew had disappeared two or three weeks earlier, right in the middle of lambing, and Rachel was at her wits' end. She appealed to the family for help. We all discussed what we could do, and as I had retired some months earlier I agreed to move in with Rachel temporarily to help out. I stayed until early in 2008, then came back here. Coombe Farm was on the market by then, we had sold pretty well all the stock, and Rachel did not need me any more. Rachel moved to York, nearer to her work at the hospital, and we kept in close touch until September 2011, when she wrote to me saying that she was going to make a fresh start and not to worry if I didn't hear from her for a while. She thanked me for all my help. It read like a valedictory.'

'Were you surprised or upset?'

'Not surprised as such.' He picked his mug up again and took a sip. 'I had encouraged her to take her time in deciding what she wanted to do with the rest of her life. I had argued that such decisions are best made when the dust has settled, not in the midst of a crisis. So no, it didn't surprise me that, after a period of reflection, she had decided to make a change. I was grieved that she decided to cut her ties with me and the rest of the family, but it is her life after all. I just hoped that the separation would be temporary. That once she felt settled again, she would get back in touch.'

'So you can't cast any light on where she may be living now.'

'No. As I said, the last letter I had from her came from York. You may have a copy if you wish.' He proffered a piece of paper. 'The last contact was the email saying she was buying a boat in Norfolk. I understood it to be a substantial boat, not a dinghy, but I have no idea where it was or is moored. I have emailed her many times since, but no reply.'

'Back to 2007 then. When you arrived at Coombe Farm, what traces were there of Matthew?'

'Only his car, oh and some overalls and wellies, which I used when working on the farm. I think there were a few odds and ends of other clothes too, but most of his smarter clothes had gone with him. Or so I thought.' He put the mug down again with a crash.

'Look, mine was not a criminal practice, so these procedures are new to me, but I am not stupid. You have found Matthew's remains on the farm and the papers are calling it a suspected murder. Clearly Rachel has to be a suspect.'

'I am afraid so, yes. Do you think she would be capable of killing her husband?'

'I don't know. I suppose any of us is capable of killing if pushed to the edge, but I don't know how far she was pushed. You must remember I had seen very little of her during her marriage to Matthew. My impression was that Matthew was a bully and quite possibly violent to her. He was certainly controlling and made her life a misery. He undermined her and destroyed her self-esteem. Most of the things she used to enjoy doing, he put a stop to. Was that enough to push her over the edge? I don't know. I don't want to believe that my sister was capable of murdering her husband and hiding his body, but I honestly don't know.'

'For a man who saw little of the marriage, you seem to have a very clear idea of Matthew's behaviour.'

'I am judging largely by effect. The changes in Rachel during her marriage and after it were marked. Before she married she was happy, outgoing, confident. She was an accomplished singer and sang with several choirs and smaller groups. During it she lost weight, became quiet and nervous and deferred to Matthew all the time. She stopped singing. We all noticed it. And we all noticed the barbed jokes and asides that Matthew used to keep her in her place. After he had gone, she started to recover the woman she had been.

'When I was practising as a solicitor,' he added, 'I did quite a lot of divorce work. It was a behaviour pattern with which I was depressingly familiar.'

'And while you were at Coombe Farm, did you have cause to visit the disposal pit?'

'I've been trying to remember. I don't think so. I knew where it was of course, but we were towards the end of lambing and I don't remember any casualties during my time, so I would have had no reason to go to it.'

'And the smell?'

'At that time of year, there would always be a bit of a smell until the rats and bacteria dealt with whatever had been put down there. If I'd noticed anything, I would have thought nothing of it.'

'Not even with Matthew unaccounted for?'

'I thought he'd gone off with another woman. Or possibly fled a debt collector. Rachel told me he had wanted to re-mortgage the farm. He appeared to have been spending Rachel's money, I know she had to take steps to stop that. So I thought nothing more of it. If I thought of Matthew at all during 2007 it was to hope he wouldn't come back and spoil our family Christmas and the rest of Rachel's life.'

'Thank you Mr Treadwell. I don't think we have any more questions at present, but if anything else occurs to you, or Rachel gets in touch, please do let us know. We will have your answers typed up into a statement and one of the local officers will bring a copy round for you to sign. Thank you for your time.'

Geldard and Peter stood up to leave and Edgar accompanied them to his front door.

'If you do find Rachel, can you let me know?' he asked. 'I would very much like to see her again.'

Back in the car, Peter and Geldard looked at each other. 'Do we believe him?'

'I think so. Yes.' Geldard put the car into gear and glanced behind him before pulling away. 'I think he was being very careful and precise about what he said to us and I do think he was being truthful. I also think that he is very much afraid that his sister did it.'

8

Rachel – New Beginnings

Once I started to look around me again, a vacancy for HR team leader in one of the newly created Community NHS Trusts caught my attention, this one in Norfolk. I thought it might make a pleasant change from a hospital, and put in my application. Given the nearly four-hour drive from York to Norwich, I decided to take a few days' holiday and booked myself a room in the Maid's Head, near Norwich Cathedral. My interview was on Thursday morning, so I went down Wednesday night and settled myself for a few days' break.

The interview seemed to go well. I dressed formally in black trousers, white shirt and long-line black and white dogs-tooth jacket. I always feel more confident when I know I am looking smart, even if the work environment proves to be relatively casual. I needed the boost. This felt like the first big decision I had made for a long time. Perhaps the first decision since I said yes to marrying Matthew. It was a milestone and it felt like it.

I had correctly anticipated most of the questions and had mugged up on the employment law areas where I felt weakest, so I was pleased with how it went. My potential colleagues seemed friendly and passionate about what they did, so I left knowing that if I was offered the job it was one I would accept.

It was a good way to start my little holiday. I celebrated that evening with a half bottle of Prosecco and an excellent supper at a little wine bar I found in St George's Street, not far from the river. That gave me an idea for an outing the following day, and Friday morning I boarded a boat for a cruise on the Broads. That impulse changed the rest of my life.

The Broads fascinated me, to the point that I spent my whole four days exploring them; rather inadequately by car, more thoroughly by hire boat and even, one afternoon, by canoe. By Monday lunchtime I had come to a decision. Whether I got the job or not, I wanted to come and live on the Broads. And I meant on the Broads, not by them. I couldn't see the point of an expensive house that would flood in bad weather. I had seen some very swish boats that were more than big enough for a single person to live on. Not much smaller than my flat anyway, and with even better views. I spent my last afternoon at the Norfolk Yacht Agency in Brundall and went home to York with fistfuls of brochures.

By Christmas I was the very proud owner of the *Edith Cavell*, a Broom 50 currently lying at Brundall but soon to be moved by me (!) to new moorings. I absolutely couldn't believe my luck. As I had anticipated, the *Edith* had more space than my flat, with three bedrooms, a lounge, kitchen diner and two shower rooms. If you regarded the top deck seating as the equivalent of a conservatory, I had everything I could possibly want. Admittedly storage space was limited, particularly if you had been used to overflowing into a garage and farm buildings, but I promised myself I would embrace my inner organiser and strip my life of unnecessary 'stuff'. In fact, instead of Christmas shopping in York I embarked on a whole month of de-shopping, getting rid of a whole heap of fancy clothes, surplus office wear and ornaments that I would never need again. When I moved on to the *Edith* I genuinely had only what was useful or beautiful. Oh, and one addition that was both. I paid a visit to Dogs Trust at Snetterton and found my new best friend in Brizo, a collie-cross-spaniel bitch.

The one small fly in the ointment was the job. I didn't get it, so in November, once my offer on the *Edith* was accepted, I went down to Norfolk again and did some more looking around. The *Edith* took less than a quarter of the cash from the farm, so I still had a cushion of savings, but I needed a job to pay for living expenses, boat maintenance and mooring fees. I wasn't stupid and I did my sums, but it didn't have to be a well-paid job nor even a permanent one. What I was looking for was a place I could moor the *Edith* and have access fairly close by to work of some kind. I found what I was looking for at Ludham. There were shops, pubs and cafes. There were some idyllic moorings down Womack Dyke, accessible by a boat like the *Edith*. I put my name on the waiting list and made the final payment on my new home.

At the end of December, I moved permanently from York, collecting Brizo en route. One small hire van was all I needed and I arrived at my temporary mooring in Brundall at the tail of the year. Brizo and I celebrated our New Year and new beginnings tucked away snugly in the lounge of the *Edith*, all curtains closed to hide the fireworks and music on to drown the noise. We were both very happy.

In mid-January I heard I had made it to the top of the waiting list for a mooring in Womack Water and hired some help from the Norfolk Yacht Agency to take *Edith* there. This was my training run, and very exciting it was too, down the Yare, across Breydon Water, through the narrow bridge at Great Yarmouth, then up the Bure. We paused at the Bridge Inn at Acle for lunch, then went on to the junction of the Bure and the Thurne. Apart from the excitement of passing under Acle Bridge, the lower reaches of the Bure are not very exciting. The land is very flat, the river wide, and there is not so much to see as on the smaller rivers like the Ant. However, once we turned off into the Thurne and then again into Womack Dyke, the waterways narrowed and there was more wildlife to admire. The river banks closed in, and after the first stretch between fields of wheat, I was sailing between trees and tall rushes. As I got closer to Ludham the trees closed in still more, sheltering the water from the breeze and providing both privacy and security. I began to feel…the only word that comes to me is safe. Here was a world protected from both prying eyes and rough winds. The only other time I had felt like this was in a walled garden, only here my walls were green and growing.

Brizo found her spot on the foredeck as figurehead, and viewed all the bird life with an acquisitive stare from her mismatched eyes; one blue, one brown. The heron, stalking the bank like a pterodactyl left over from pre-history, got particularly close scrutiny. Let nobody say that Brizo lacked ambition.

I was glad of the taciturn Richard's assistance when it came to reversing *Edith* into her mooring. He showed me the correct knots to tie her up, allowing a little for the river to rise and fall; then, accepting his pay and tip with a cheerful nod, he strode off to the village for his lift to Brundall. I had found my anchorage, protected and private. I was truly home.

My new landlord was named David. He lived in a large and elegant house on the edge of Womack Water, separated from the public moorings and busy visitors' area by a thick belt of more trees. His long and well-kept garden ran down to the water side, with space for three boats to be moored there. The other two moorings were already occupied, one by a rather beautiful old yacht and the other by an elderly but well-kept cruiser, smaller than the *Edith*. The cruiser was using one of the two electric points. The second was for the *Edith*. On the bank nearby was a garden shed and a tap with a long hose fitted, to make it easy to fill water tanks. I had been advised I was paying a generous rent for the mooring, but to my mind the privacy, quiet and facilities more than justified the extra cost.

David and I had hit it off immediately. He was a quiet and self-contained man, a little shorter than me and slight in frame. Dapper was a word that sprang to mind, and I much admired his clothes sense. He carried a small brown leather handbag and had small neat feet encased in immaculate brown leather shoes. I was to learn that when the shoe colour changed to black, the bag was changed to match. He was friendly but intensely private. I was never invited into the house, which peered at the water over the tops of the fruit trees in the orchard. Equally, it was made plain to me that he did not expect to invade my privacy either. So long as I paid my rent on time and kept the *Edith* and her surroundings in good order, neither of us would interfere with the other. A private footpath led through the belt of trees to the public staithe, its parking, shops and cafe. David showed me where to leave my car and explained that would be my landward access to the mooring. I would not need to approach his house except in an emergency. It couldn't have suited me better.

My first few weeks at Womack Dyke were spent settling in. I made a sort of day kennel on the upper deck for Brizo. Basically it was a sheltered corner, with a soft bed conveniently placed for a tether to be fixed to a handrail, just in case I needed to restrain her from wandering off. I had already discovered that the collie in her expressed itself as a spirit of independence and adventure. Luckily, the spaniel liked home comforts and food, which so far meant she had always come when called. I put a second memory-foam mattress for her in a corner of what Richard had assured me was called the saloon not the sitting room. I got the clear impression that only describing the prow as the pointy bit would have called forth more scorn than this error in taste.

The next step was to arrange my very limited collection of books on shelving in the saloon and sort out the Wi-Fi. Taking advice from a much more expert sailing family who had briefly tied up on the public moorings during an out-of-season winter break, I achieved a limited and rather slow connection.

My now (very limited) collection of clothes fitted neatly into the cupboards and wardrobes of two bedrooms. Incidentally, I found it much easier to de-clutter when selecting what I wanted to keep, as opposed to selecting what I might want to throw away. Selecting the minimum and dumping the rest was much more efficient process.

It was at the beginning of February that I met Philip. I had been prowling round the little yacht chandlery by the public staithe, making a mental note of what I could buy there for the *Edith*, and also checking the limited display of paperbacks. They were clearly aimed at the tourist market and not a very exciting selection. My reflex thought, 'I'll have to shop on Amazon,' reminded me that I first needed to work out where I could have post and parcels delivered. I certainly didn't want to bother David with any of that. I decided to pop in to the little coffee shop and treat myself to a cappuccino and cake, which is when Philip and I got chatting.

It was a cold day, as you'd expect in February, but sunny, and, warmly wrapped as I was, I decided to enjoy the sun at one of the tables on the green. When he brought my cappuccino over, he had two mugs in his hand.

'I hope you don't mind if I join you for a few minutes,' he said. 'I usually take a break round about now. I've seen you around a few times this last few weeks. Have you recently moved to the village? I'm Philip by the way, and I run this little lot,' and he waved an arm vaguely round the small visitor centre, which included the cafe, boat supplies, pump-out station, and some boat maintenance facilities. He was a slim man with dark hair attractively touched with grey at the temples, and neat hands. I found him deft in everything he did, whether it was tidying up loose coils of cable, putting items away on his shop shelves, or writing notes to himself. I realised this was my first social approach from a man since Edgar had left the farm, and certainly the first from any man not a relative. I found myself rather confused and bashful. I was out of practice at this, even just to say hello.

'I'm Rachel,' I said. 'Pleased to meet you.' If I had wanted to object to his company it was now too late, as he was sitting down, blowing on his black coffee.

'I'm living on a boat here.'

'I see,' he said. 'You do know don't you, that you can stay at a mooring, living on the boat, for a maximum of eleven months out of twelve?'

'Yes of course. I was planning to do a little touring each year. But I do expect to be here most of the time.' I realised I sounded like a weather announcer, commenting on an incoming cold front, but I couldn't seem able to shed the formality. 'In fact, I'll be looking for a job, or a couple of jobs, locally. I'd be very grateful if you could mention my name, if you happen to hear of anything of course. I've done a lot of office work, but I have also worked in cafes, restaurants and shops in my time. I don't mind what I do.'

'Provided it is legal, decent, honest and truthful?' He grinned.

'That's right,' I said 'and modestly lucrative.' I cringed, realising I still sounded like the BBC. Luckily, he didn't seem to notice.

'I'll keep my ear to the ground,' he said. 'I may have some part-time work myself. In the summer I could use a pair of extra hands in the cafe, but it wouldn't be full-time and wouldn't be all year round. Interested?'

'I am interested,' I said, 'and thank you.'

That afternoon I went up into the village to see what else might be possible. There was a pub, several cafes, and a number of shops that clearly catered mainly for visitors. I decided to get some cards made up. I could put one in the Post Office window for a modest sum, and the rest I could distribute around the main businesses. While I was in the Post Office I also spotted an advert for a bicycle. That would be ideal for getting around in the village and would save me taking the car out every time I wanted some groceries or a trip to the pub. I noted the number and went back to the *Edith*.

Over the next few weeks I distributed my cards around the village and in the process made the acquaintance of a number of friendly locals. Contrary to the Norfolk reputation, I found them open and welcoming. Amelia in the Post Office was particularly chatty, although demonstrating a slightly disconcerting enthusiasm for finding out about my past. In general I felt that was best left buried. My aim was a new start, a new life, a new name and a new future. The past needed to stay where it was, in the past.

As we got closer to Easter, my card started to bear fruit, and by the time the tourist season was in full swing I had three regular jobs. Five mornings I worked for Philip, mainly in his cafe serving coffees and cake, but occasionally in the shop. Friday and Saturday afternoons I worked in the tea shop in the village; Thursday and Friday nights behind the bar in the pub.

That made Friday a long and busy day, but the cash in hand kept me fed and electrified and I even saved a little towards mooring fees and other maintenance charges for *Edith*. I was keen that I didn't raid my savings accounts unless absolutely necessary. My main worry was how to look after Brizo on a Friday, but I enlisted the support of a dog-mad teenager in the village with ambitions towards veterinary nursing. He wasn't allowed pets at home, so was more than happy to foster Brizo on Fridays. This meant, if anything, that Brizo got more attention and better walks on a Friday than any other day of the week. It was particularly touching therefore to be greeted by her on my every return as though I was the most wonderful, magical being in the world. After the putdowns and control freakery from Matthew, the sheer joy of coming home to an always loving, always accepting, generous heart like Brizo's was sheer joy. The fact that she was a dog, not a man, was immaterial.

Occasionally I got emails or text messages from the family. They were usually from Edgar, usually asking when I would ring him, and when would I go up and see him. I felt especially guilty about Edgar, who had been such a help during that last year on the farm. Without him I wouldn't even have got through that last lambing, let alone managed to sell the farm and move away. However, I couldn't surmount the reluctance to have anything to do with the life I had left behind. On the few occasions I started to think of Matthew, I always found my mind shying away like a nervous colt. Sometimes I woke in the night in a cold sweat, dreaming that he was still with me, that he was still controlling my every move, that I wasn't allowed to see people, work in pubs, and especially not sail the Broads.

'What was this madness,' the dream Matthew would ask, 'that I thought it right to waste money on a tacky fibre-glass boat with mock leather upholstery and a microwave for God's sake! How could I do any proper cooking without a range, or an Aga?'

The enormous relief to find, on waking, that a present Matthew was a nightmare and an absent Matthew was reality was what kept me sane. I wondered sometimes why I didn't feel more guilt. The more I thought about it, however, the more the nightmares came back, so I learned to join the nervous colt in shying away from the uncomfortable thoughts. And gradually, as time passed, that whole life took on the aura of a nightmare until I began to wonder if I had dreamed it all. I had read about the phenomenon of 'recovered memory'. I seemed to be experiencing the reverse, a lost or discarded memory that became more and more elusive over time.

9

The Hunt for Rachel, July 2015

With the identification of the skeleton as Matthew Wade, finding Rachel became still more important and senior management made it clear they were becoming impatient with the slow progress. The pressure was on and Geldard knew it.

'Rachel's movements immediately after the sale of the farm in 2008 were quite easy to trace,' said Fiona, perched in the corner of the Ops room. 'In May 2008 she moved from Coombe Farm to Flat 5, Ouse View, Castlegate, York. She carried on working at the hospital and according to their records her salary continued to be paid until November 2011. The one change was that from 2007 to 2011 her salary was paid not into the Wades' joint account but into a current account still in her maiden name. We're checking the details, but it seems that the proceeds from the sale of Coombe Farm, once all loans were paid off, were deposited in that current account. She created a savings account associated with the current account and that is where the money sat until November 2008.'

'How much are we talking about here?' asked Gary.

'I checked with the agents,' said Peter, 'and if you add together everything she got from the parcels of land sold separately and what's now known as Coombe Farm, she must've got around £700,000. However, there were a number of small loans and debts, so she seems to have banked around £600,000.'

'And what happened after 19 November 2008?'

'That was the point when she moved the money. She divided it eight ways. Seven lots went off to seven different building societies or similar and the rest stayed in her current account. Odd move I thought.'

'Safety.' Peter turned round from the noticeboard where he had been pinning up some relevant details. '£50,000 was how much was protected by the Financial Services Compensation Scheme in 2008. She was lucky she hadn't lost any when the banks all fell apart earlier that year. So my guess is she was making sure that she didn't lose it in the event of any further crises.'

'Nothing particularly suspicious in that,' said Fiona. 'However, nor does it make it particularly easy to work out what she did with it after that. There are now seven other accounts to chase up as well as the original current account. What is clear from the hospital records is that she left her job there at the end of 2011. She gave up the lease on the flat in Stonegate at the same time but we're not sure yet where she went. She'd obviously stopped using the name Rachel Wade and gone back to Rachel Treadwell, but so far we haven't found anyone under either name. The 2011 census turned up some possibilities but so far nothing obvious. Until we get some answers back from the seven building society accounts we are stymied.'

That evening Gary took up the offer of a pint in the Stone Inn with Ben. The discovery that they had some colleagues in common, together with Ben's complete dissociation from Matthew Wade, decided Gary in favour of unwinding with a like-minded near colleague. Gary got to the Stone Inn first and bought his pint of Theakston's Old Peculier at the small bar. At this time in the evening it was relatively quiet and he was able to take a seat at a small table by one of the windows overlooking the main street. A trailer loaded with straw went by, navigating the sharp bend by the pub with some difficulty, and Gary wondered how often the pub had bales of straw brushing the windows. Perhaps this explained the lack of hanging baskets. On the other hand, perhaps it was just that the Stone Inn didn't lend itself to such frivolities. It was clearly a serious pub for serious drinking by locals. The floor was stone, tables were topped by naturally, as opposed to artistically, distressed copper, and the walls undecorated by anything so southern as either plaster or paint. On the whole, Gary approved. The seats were comfortable albeit showing signs of similar distress, and the beer was good. When he checked the menu he was surprised to see, alongside the pub staples of pies, chips and burgers, the offer of double trout and chips.

Ben arrived, also with a pint of Theakston's in hand.

'I saw you'd already got a drink,' he said. 'The next one's on me. Admiring the menu?'

'Intrigued by the double trout and chips,' said Gary.

'That's because there's a trout farm in the village, and they let the pub have the little-uns cheap. There's no one round here who would be satisfied with one small trout, so double trout and chips was the obvious solution.' Ben sat down at the table, resting his elbow on the wide windowsill. He took a large swig from his pint and wiped the foam from his lip.

'So, tell me about your boss.'

'Greg Geldard? What do you want to know?'

'He's not your usual Yorkshire DI, I imagine. At least, he's not the usual DI we get in Norfolk. What's his background?'

'He's an off-comed-un obviously.' Gary took another swig of his beer. 'He's one of your graduate entrants. Joined the Met fresh from a degree in psychology. Ambitious definitely, but not one of your academic let's not get our hands dirty types. I met an old friend of his from his student days once. It seems he was quite a wild lad on and off the rugby pitch, and for someone who, for whatever reason, was living in a teetotal Methodist Hall of Residence he had a legendary line-up of empty wine bottles on his pelmet.'

'Not one to abide by the rules?'

'Not always. But, the thing I find with Greg Geldard is that he plans. If he breaks a rule it's never by accident. I think his wild student days were part of his life plan. Taste the excitement, get the degree that would be relevant to his police career, then a haircut and overnight transformation from hairy wild man to police officer. Onwards and upwards ever since. At least, until he met Isabelle here in York.'

'Isabelle?'

'His wife. As you'll know, some tactical moves between uniformed and plainclothes, and between forces, can really accelerate a career if that's what you want. Greg's quite open about what he had in mind until he met and fell in love with his Yorkshire songstress. And jolly crabby he gets too, when she's away on a tour. I think his original aim was a leapfrogging promotion back to the Met as a Detective Chief Inspector. Now he seems to have stalled at Detective Inspector.'

'A spectacular resolution to the current problem would suit him nicely then?'

'And not just him. But not to the point of poor process if that's what you're worried about.' Gary looked at Ben sharply.

'Well, obviously I'm concerned about Tristan. She's an old friend. But I'm sure the evidence will put her in the clear. On which topic, getting any further with the bones?' Ben asked.

'Not much,' said Gary. 'You already know from the papers that the skeleton's been identified as Matthew Wade, but we still haven't found Rachel.'

'And she has to be a person of interest.'

'Of course. And her movements following the sale of the farm might be thought to be suspicious. Not obviously so, and there may indeed be a perfectly innocent explanation, but it hasn't made her any easier to trace.'

'Bank accounts? Census?'

'Tried all the above. The info's coming through but it's slow. And to be sure about her movements, we need detail from all her accounts. What's slightly more worrying is that she doesn't figure in the 2011 census, at least not as far as we can see. She went back to her maiden name after she sold the farm. That wouldn't be surprising if she was perfectly innocent and still under the impression she had been deserted by her husband. On the other hand, perhaps that was the first move towards hiding her steps. We haven't found her registered with any utility companies neither.'

'She is the obvious suspect.' Ben downed the rest of his pint and looked at Gary's rapidly emptying glass. 'Ready for another?' he asked, 'and how about some food?'

'Don't mind if I do,' said Gary, 'the wife's out with her old school friends tonight so there'll be nowt on offer at home. And I need summat to soak up this beer. But aren't you eating with Tristan?'

'She's got a meeting of the Dairy Goats Association. She wasn't going to go, given all the kerfuffle, but I encouraged her that a break away from the farm talking about something other than death would be a good thing. An evening discussing milk yields and cheese-making is just what she needs. Want to try the double trout and chips?'

'I think I'll pass on the trout,' said Gary. 'Not really a fish man meself. How are the pies?'

'How are your pies, Jenny love?' said Ben to the lady behind the bar. She flipped him with a, luckily, clean beer mat and said, 'You know all about my pies, Ben. You have my steak and ale every time you visit.'

Ben looked over at Gary with a raised eyebrow and turned back to Jenny. 'Two steak and ales it is then, Jenny, with chips and veg and plenty of extra gravy.'

'No bother,' she said. 'I'll bring it over when it's ready.'

Gary went back to the table with two brimming glasses of Old Peculier, knives and forks tucked in his shirt pocket.

'You'll enjoy the pie,' he said to Gary. 'The meat comes from Asquith's up on the hill and Jenny makes the pastry herself. The gravy is proper stuff too. None of that powdered rubbish here. Oh sorry.'

He realised that Gary was on the phone, his right index finger pressed into his right ear, the phone pressed to his left. He was clearly struggling with the lack of signal inside the stone-built inn and with a raised apologetic eyebrow he went outside. Ben sat down with the two beers and picked up one of the old newspapers lying on the table beside him. It was open at the page that reported the sensational findings at Coombe Farm, and he grimaced as he found himself reading some of Sharon Dyble's flights of fancy.

Gary came back in, accompanied by a gust of warm, chaff-laden air and the noise of another farm trailer rumbling past the pub.

'We've got something back from one of the building societies,' he said. 'Late in 2011 she emptied the account and the money went to a company called NYA. Ring any bells with you?'

'The only NYA I know,' said Ben, 'is the Norfolk Yacht Agency. It's never that!'

'It is too,' said Gary, then changed the subject as two plates laden with pie, chips and peas and the specified boat of extra gravy arrived at their copper-topped table. By the time Jenny had added sauces, salt-and-pepper and a portion of battered onion rings there was little room for anything else.

'Onion rings on the house,' she announced. 'Enjoy, gentlemen!' and sashayed back to the bar where a couple of locals were now awaiting her attention.

Adding salt to his chips with generosity and little thought for his blood pressure, Gary looked over his shoulder at the new arrivals. For the moment they were busy exchanging insults with Jenny and ordering their beer, but he took the precaution of lowering his voice.

'It seems the lady bought herself a boat,' he said to Ben. 'What sort of a boat would you get for £50k?'

'Back in 2011? Quite a decent one I would have thought. But of course, she might have spent more than £50k. It will be very interesting to see if any more money went from savings accounts to boat-buying. In my time, and still today, the Norfolk Yacht Agency sells all sorts of boats, from little Broads boats to fully sea-worthy cruisers. One of the latter would easily take her across the Channel and anywhere she chose. Perhaps she was leaving the country.'

'Rather elaborate,' said Gary, around a mouthful of excellent steak and ale pie. 'Why not just get on a plane? No one was after her. No one was even looking for Matthew much.'

'The wicked flee'eth where no man pursueth. Sorry. Put that down to my churchy upbringing. But it is true that a guilty conscience can make you behave oddly.'

Gary was clearing up the last of the gravy and peas from his plate.

'Smashing, love,' he called across to Jenny at the bar. 'Will you marry me?' Then to Ben, 'It seems we're going to be in touch with your mates in Norfolk again. We might even manage a trip down. When do you go back?'

'Sunday. The wife is joining us on Friday, then we both need to be back for work Monday morning. If you keep me posted, I'll ask around a bit. Informally of course!' he said hurriedly. 'But as a first responder I get over most of the county. I am even up and down the Broads quite a bit with one of the inshore lifeboats. If there's anything you'd like me to keep an eye open for, just let me know. Meantime, do you want a pud? Jenny does a mean syrup sponge and custard.'

'Better not.' Gary slapped an ample midsection. 'Better get back to the office and see what else we can rustle up. Keep in touch.'

Ben had one more pint and a chat with Jenny at the bar. She was a friendly, expansive woman in her mid-forties with mid-brown hair piled on top of her head so that she didn't have to keep sweeping it out of her way as she got hot, dashing between the kitchen and the bar. Ben marvelled that she managed to keep the bar going and did most of the cooking too, while scarcely breaking into a sweat. Her husband Dan dealt with barrels and helped out serving when necessary, but help in the kitchen was limited to a succession of skinny teenagers mainly washing up and dishing out.'

'Can't I tempt you to a syrup sponge, love?' she said. 'Sorry to hear about all your trouble up on the Coombes. It is a bit rough for Tristan, buying a smallholding in all innocence and then finding herself stuck with a corpse.'

'Not tonight, Jenny, thank you. And I'll pass on your good wishes to Tristan. She'll be glad to know she has some support in the village.'

'Course she has. Tell her to pop in here anytime she's feeling a bit down and I'll be happy to have a chat and a drink with her, on the house of course. And tell her not to take any notice of that Sharon. We say the noise she makes is like the bleeping sound as comes from a reversing lorry. Really irritating, but it does warn you to get out of the way.'

Making his way back up the hill on foot, Ben paused where Coombe Road turned off Main Street by the old churchyard. He could hear the noise of the water flowing through the beck at the bottom of the dale. Judging from the calls to his left, one of the ewes had lost her lambs and was announcing the opening of the milk bar. The hill was steep and even taking it steadily he was out of breath by the time he got back to the farmhouse. He paused by the fence that divided the farmyard from the paddock and took a moment to enjoy the view across the Vale of York. As darkness fell, he could see the twinkling of lights in the middle distance where a busy road crossed the Vale. The time when most of the view would've been lit by burning straw had passed. As he turned to go back into the farmhouse, Tristan drove in from the lane and parked by the garage.

'Any news?' she asked.

'Not much, although what there is, would you believe it, seems to point to Norfolk. I'll do some looking about when I get home.'

10

Rachel in Norfolk

By the autumn of 2012, Brizo and I were as comfortable on the *Edith* as though we had never lived anywhere else. The joy of waking up to the water lapping inches from my bed and the gentle snores from the dog on the floor; the simple pleasure of eating toast on the upper deck while the cold morning mist drifted across the waters of the Dyke; even the effort of lifting the bike from her spot on the after deck to the track by the mooring and pedalling up to the village for supplies of milk or bread; all of these things filled my new life and reinforced the barrier between Rachel today and Rachel Wade.

Philip grew on me, slowly but surely. At the beginning he was the helpful owner of several boat-related businesses, a friendly boss and then, gradually, friend. At the end of the morning in his cafe, cakes and pies would come my way.

'No point saving them till tomorrow,' he'd say, 'can you use them?'

At the end of my first year he started dropping by for little chats. He never came any further than the upper deck, would never accept anything more than a cup of coffee, or maybe a piece of his own cake, but always had some useful suggestion or something helpful to say. On several occasions he gave me a hand with small tasks that were easier with two pairs of hands. On another occasion, he helped with the Wi-Fi, and he offered a solution to my problems when the electrics packed up temporarily. Gradually, very slowly, we developed the habit of a final cup of coffee together at the end of each morning in the cafe, before the afternoon shift took over the customers.

Philip's face became as familiar to me as my own. I could have traced from memory every line from his nose to the corners of his mouth, every unevenness of shade around his temples, where the grey locks often flopped and shielded the skin from the sun. Had I been able to draw, I could have depicted a sequence of facial expressions with total accuracy, from the smile of greeting when I arrived, through the frown of concentration as he did the accounts, to the intent and focused look that he accorded my every comment. And yet I knew very little about him other than his life at the visitor centre and his face. I knew he had two grown-up sons but not whether he still had a wife. One of the other waitresses said he lived in a cottage in Ludham but I didn't know where and I never asked. I accepted our growing friendship with a complete lack of curiosity. The gentle, almost casual contact that we had suited me fine. Perhaps my lack of curiosity regarding his life was stoked by my reluctance to share any of mine. In any event, it came as quite a shock the day when he popped over to the *Edith* and mentioned an afternoon performance of Shakespeare by a visiting company, to be performed in the garden of the village hall, and suggested that I might like to accompany him. Apparently the play to be performed was *Twelfth Night*, and we had been discussing that very play the week before. I now wondered if it was Philip who had raised the subject in the first place and whether he had intended all along to invite me to the performance. I refused without a second thought. He smiled, said no problem, and went away, just as he had always done.

I was surprised by how much this mild and inoffensive invitation frightened me. I couldn't quite decide why. Yes, I wanted to keep my distance from people. Friendship was fine. I thought I was quite good at friends, but not so good at being intimate. But what I felt now was definitely fear, and an almost overwhelming desire to run away. Or at least, to put space between me and the challenge.

'Don't be ridiculous,' I told myself at one moment. Then at the next, 'Why couldn't he have left things as they were?'

I had liked having a friend. I liked living alone. Now it was all spoiled.

That evening I rang the pub and the cafe and explained that I would be away for a couple of days. I left a note for Philip, released my moorings and sailed off. I didn't go far. I dropped my mud-weight in the still waters of South Walsham Broad and stayed there the whole weekend. On Sunday evening I deliberately returned just as the light was failing and long after normal closing time. I thought, to my relief, that the cafe was locked up and silent. I moored the *Edith* back in her private spot and plugged into the electrics with a considerable feeling of satisfaction. Makeshift barbecues and cold food had palled quite quickly.

I had just settled down for an evening watching TV, with Brizo curled across my lap, when I heard steps on the wharf and a familiar knock on the hull.

Philip hadn't climbed aboard, as had been his normal custom, but was still standing on the wharf. He was holding an immense bunch of flowers, for which a moment's thought would have indicated I was going to struggle to find vases.

'An apology,' he said, 'at least, it was meant as such, although I realise, with hindsight, that they're probably just going to be a pain in the neck.' He smiled at me a little uncertainly. 'I think I offended you, and I never meant to. I just wanted to say that the invitation to the picnic and *Twelfth Night* was just that. If anything, I was thinking of it as a slightly extended coffee break. I'm sorry if I got it wrong. And I'd be more than happy to go back to just coffee if that was what suited you.'

I couldn't help but smile.

'You'd better bring those aboard,' I said, 'and help me find enough jugs to put them in. Would you like a coffee? Just a coffee!'

Philip smiled back. 'Just a coffee would be fine,' he said and for the first time came down the steps into the saloon.

After that weekend, which in my own mind I labelled 'Shakespeare and Flowers', my relationship with Philip continued steadily. And 'relationship' was how I started to think of it, despite my fears. They were still there, hidden away in my secret place, but on the surface Philip had succeeded in reassuring me. And on the surface was where my life carried on. We still had a regular cup of coffee at the end of the mornings I worked in his shop. He started to come round to the *Edith* fairly regularly in the early evenings when his shop closed; in the beginning just for coffee, but eventually coffee segued into supper. It all happened so gently and naturally I hardly noticed. Coffee-and-cake became coffee, cake and sandwiches; then coffee and lasagne, and eventually supper and wine.

One threshold it took me a long time to cross was to allow Philip to stay the night. Not that he ever asked or made a move in that direction, but I did feel the social pressure as an evening drew to its close. Of one thing I was absolutely certain: I would never again have a husband or a live-in partner or anyone who could apply the same sort of pressure on me as had Matthew.

The step that took me over that threshold was a cruise on the *Edith*. Philip had, on a number of occasions, expressed a wish to visit some other parts of the Broads by boat. Eventually, I began to feel that I had little choice other than to offer to take him. We began with day trips and enjoyed them so much that we began to plan a longer visit to the southern Broads in the autumn. I began to feel very awkward indeed about owning a boat with several bedrooms and Philip discussing where he might stay in a pub or guest house at our destination.

One night at the end of supper, clutching my wine glass so tightly I threatened to snap the stem, I summoned up my courage. Ignoring all the uncertainties and inner warnings, I said, 'Philip, you are welcome to stay on the *Edith* when we go south to Beccles. But I need to make something clear. I'm inviting you as a friend, a valued friend, and the bedroom in the prow would be yours.' I looked at him, hoping I had made myself clear. He looked back, holding up his wine glass and looking at me through the remaining liquid, one eye distorted by the refractions in the glass.

'Thank you, Rachel. I really appreciate the invitation and I understand.'

That trip went well enough, but I was surprised by how awkward it felt having someone else sleeping on the boat. That night Brizo slept with me rather than on her bed in the saloon, and I woke at every movement in the prow. Thank God for the two shower rooms! At least I didn't have the embarrassment of meeting Philip before breakfast. We had a great time sailing the boat together, laughing, joking, relaxing over the newspapers after a pub lunch and enjoying the sights and sounds and, in Brizo's case, smells of the Broads. During the day we fell into our usual friendly banter. The evenings, however, got more and more awkward the later it got, until eventually Brizo and I retreated to our safe place in the stern and left Philip to put himself to bed in the prow.

Philip gave no indication that he shared my uneasiness to any degree. Indeed, when he left the *Edith* at Womack Staithe at the end of the trip I discovered he had left his razor and toothbrush in the guest shower room. I found them when I stripped the bed in his room and started to give the *Edith* her end-of-trip clean-up. I stared at them, unable to make my mind up whether he had left them behind on purpose like a cat marking its territory, or had simply forgotten them as he packed up to return to the cafe. When I went along for my morning shift the following day I took them with me.

'You left something behind yesterday,' I said. He took them from me with a quizzical look.

'They're spares. I didn't think leaving them would be a problem.' And he looked hurt.

'No problem. I just thought…' My sentence tailed off and I went to work, feeling embarrassed and guilty.

Two weeks later he suggested another long trip. I agreed, although feeling a little doubtful, remembering my concerns in the night. To be honest, I was also feeling a bit manipulated, but if I articulated that to myself, I felt silly again. I had enjoyed the trip – at least all the daylight parts of it. We had fun, we enjoyed ourselves. What was I fussing about? This time, when he brought his things on board he did it with a bit of a flourish.

'I thought I'd only have to bring them back again,' waving his toothbrush and razor. This time when he left them in the shower room at the end of the trip I left them there. I didn't feel able to return them to him again.

That Christmas I was invited for the first time to Philip's bungalow in Johnson Lane. The village of Ludham trailed down towards Ludham Bridge with a long double row of cottages and bungalows and the second pub, the Dog. Philip's was one of the small square bungalows about halfway between Ludham Church and Ludham Bridge. Inside, it surprised me with its spartan decor. I hadn't seen Philip as a minimalist, but the bungalow certainly contained the absolute minimum of 'stuff'. I wasn't allowed to see much of the kitchen. When I offered to help with Christmas lunch Philip shooed me out and sat me down in the living room with a glass of bubbly. I just got a glimpse of IKEA-style plain kitchen cupboards and then the door was firmly closed in my face.

I wandered round the sitting room. At one end was a plain glass-topped table and four chairs. The table was set for a four-course lunch for two, with a centre-piece of holly and ivy. There was a square leather sofa and two very geometric leather chairs set around a glass-topped coffee table. Apart from a TV and a music centre in one corner that was all there was. The floor was stripped pine boards, the walls painted pale grey, the woodwork white, and a square white carpet lay before the wood burner in the fireplace. Much as I missed Brizo and felt bad about leaving her on her own on the boat, I was glad I'd not brought her with me. She would not fit in this environment!

Lunch was excellent. We started with smoked salmon and crab cocktail. Our second course was a twice-baked cheese soufflé, then we had a pause before the main event of roast turkey and all the trimmings.

'I have cheated on the pudding,' announced Philip. 'I am afraid that's just a plum pudding from Marks & Spencer.'

I smiled. 'That's fine. I haven't made plum pudding in years. I don't think many people do now.' I kept to myself the reflection that the crab cocktail, turkey crown and all its trimmings had also come from Marks & Spencer. I recognised them. If Philip wanted to take credit for some skilled reheating and putting on plates, that was fine by me. It was a mild enough deception after all.

After lunch and the Queen's speech we settled down with a glass of brandy by the fire; but when Philip got out his Monopoly set, obviously planning a lengthy game, I became uneasy.

'I am sorry, Philip,' I said, 'but I will need to leave soon. I need to let Brizo out for a walk and give her her supper.' Philip looked hurt.

'I would've thought you'd be staying the whole day. Surely Brizo would be all right.'

'No I'm sorry, I can't leave her shut in much longer. It's not fair.'

'You could have arranged for someone to let her out.'

'Not on Christmas Day, surely you see that.'

'But I just thought, given all the trouble I had gone to, that you would have made some suitable arrangements. She is just a dog.'

I thought it was time I went and gathered up my belongings.

'Thank you for a lovely lunch, Philip. I'm sorry to disturb your arrangements but I do need to go. It's been a lovely day. Anyway,' I said, trying to lighten the atmosphere, 'if I don't go home soon I'm going to be drunk in charge of a bicycle.'

I pedalled off feeling guilty. Thankfully, although the skies were heavy and grey I was spared both rain and snow. The road was almost empty of traffic at that time of day. Most people, I imagined, were enjoying an afternoon nap or, if children, were playing with their new toys. I was surprised when I heard a vehicle behind me travelling at speed, and very alarmed as it got closer. The road was not particularly wide just there and I was worried at the pace it was going. Glancing over my shoulder, I was doubly surprised to see that it was Philip's car. After all that he had drunk that day, there was no way he should have been behind the wheel. I stopped on the verge and put my left foot down. It was lucky I did, as the car came past so close I fell into the hedge. It screeched to a halt in front of me and Philip leapt out.

'I am so sorry, Rachel. I am so sorry. Are you all right? I was just coming to see if you'd be willing to come back. I'd planned such a pleasant evening.'

I picked myself up, dusting myself down and pulling twigs out of my hair.

'I'm fine, but you really shouldn't be driving. I suggest you leave the car there and walk home.'

'But, Rachel…'

'I'm sorry, Philip. I explained. I really do need to go home.' I got back on my bike and left him behind me in the road. I didn't stop to see whether he got back in the car. I was sick and I was shaking. It felt as though he had knocked me off the bike on purpose. All sorts of old nightmares rose up in my mind and the tears welled so that I could hardly see where I was going. I had never been so glad to get back to the *Edith* and Brizo. We went for a walk through the woods, along the tow path by Womack Dyke and then back home for Brizo's tea and a scratch supper for me. I was extra careful about locking up the boat that night. This was another night Brizo spent sleeping with me.

11

Edgar and Coombe Farm

Saturday was Chris's day off, so Ben was giving Tristan a hand with the morning milking while Paula planned a slap-up fried breakfast for the three of them. The kitchen window faced the drive, looking down over the silage bales to the Vale of York, so Paula was the first to notice a small red car coming up Coombe Lane and turning in at the farm entrance. The car pulled round the garden wall and parked in front of the garage as though the driver knew where he was going. After a short pause the door opened and the occupant got out a little stiffly. It was an older man, dressed very smartly in a tweed coat with velvet lapels and dark trousers, probably in his seventies and, judging by the way he moved, with some problems in his knees or hips. He levered himself out of the car then leaned on the roof as he pushed the door closed. Still leaning on the roof, he looked around the farm and particularly at the goats in the paddock behind the house.

Paula put down the bowl of eggs that she was beating and went to the back door.

'Can I help you? I'm afraid Tristan is still busy milking.'

The gentleman looked round. He was thin but not fragile, with a countryman's face and thin, fluffy grey hair brushed back under his flat cap. His eyes were blue, he had a pleasant smile and when he held his hand out his handshake was firm.

'Pleased to meet you. I hope I'm not going to be a bother but I can assure you I'm not from the press.' Paula laughed.

'I thought you probably weren't. Was it Tristan you wanted to see? I'm a friend of hers. My name is Paula. Paula Asheton.'

The man took his cap off and scratched his head with the peak.

'Well I suppose it is Miss Smith I ought to see but truth to tell, now I'm here, I am not really sure why I came. My name is Edgar Treadwell. I lived here for a year or so with my sister just after Matthew disappeared. We all thought that Matthew had run off with another woman, but now,' and he waved a vague arm around the farmyard, 'now I don't know what to think.'

Paula saw that under the gentlemanly manner was a layer of confusion and concern.

'I think you'd better come in. Come in and have a cup of tea. Tristan will be back as soon as the milking is finished. Did you have any breakfast this morning?'

Edgar sat at the kitchen table with a bit of a bump and looked around him.

'You're very kind,' he said. 'No, I didn't have much before I came out. Didn't seem to have much appetite really.'

'Then have some breakfast with us. You probably know the routine. We are about to have second breakfast and there's plenty for four. Here's Tristan now.'

Tristan and Ben both came in, laughing about the antics of the goats.

'You need to come and see Noemi's latest trick,' said Ben as he came through the door, and then stopped when he saw the stranger at the table. Edgar got to his feet, leaning on the table edge, and held his hand out to Tristan.

'I'm sorry to bother you, Miss Smith, but I've been contacted by the police and I've read the papers too. I couldn't stay home any longer. I'm Rachel's brother and I lived here with her when Matthew disappeared. We all thought he'd run away with another woman,' he repeated. 'I really thought he'd run away.'

Ben waved him back to his chair.

'Let's all have breakfast,' said Paula, 'while it's hot, and then we can talk.' She shot a look at Tristan, who pulled out a chair next to Edgar and sat down.

'I'm very pleased to meet you,' she said. 'I met Rachel when I bought Coombe Farm but only the once. Do you know where she is now?'

'Not precisely,' said Edgar. 'She rather shut us all out of her life when she moved away. After she left York we didn't even have her address, other than a boat in Norfolk. I rang her mobile and sent emails and text messages, but apart from a few short messages early on never got much of a response. I haven't heard much from her for a few years now. I wondered if you might know something, Miss Smith.'

'Call me Tristan.' She passed him a plate piled high with

a good Yorkshire fried breakfast. 'And get yourself round that. Everything looks better on a fried breakfast.'

Edgar thanked her, taking the plate and starting to eat.

'And no further discussion until we have finished breakfast,' she said, 'we've plenty of time for a chat afterwards.'

Dishes all piled in the sink and more tea poured all round, they all four sat at the kitchen table. Edgar poured sugar into his tea and sighed.

'I gather they're sure it's Matthew?'

Ben answered for all of them. 'Yes. Matthew's dentist from Cambridge has confirmed the identification. Do you know if Matthew had any other family?'

'Not any more.' Edgar sipped his tea. 'His father died shortly after they married and his mother died not long after that. I vaguely remember a cousin at the wedding but we had no contact with them for years. It's Rachel I'd like to find. I can't believe what they're saying about her. I suppose it's what they always say, murder tends to sit close to home, but I can't believe it of Rachel. Although from all accounts she'd had plenty of excuse. Right little shit that Matthew, if you'll pardon me, ladies.'

'They weren't getting on then?' asked Ben. Paula frowned at him and shook her head.

'That's a difficult question to answer in a word. I never saw them quarrel, but as I explained to the police, I thought Matthew was a controlling bully. It wouldn't surprise me if he was a wife beater too. I spent most of my career as a solicitor dealing with divorce cases,' he explained, 'and I learned to spot the signs. It was very distressing to see them

129

in my own family; the put-downs, the snide remarks, the loss of contact with family and friends, the behavioural changes I saw in Rachel. We discussed it as a family and compared notes. Unfortunately, there wasn't much we could do, since Rachel wouldn't talk to us about Matthew. The one really good precaution had already been taken by our grandfather when he put the deeds to Coombe Farm in Rachel's name alone. He never said anything to the rest of us, but he was a wise old bird and I think he'd already suspected what the rest of us only saw later.

'Anyway, Rachel certainly changed very much after she married and she changed back again after he disappeared. She was a lively happy girl when we were children. All the time she was married to Matthew, she seemed to get more and more subdued. And thinner. And I did notice she could do nothing right. If she cooked, it wasn't gourmet enough; if she dressed to go out, she wasn't smart enough; if she went shopping, either she bought the wrong things or she spent too much. If she went out with friends she was needed on the farm. She missed a lot of family get-togethers around that time, but I saw enough to realise he was bullying her. By the time he disappeared she had no self-confidence left at all.'

'Did Matthew have any enemies?' Ben noted the scowl on Paula's face and added, 'It would seem he wasn't a very nice man. People like that make enemies.'

'Not that I know of. In fact, he liked playing the squire around the village, and was very generous with money he hadn't got. Always buying drinks in the pub, you know the sort. Not that he had much respect from the village either.'

Edgar looked at Ben very straight. 'Your average Yorkshire-man can see through bullshit like a laser through jelly. Most of his neighbours had little time for his carry-ons, judging by what they said to me after he'd gone. Now,' he said to Tristan, 'I've probably trespassed on your time for long enough and you've been very kind. Thank you for my breakfast too.' He stood up. 'I'm not really sure why I came, but I'm glad I did. If you hear anything of Rachel, please pass her address on to me. I would very much like to see her again.'

'We surely will,' said Tristan, looking at Ben. 'But while you're here, would you like to look around the farm?'

'Thank you, but no, not this time. I'm not sure I'm ready for that today. But if I might come back some time?'

'Of course,' said Tristan, as she saw him to his car.

When they had seen the old man off, Tristan, Ben and Paula went back into the house. Paula automatically cleared the dirty mugs into the sink and they sat down at the kitchen table again.

'I could see you glowering at me,' said Ben, 'but I thought there might be some useful information to be had.'

'You were in police mode,' said Paula, 'and I thought that nice old man had troubles enough on his mind at the moment. He's afraid that his sister murdered her husband, and your questions were leading him to believe that was highly likely.'

'I'm afraid it is. The skeleton was Matthew Wade, he disappeared from the village and his wife didn't report him missing, and information is accumulating that suggests he was bullying and abusive. He also seems to have been spending

131

money that was largely earned by Rachel or from Rachel's property. In other words, she had plenty of motive, and every opportunity to dump the body in the waste disposal pit.'

'Well I still think you were hard on poor old Edgar. You could have been a bit more sensitive.'

Tristan was staring out of the window, silent. She watched as two pigeons balanced themselves precariously on the edge of the cattle trough in order to drink. They shuffled about, jostling for a position that gave them access to the water but didn't take them too close to the goats drinking at the other end. She could see Heidi eyeing them up and thought it likely that unless they drank swiftly one of them was going for an early bath. There was a squawk and a flutter of wings as Heidi made her move.

'What do you think, Tristan?' asked Paula.

'I am afraid I'm being selfish,' said Tristan. 'I'm sorry for old Edgar, but if it's a choice between suspicion falling on the previous owner of this farm who is highly likely to have murdered her husband, and suspicion falling on me, I know where I would prefer it to lie.'

Paula felt somewhat abashed. 'Of course, the whole idea of you having anything to do with it is just so unlikely that I never stopped to think. What happens next?'

'Let's just sum up what we think the police know,' said Ben. 'First, they know the skeleton is Matthew Wade. Second, the forensics suggest he had a blow to the head before he died that could have caused his death. Third, they know the body would have skeletonised very rapidly in the circumstances in that pit, so they can't know for sure when it was placed there. However, given that Matthew was not seen in the village after early March 2007, there is little reason to think that he didn't go in the pit more or less straight away. In some ways, what there is no evidence of is just as interesting. There seems to be no evidence of him having an affair or of having left home with someone else. And so far, no evidence of him living anywhere else for any length of time after his last sighting in the village.'

'What about the bank statement details that Edgar was talking about? What about him spending money after he left the farm?' asked Paula.

'You need to be more precise about what the evidence is telling us,' remarked Ben. 'All we know is that debit cards were used. We don't know by whom. It's perfectly possible that Rachel paid a visit, or even several visits, to London and did the spending herself.'

'Except that it was lambing time,' pointed out Tristan. 'There's no way she could have left the farm for any length of time. Even if she was prepared to neglect her livestock, someone would have known; and after only a few weeks Edgar was living here himself and he vouches for the fact that she was here at the time money was being spent by Matthew. So if someone other than Matthew was using those cards, is it likely that Rachel could have had an accomplice?'

'An accomplice is always possible, but not very probable,' answered Ben. 'She'd be putting her future in their hands. And what would be in it for them? There's no evidence that Rachel had any significant relationships other than with Matthew. When she needed help in 2007 she called on her family. As for what next, the last bit of information I got off the police was that Rachel spent £70,000 with the

Norfolk Yacht Agency at Brundall in 2011. That fits with what Edgar said about a boat.'

'Norfolk! Well, that's a bit of a coincidence. Perhaps you could do some looking around when we get home.'

'Perhaps I could, provided I can do it without stepping on anyone's toes. I might have to look a few friends up when I get home.'

12

Rachel, Norfolk 2012–13

That year, as in the last two, I saw the New Year in with Brizo. On New Year's Eve I unplugged my electrics and left my private mooring behind. I decided this was one evening when I wasn't going to worry about unwanted, or for that matter, wanted, visitors. Early in the frosty morning I quietly slipped my moorings and sailed down the dyke past Womack Staithe, then turned sharp right to loop behind the island to the public moorings hidden on the other side. As I had expected, I had the place to myself except for wildfowl resting on the bank and exploring the still waters. A swan looked at Brizo very much askance, then waddled into the water and sailed gracefully away. The ducks were braver, or greedier, and swam up to the *Edith* looking for scraps. Without an electric supply, other than from the battery, I couldn't use the TV or the microwave. But I had plenty of diesel so the hot water and heating were on, and I had light, books, and the gas stove and cooker. And Brizo of course. She was delighted with the change in her circumstances and lay on the forepeak, watching the ducks and coots. The frosty weather didn't seem to bother her at all, but she did deign to come inside when I announced that breakfast was ready.

I had decided to treat myself to a New Year brunch; eggs Benedict, followed by croissants with blackberry jam from the farmers' market. Brizo had her normal biscuits breakfast, then sat with tongue lolling while she waited for her share of mine. Her blue eye always seemed especially bright when fixed on food, while her brown eye was especially pleading. From her perspective it was a winning combination.

'Right, Brizo. Your turn now, Jack Spratt's wife.' She always got the fat I fussily trimmed off ham or bacon, plus an extra bit just for love. Then she got a lick of my plate, with particular enthusiasm for the smears of hollandaise, and finally the corner of croissant I didn't quite finish. Both of us replete, I put the dishes in the sink to wash later and looked over my supplies for supper.

Given my limited non-electric facilities I had settled for easy options. Like Philip I had resorted to Marks & Spencer to do the heavy lifting. Smoked fish soup to start, then duck terrine with French toast, fillet steak and salad for the main event, profiteroles for afters. I was very pleased with my arrangements.

'Just because it's just the two of us, Brizo, no reason why we shouldn't celebrate.'

We spent part of the afternoon just pottering along the bank. I had to keep Brizo on the lead around the wildfowl, but she was delighted to have a new lot of sniffs to explore.

I saw one boat through the trees, as it passed down the dyke to the staithe; otherwise I passed my day in blissful and safe isolation. By mid-afternoon we were cosily ensconced in the *Edith*'s saloon, a glass of sherry in my hand, a bone in Brizo's teeth and a new book awaiting my attention. I had been saving the new Simon Serrailler book for some months. It had come out in October last year, but somehow escaped my attention at the time. Now it was the perfect self-indulgence for a solitary New Year's Eve.

Around six o' clock my mobile rang. Rats! I'd forgotten I was not totally uncontactable. The ID was Philip. I hesitated but ignored it. Right in the middle of my supper it rang again. This time it was Edgar. I ignored it again, but made a mental note I would text in the morning to wish him Happy New Year. I still felt guilty about Edgar. The third time it rang there was no caller ID. I hesitated, then answered it but didn't say anything. It was Philip.

'Rachel? Rachel, where are you? Please speak to me. I am sorry about the other day, but I had made a great effort to make everything nice for you. Rachel?'

'I'm sorry,' I said. 'I have very poor reception. I can't hear anything. Please try again another day.' And I rang off.

The call put me on edge, and I found I was listening for a dinghy or a motor boat. There was no other way to reach me at present. After a while, I relaxed and listened to the sound of waterfowl on the bank and in the water. Then I tensed. I was sure I could hear the sounds of oars dipping slowly and quietly. The air was very cold and still and sounds carry a long way over water. Perhaps I could hear someone by the staithe? But no, the oars were coming closer. The sounds got louder. My phone rang again. The same number. Then a voice from the river.

'I know you're there, Rachel. I know you're there.'

Brizo barked, and I couldn't hear anything else. She barked again, and I locked the saloon door with shaking hands. Then I put my hand over her muzzle.

'Shh Brizo.' She was quiet for a moment, then pulled free and barked again. One sharp bark. Then silence again. I listened hard, but couldn't hear anything else. Carefully I pulled the curtain to one side. And screamed. There was a face, a mask staring in at the window. Brizo let loose a fusillade of barking and went wild at the window as I dropped the curtain and fell back onto the sofa. Our movements were making the *Edith* rock at her moorings. I couldn't tell whether anyone had climbed aboard.

Eventually Brizo fell silent and I listened tensely. I could hear nothing. After what felt like hours, but was probably only fifteen minutes or so of silent waiting, the *Edith* also became still. I crept to the next window along and squinted sideways to where the face had been on the rail. Nothing. I looked at the water. Also nothing. Not even a mallard or a coot. Brizo was quiet now and seemingly not worried. She sat down for a vigorous scratch behind her ear. I listened some more, then, taking my cue from Brizo, I stealthily unlocked the door and peeked out. Nothing. Then after a breathless pause, the sound of fireworks at the staithe frightened the life out of me. Brizo started barking, but for a different and obvious reason. So we both retreated to the saloon and I drew the curtains together. Then I went to bed; Brizo and I together again.

*

After breakfast on New Year's Day I returned to my mooring, somewhat warily. Around tea time Philip turned up, waving from the bank.

'Happy New Year, Rachel. I have a New Year's present for Brizo.' He flourished a long and oddly shaped parcel. 'Actually it was meant to be a Christmas present but you set off in such a hurry I never got to give it to you. That's why I chased you down the road. But I admit,' and he spread his hands as much as he could while still holding the parcel, 'driving was poor judgement on my part. Still, she can have it now.' He stepped aboard the *Edith* and I backed off down the deck.

'What about last night?'

'Last night? I admit I spent last night boringly and virtuously home alone. I even went to bed early.' He looked at me, head on one side. 'I did try to ring you once, but didn't get an answer. I assumed you had gone out on some mad social whirl.'

'You rang just once? And what about the trip round my boat?'

'Sorry. Not me. I was watching the modern-day equivalent of *The White Heather Club* from my bed. Did you have someone wandering round the *Edith*?'

I hesitated.

'Someone came to the boat and peered in wearing a fright mask,' I said, as we both went down into the saloon.

The remnants of my supper were still by the sink, including the empty bottle of sherry and the half-empty bottle of Chianti.

'Looking at the empties, are you sure you didn't dream it all? Come on, let Brizo have her present.' I shut up, and

139

Brizo enthusiastically unwrapped her parcel. The present was a tennis ball thrower. She already had one, but I didn't say anything and we both said 'thank you' very prettily as we went down to the staithe, where there was space for her to try it out. Had I imagined everything? Yes I'd had a drink or two, but I hadn't been drunk. And Brizo had barked. 'Brizo would bark at a bird,' I told myself, and pushed my misgivings out of sight.

After the bank holiday, our routines went back to normal. We did our winter stock-take at the shop, and the tea shop near the church closed for a couple of weeks for refurbishment. I thought at first this was going to cut my income, at least temporarily, but they were very happy to have an extra pair of hands painting, cleaning up, and eventually fitting new chair covers. Philip and I reverted to our coffee and cake on the mornings that I worked in the shop, and we had supper together a couple of times a week. The memory of my scary New Year faded, until I concluded I must after all have imagined the mask and the oars. I was confused and stopped thinking about it.

It was late spring when my trusty little car decided to give up the ghost. She had been making funny noises for a while, but being a firm believer in the principle that anything oily required a Y chromosome, I had ignored it. Now the disease was terminal. According to the man-who-knows, the gear box was shot and even if the engine had not seized, that would probably have consigned it to the knacker's yard anyway. Plainly I needed a new car, and equally plainly that meant recourse to one of my savings accounts.

Philip was very concerned about the demise of my little Ka and very worried that I would not be able to replace it. He kept offering to run me around, and saying that I didn't need a car really, he would always be happy to take me places. I said something vague about having a bit put away, and accepted a lift to a Ford car agency in Norwich to look at second-hand models. There I picked out another used Ka, and made the arrangements with the agent to collect it the following week, paying cash. I was rather discomforted by Philip hanging around at my shoulder, reading my paperwork, but couldn't think of a polite way to get rid of him. I tried very hard to go to collect my car on my own. I picked a day when I knew he was busy and booked a taxi, but as soon as he got wind of the arrangement he cancelled everything else and insisted on taking me. Remembering the fuss on Christmas Day, I decided it was probably easier to go with the flow, and accepted with as good a grace as I could muster.

I had to call at a branch of Nationwide to collect the cash, and he insisted on accompanying me there too, arguing that I shouldn't be wandering about unprotected with large sums in cash. Unfortunately, his protectiveness included keeping close to my shoulder again. Even the lady at the till was disconcerted by his closeness and asked him rather sharply to give me more space.

'I'm a friend,' he said. She looked at me and said nothing further. What could I say? I wasn't comfortable and I was pretty sure he managed a squint at my passbook and the total in it.

A month or so after I bought my car, Philip turned up at the *Edith* with a bottle of champagne and truffles. I felt mean for thinking that they looked like another special offer from his favourite store.

'I know it looks like a celebration, which may be a bit presumptuous of me, but I'm hoping it will be a celebration,' and he smacked the bottle down on the saloon table with something of an air of triumph combined with trepidation. 'I've been working for some time on the possibility of expanding the shop into a proper cafe with an al fresco eating area for the summer. I've got all the ideas, I'm pretty certain I've got the planning permission, so all I need is the capital. I'm inviting you to come in with me and become a partner in the new Womack Cafe.'

I sat down with a bump and stared at him. All my instincts were to say no. The ghost of Grandfather Treadwell rose in my mind, his finger wagging, his expression stern. He protected me once, it was up to me this time.

'I'm sorry, Philip,' I said, 'but I don't have that sort of money. Perhaps you'd better save the champagne for an occasion when you are genuinely able to celebrate. I really do wish you well, and if I can help in any other way I will,' I looked at his lowering brow nervously, 'but I don't have the money to invest.'

'You had enough to buy the car with cash,' he pointed out and his expression and tone both dripped with acid. 'If you don't want to help me out just say so. I thought I'd earned some generosity from you and certainly some honesty. But I know you've got the cash. I was with you in the building society, remember? If you don't want to lend to me or don't trust me, just say so.' And he flounced off.

Part of me seriously considered telling him to sod off.

'Did I need this hassle?' Then I thought some more. Was I being unfair? He was, after all, offering me a share in his business. Should I have been a bit more gracious? Explained better? I chased after him along the path to the staithe.

'Philip, Philip!' I was panting, both with the effort of running and the stress of having to say no. 'I'm sorry, Philip. I genuinely don't have enough spare cash to be able to invest in somebody else's project.'

'I thought it was something we would do together, a joint project.' And he stormed off. 'You can be very hurtful sometimes, Rachel,' he shouted back over his shoulder.

We still hadn't made it up when we met in the cafe the following day. There was no coffee and cake, no chat, no friendly banter. I went home to the *Edith* rather depressed. Philip could be a little demanding, but there was no denying I enjoyed spending time with him. I enjoyed our days out. But if it was going to be like this, perhaps it was time to move on.

That evening Philip surprised me by coming round, again with a bottle in his hand although this time it was Chianti.

'I thought we needed to make up,' he said. 'No matter how you hurt me I am still your friend.' He poured me a large glass and as he did so spilled some on the saloon table. 'Oh sorry. If you get me a cloth I'll mop it up.' I went to the galley, came back with a cloth and we drank the Chianti. I wasn't really in the mood and was drinking rather slowly, but when he finished his glass he topped mine up as well. When he left I had part of a bottle and a whole glass still in hand.

'I'll see you tomorrow. It'll be all right, you'll see.'

That night I slept very heavily indeed. In fact, I fell into bed almost comatose, forgetting to shut Brizo in the saloon, forgetting even to clean my teeth. As it turned out that was lucky. The bit about Brizo I mean, because I woke in the early hours of the morning to her barking right in my face and a strange orange glow coming through the windows. I really struggled into consciousness but as I did so became aware of a dreadful snapping and crackling noise. The orange glow was getting brighter and brighter as I rushed onto deck. The garden shed on the bank only a few metres from my mooring was alight. As I watched, an orange sail of fire plumed into the air and drifted off, snapping. There were muffled explosions as what I assumed to be cans of paint heated up and blew their lids off, and the glow got brighter and brighter. The heat was intense. I was at serious risk of losing the Edith, Brizo and everything I had. My heart couldn't have beat faster if it tried and my hands seemed to have a life of their own, shaking with a tremor I couldn't stop.

I had no time to think, just time to react. I rushed into the galley and grabbed a carving knife from the magnet on the wall, then hurried on deck and, with frantic energy, severed the three mooring ropes holding the *Edith* to the wharf. I did the one nearest the fire first, before things got any worse, and even as I did so I could feel my fringe frizzling and my skin crisping in the heat. As I moved on to the second I wondered if I was being stupid. Should I grab Brizo and jump off the far side of the *Edith* into the water? The second rope came free and I moved on to the third, just as there was a big bang and a Calor gas bottle blew a jet of fire clear over the *Edith*'s bows. Then the third mooring rope gave way and without bothering to start the engine I used my foot to push us hard from the bank. The *Edith* drifted out into the centre of the dyke and, my hand still shaking, I turned the key. Thankfully the engine started almost immediately. As we chugged down the dyke I got my phone out. A bar or two of signal thank God and I dialled 999.

'Fire,' I said when asked which service, and then, 'there's a fire at the private moorings at Womack near the village of Ludham.'

'It's all right,' the voice said, 'it's been reported already. We're on the way.'

I could've sailed round to the public moorings and tried to tie up there with what bits of rope I'd still got on the *Edith*, but I was shaking so hard I wasn't sure I'd be able to reverse her in safely. I decided to move well away from the fire into the centre of Womack Water and, still shaking, I dropped the mud weight from the prow. We swung there in a small cocoon of silence as all hell broke loose on the bank. Lots of people were standing around. One or two had hoses dribbling, but the intensity of the fire was such that it was plain they would be no use at all.

In about ten minutes the fire brigade arrived; two huge engines and about ten men. Their complete focus was impressive. Ignoring the chaps on the bank with their dribbling garden hoses, and the well-meaning sightseers in pyjamas trying to give them directions to a fire that could be seen for miles, they unrolled hoses in a direct line towards the burning shed. Anything in their way was trampled underfoot as they took the quickest, most direct route.

'Get some water on that,' shouted the chap in front, 'and get these folk out of harm's way.' The onlookers were herded back, they swiftly pointed hoses at the flames and I saw them talking to David, the owner of the mooring. I discovered later that they were asking for details of what was in the shed, whether there was anything explosive, poisonous or highly inflammable. The main problem was the paint and the big whoosh I'd seen from the Calor gas bottle attached to the barbecue. In less than an hour the fire was out, the embers steaming, and all that was left of what had been a substantial garden shed was a pile of ash and rubble. Anything plastic, anything wood, aluminium or paper had disappeared in seconds. There remained only some mangled metal tools, the business end of a garden fork, a wheelbarrow with no wheel or handles, and a ladder with no treads.

I was still dazed and confused. I couldn't make out whether it was the smoke that had got to me, or the after effects of panic, or whether I was just tired from the stresses of the day, but I didn't think I had ever felt so stupid and thick-headed. As I went back into the saloon I noticed that I had never finished my glass of wine and the rest of the bottle was also still on the table. I hadn't enjoyed the wine and judging from the quantities left, it wasn't alcohol that was making me stupid. I tipped the remainder over the side of the boat, with apologies to the ducks, and went back to bed.

Early the following morning I cautiously returned to my mooring. David, my riparian landlord, was waiting for me.

'What happened to you last night?' His tone was uncharacteristically unfriendly as he stood on the bank with arms crossed.

'I woke up to find the shed alight,' I explained. 'I cut the *Edith* free and then rang the fire service, but they were already on their way.'

'Yes. By the time I rang, someone in the village had seen the glow and rung them too. As you know I sleep on the other side of the house, so I didn't see anything until it was all well alight. What happened?' He still sounded angry and suspicious.

'I've no idea, David. I'm sorry if you think I should have rung first and worried about the *Edith* second, but at the time I just wanted to get her clear. I didn't think her diesel and gas tanks going up would help anything.' I was beginning to feel rather irritated myself and took a deep breath. Two of us getting stroppy wasn't going to help. But after all, it was his shed that had nearly sunk my boat and killed me and Brizo.

'How did it start? Do you know?' I asked.

'No idea. I was hoping you could tell me.'

'Me? I had supper and went to bed as normal. There were no naked flames on the *Edith*. Not even a candle. Not even any heating on.'

'Philip Sayer seems to think you were a bit under the influence when he left, and that you might have thrown lighted candles onto the bank.'

I gasped and sat on the edge of the coaming.

'That's complete rubbish,' I said. 'I've never thrown *anything* over the side of the boat let alone a lighted candle. I've been here three years, David. When have you ever known me make a mess or leave waste about? We didn't even have any candles lit last night. In fact, I don't think I've got any!'

David sighed and unfolded his arms, which I took to be a good sign.

'Well I don't know what happened,' he said. 'Something started the fire, so I can only imagine a tramp got in or something like that. The fire inspector said it looked accidental, but anything inflammable has gone, so it's impossible to see if someone may have been dossing there. At least no one got hurt and I am insured. I wouldn't have said anything, but Philip seemed so sure you might have been involved.'

'I've no idea why he would have said that!' I was still indignant.

'Well he's an odd chap, Philip. Gets bees in his bonnet.'

13

Early Warnings

I was still thinking about the bees in Philip's bonnet when I went to the tea shop for my half day of waitressing. As luck would have it, it was a quiet day, so there was plenty of time to catch up on the hot topic of the fire. Late afternoon, when the shop was empty of customers, I kept getting the feeling that Amy, the proprietor and my boss, was trying to raise a delicate subject. Amy is a generously proportioned lady who looks exactly right to be running a tea and cake shop. All her bulges are comfortable, her face often seems floured rather than powdered, and her long, white fluffy hair, caught up in a bun at the back of her head, makes her look like a particularly motherly primary school head. She could be any age from fifty to eighty but is actually at the lower end of that spectrum.

Eventually she suggested we shut up early and sit down with a cup of tea.

'There's something I've been wanting to say to you, Rachel,' she said, 'or to ask. I apologise if I am trampling in where angels fear to tread, but I'm worried you may not know what you are getting into. You don't have to answer me if you don't wish, but are you and Philip Sayer an item?'

I didn't say anything straight away, but she looked at me over her half-moon glasses and said, 'Yes I thought you were getting in deep. I'm sorry to be an interfering old besom, but I just wanted to warn you.'

'Warn me!' I was astonished.

'Yes.' She took her glasses off and scratched her head with them, before balancing them on top of her white bun.

'This is going to sound so interfering, so dog in the proverbial manger...'

'So you keep saying.'

'...but I am worried about you.' She overrode my further protests. 'A few years ago I was very good friends with Philip. Very good,' she said with emphasis. 'Until he asked me to mortgage my tea shop to fund a development at his shop on the staithe. I wasn't willing to sacrifice my independence and he didn't take my refusal well.'

'You fell out.'

'Well, not exactly. He was angry for a short while, then he was friendly again, but I found a lot of things started to go wrong for me. Suppliers let me down, and then claimed I'd cancelled the order. I had a power cut on a very busy bank holiday. My car tyres were let down. People I thought I knew well suddenly started cold-shouldering me and I found that unpleasant rumours were circulating.'

'And you blamed Philip?'

'I don't know, Rachel. For a while I thought I was getting dementia; you know, forgetting what I had done. It was really scary and depressing. But then you came on the scene, Philip switched his attentions to you, and things started going right for me.'

She put her glasses back on and looked at me over them again. 'I'm just telling you how it felt for me. And saying to be careful.' She stood up and started collecting dirty dishes together. 'The truth is, bad things seem to happen to people who upset Philip Sayer. I don't want anything worse to happen to you.'

'Worse?'

'Worse than nearly losing everything you have in a fire.' She hesitated. 'I really shouldn't say this, but there are others in the village who might, so I'll go ahead. Philip's first wife died suddenly. There have been rumours ever since.'

'Oh no, that's ridiculous!' I scoffed, then shut my mouth tight on the words that might have followed.

I was very thoughtful when I went home to Brizo. The fall off my bike, the mask on New Year's Eve, the request for 'investment', the fire. No, surely they were all coincidence. People just didn't behave like that in real life. Did they? Then I thought about how I had felt the night of the fire, and remembered the bottle of Chianti that I hadn't drunk.

The following day I went to work for Philip pretty much as normal. There might have been no disagreement about investment and little was said about the fire except:

'You must have got such a terrible fright. What an awful thing to have happened. So scary for you, with the boat being so close to the fire, and Brizo and all.'

'Yes it was.' I was uncharacteristically short with him. 'But what do you think you were saying to David about me being drunk and throwing candles on the bank? You all but accused me of starting the fire. I most definitely was not drunk and you should know that. I don't take risks on the boat. I can't imagine what that was all about.' I was flushed with the energy of standing up for myself for once. Actually, it felt good. Perhaps I should do it more often.

'Rubbish,' he said. 'You must have misunderstood him. You don't even have any candles do you?' and he swept off to finish the stock-take. I served a customer looking for a map of the Broads and sold them some rolls and coffee while I was at it. Then I cleared up the picnic tables and set everything ready for the afternoon. Philip and I had our end-of-morning coffee together as normal. I was stiff with him to begin with, but it's hard to carry on being stiff when it has no effect whatsoever on the other person. Also, I was confused. Had he meant to do me harm? Or was Amy completely barking in assuming everything that had gone wrong for her was down to Philip? Which of these two, pleasant, friendly people was hiding something else entirely? Philip was pleasantly chatty about the forthcoming village show.

'Are you entering anything?' he asked.

I laughed. I actually laughed.

'Well, there isn't much scope for growing or baking on a boat. I might manage some biscuits and a flower arrangement. At least I can buy the flowers for that. Or perhaps I'll have enough strawberries from my hanging baskets to enter in the soft fruit class. Provided they survived the scorching of course.'

I have to admit I had been quite proud of my productive hanging baskets. I just had the two dangling from the corners of the cabin, and I'd decided that if I was going to have the faff of watering them daily, then it was going to be worth my while. I planted them with strawberry plants bought from the farmers' market, and had been thrilled that they were both decorative and edible. Now, they looked a bit sorry for themselves.

'You should get an allotment,' he said. 'Since you can't have more than pot plants any other way. Why don't you talk to the Parish Council about getting your name down for one?'

'Oh I don't think so,' I said. 'That might tie me down a bit. I like the feeling I can just up and off with the *Edith* if I want to. I don't,' I added hurriedly, as his brow darkened. 'But I do like the sense that I could if the spirit moved me.'

He finished his coffee in a gulp that must have burned his mouth, and walked off silently. I looked after him with my mouth open to call his name, then shut it. Perhaps I was learning a little. After all, I had been careful to make no commitment to Philip. That was one resolution I had kept. One resolution I needed to keep.

A couple of evenings later, Brizo was under the weather. She seemed listless and apathetic, very unlike her usual energetic self. When she wouldn't even eat her tea, nor come for a walk, I got seriously worried and rang the out-of-hours number for the veterinary surgery.

'Bring her in straight away,' they said. 'We have a late clinic at North Walsham. Can you get to it?'

'Yes,' I said. 'How do I find it?'

'Beside the village hall,' they said, and gave me the address.

I persuaded Brizo into the car and drove to North Walsham, my heart in my boots. If anything happened to Brizo I would be bereft indeed. She was my companion, my best friend, my support; I found tears on my face as I drove.

Thankfully the vet was ready and waiting for me when I got there, and took me straight into one of the consulting rooms. Brizo didn't even make a fuss about being lifted onto the table, but squatted there looking dopy and miserable. After a lot of listening, taking temperatures and examining skin, eyes etc the vet, a recently qualified young woman with a lovely manner, stood up.

'I'm going to ask Jeff for a second opinion,' she said and whisked out of the room. I felt even more panicky, and stroked Brizo while we waited, wiping tears from my face. Jeff came in briskly.

'Hey now,' he said to me through his bristly red beard, 'no need for that yet.'

He repeated the temperature and blood pressure checks.

'Could she have had access to any pills of yours?' he asked. 'Particularly sleeping pills or the like?'

'No,' I said. 'Just about the only pills I have on board the *Edith* are ibuprofen for me and some worming tablets for Brizo. And they're all locked away in a cupboard in the bathroom.'

'Has she stayed with anyone else?'

'Not recently. She's been with me or else on the boat on her own for the last few days.'

'And you noticed these symptoms when?'

'Just this evening.'

He looked at the young vet, 'Katharine', it said on her name tag, and nodded.

'I think you're right, Katy.' Katy looked greatly relieved in one sense, but still worried in another. Then Jeff looked at me.

'We think Brizo has been doped with something like sleeping tablets. It was a good call of Katy's because it's harder to spot than you would think. Different dogs react differently, and a lot depends on which drug too. Sometimes dogs get excitable and restless, and sometimes they get dopy like poor Brizo here.'

'Is she going to be all right?'

'I think she'll be fine. But I'm going to suggest we keep her in overnight. We can monitor how she gets on and if there are any problems we can deal with them. But I think she'll just need time to sleep it off,' he added, seeing my look of panic. 'I'm going to suggest some blood tests so we can check the markers for kidney and liver function, but she's not had a problem in the past, so I don't anticipate one now.'

We settled the still-sleepy Brizo in a cage under the watchful eyes of the duty vet nurse, then Jeff saw me to the door. He stopped me just as I was about to leave.

'If you're sure you have nothing that could have caused the problem, and Brizo is always supervised or on the boat, you need to consider how this happened,' he said. 'This isn't the sort of poison that people sometimes put down for rats or mice. In one way that's a good thing, because the warfarin type poisons can be very nasty. On the other hand, this could be a malicious act, and we don't want it to happen again do we? Is there anyone who could have it in for you or Brizo?'

'No,' I said without thinking. 'No one. But what can I do? I work. I have to leave her sometimes. If I am away all day she stays with a dog sitter, and I have total confidence in them. If it's just a short time, then I lock her on the boat. I'm always nervous of her being stolen, so she's never left to just roam.'

'Is she safe on the boat?' he asked, leaning on the bonnet of my car and scratching his wild beard. 'I don't want to be alarmist, but what if it sank?'

'That wouldn't be a problem,' I said, smiling for the first time for some hours. 'There's only about two to three feet under the keel of the *Edith* and she has a flat bottom. If she sank, Brizo would be fine in the upper parts of the boat even if the lower areas got wet.' My smile faded, as I thought about the fire of a few days ago. That would have been another matter if I'd not been on board.

'I will think about it,' I promised Jeff. 'I just want Brizo well and safe.'

He waved me off as I pulled out of the car park and set off back to the *Edith*. It felt very strange that night, home alone. Every time I stood up I expected Brizo to follow me from one part of the boat to another. Every time I looked down I expected to see a furry shape close beside me on the cabin floor. It was probably the second longest night of my life.

In the morning I texted Philip to say I wouldn't be in for my morning shift, apologising for the short notice and explaining that Brizo was at the vets. Then I drove back to North Walsham. I was there on the dot of eight thirty as they opened the doors to the morning flood of customers for scheduled surgery. To my surprise Jeff was on duty again.

'They're working you hard, aren't they?' I said.

'Actually I'm just going off duty,' he said with a grin, 'but I had something to show you and I wanted to see your face when we reunited you with Brizo.' As he said that, another veterinary nurse came through the door to the waiting room with Brizo hauling on the lead. She rushed up to me, towing the nurse behind her, and wrapped her forepaws round my legs as she always did when I had been away for a time. She was absolutely back to normal!

'I think we can mark that one down as a success,' said Jeff with some satisfaction, as the nurse handed me the lead. 'This is what I wanted to show you.' He flourished a printout in my direction.

'This is a spec for a webcam. I think you said you have Wi-Fi at your mooring. This might help keep an eye on Brizo, and your boat when you're not around.' He handed me the sheet. Lowering his voice, he added, 'and if you're satisfied this can't have happened by accident, you should seriously think about reporting it to the police.'

I looked him in the eye and replied, 'I will definitely give that careful thought,' but knew in my heart that even with Brizo at risk, that was not a solution I wanted to adopt. I had taken some care to keep my profile low. This was not a time to draw attention to myself. If we were at risk, I needed to find another answer.

I sat in the car for a few moments, making a fuss of Brizo and checking my phone. There was a reply from Philip.

'Disappointed you would leave me in the lurch like this. Thought I could expect better. P.'

I read it twice. No 'How is Brizo?' No 'Hope she is well.' I realised that much as I liked Philip and enjoyed his company, he was never going to understand the importance a dog could have in your life.

'I suppose,' I said aloud to Brizo, 'there are dog people and there are not-dog people. Philip is the second sort.' Brizo looked at me out of her mismatched eyes and laughed at me, her tongue lolling and her head slightly on one side, as she did when concentrating hard on what I was saying. I put the car in gear and drove back to Ludham.

Before returning to the boat, I called in at the tea shop to explain to Amy that I would not be able to work my afternoon shift. I still didn't feel able to leave Brizo on the boat alone, until I had worked out a solution to my security problem.

'Oh bother,' said Amy, 'and I could really do with your help this afternoon. But is it just Brizo that's the issue?' I braved myself for another non-dog person comment. 'Because if so,' went on Amy, 'why don't you leave her in my back room while you work. She's house-trained isn't she? She'd be fine in there and you could pop in to see her from time to time. I'm sure I can find an old rug for her to lie on.' I flushed with relief.

'Oh, Amy, that would be wonderful. Are you sure that's okay?'

'A lot more okay than losing you this afternoon,' she said, smiling at me. 'Anyway, I like dogs. I can't think why I haven't thought of it before. Pop Brizo through there now, have a bite of lunch and then we can all get stuck in to the afternoon teas.'

*

Later that afternoon, as the rush for cholesterol-on-scones began to subside, Amy asked me about Brizo and precisely what had taken us to the emergency vet. I explained and she went quiet for the space of two ladies ordering cheese and ham toasties and a family in the garden outside sharing yet more cream teas with the wasps.

She came back in, wiping her hands on the tea towel tucked into her apron strings, and perched on the stool behind the counter. I guessed what was coming, and concentrated on wiping damp dishes emerging from the dishwasher.

'Have you thought it might have been Philip?' she asked, blunt as ever.

'I've thought about it, but I can't believe it.'

'Can't or won't?'

'Can't,' I repeated. 'I can't believe Philip would do anything to harm Brizo. I know he's not really a dog person, but Brizo has never done him any harm and what would he achieve by it?'

We were interrupted by a commotion from the garden. The teenage son had decided to explore what would happen if he pulled the lever on the umbrella shading their table. Naturally enough the umbrella had abruptly folded up, and the entire family of gran, grandpa, mother, teenager and toddler were now face down in the cream scones. The cries were muffled, but nonetheless indignant, all except those from the toddler, who appeared to find a face full of cream and jam entirely to his liking. Mum was inclined to see the funny side, but Grandpa, dignity seriously threatened, was demanding clean cloths, a free tea, compensation and a case to be heard at the court of human rights. Amy and I rushed out with the requisite cloths and, having restored the umbrella to its open position, I went to fetch some extra scones as a goodwill gesture. Grandpa was not much mollified, and Amy could read on my face that, after a night short of sleep and long on worry, the reply formulating on my tongue was likely to be less than tactful. She shooed me away hurriedly.

When she came back in we took one look at each other, then burst into fits of giggles, made more hysterical by the need to muffle them.

'A warning sign!' I gasped. 'What could it say? *Do not close the umbrella while under it?* We could have a full set of statements of the bleeding obvious! *Do not flush the loo while sitting on it. Do not pour the tea in your lap. Do not walk through the door without opening it. Peanut butter cookies may contain nuts!'*

Even though it cost Amy a batch of free scones, the event lightened the whole afternoon, a much-needed relief from worry. But when I was about to leave for the *Edith* we did return to the subject of Brizo's doping. Laughter had provided a space, but the problem had not gone away.

'I know you don't want to think it's Philip,' said Amy, 'and it may not be. I'm not going to go on about it,' she added, 'but just bear in mind my experience and how it compares with yours. And create a balance sheet. What are you getting from your relationship with Philip, and what is it costing you? I don't mean in money obviously, but in happiness and confidence.'

'Is that what you did?'

'In a way yes, and much later than I should have done. Which is why I'm nagging you about it.' Very uncharacteristically, she kissed me on the cheek as I put Brizo back in my car.

'Don't make my mistake,' she said. 'If the game isn't worth it, get out.'

'All very well, Amy, but even if you're right, how do I get out? According to you, you only got your life back when I turned up and Philip switched his attentions to me. Dumping him didn't solve your problem. So what do I do? Hope for another incomer of the right age and gender?'

'And bank balance,' she said soberly. 'Don't forget that too. I don't have an answer to that for you, Rachel. I think you have to work that out for yourself. But in the meantime, you are welcome to bring Brizo with you when you are working here. Incidentally, why Brizo? Where did the name come from? I've always meant to ask.'

'Brizo was the Greek goddess who protected sailors,' I said. 'It seemed appropriate.'

'Very,' she replied. 'Stay safe, and think about what I have said.'

14

Norfolk, July 2015 – Closing in

Sunday night saw Ben and Paula tackling the long drive back to Norfolk. The usual end-of-the-weekend traffic was choking the A1(M) and the A17 wasn't much better. The tedious trek between stretches of dual carriageway was undertaken more or less in silence. Paula, as normal on a long car journey, fell asleep. Ben was preoccupied by traffic, the weather was awful, and his thoughts were with the skeleton in the pit as he reviewed the list of old colleagues he could approach.

'Once a policeman, always a policeman,' he thought. His curiosity was dragging him in the direction of Brundall and questions about boats purchased some years earlier, but he didn't want to wrong-foot the official investigation in Norfolk. As they approached the dual carriageway sections of the A47 near Norwich, traffic started to speed up and Paula woke with a snort.

'Sorry. Was I snoring?'

'Only a bit. Now you are awake though, I'd like to make a phone call. Do you mind?'

'Be my guest.'

'Can you just scroll through my contacts list until you get to Jim Henning.' Paula leaned forward against her seat belt and prodded the buttons on the hands-free set until she found 'Henning, Jim' and looked at Ben.

'Press call?' she asked.

'Yes.'

'Henning,' said the voice answering.

'Jim, it's Ben Asheton. Have you time for a word?'

'Good to hear from you Ben. I'm going on duty in ten, but I have time for a quick chat. What have you been up to in Yorkshire?'

'How d'you know about that?'

'The office told me we'd had a call checking you were still in the land of the living. Somebody seemed to think you might be a skeleton in a hole in the ground.'

'I see,' said Ben. 'In view of the fact I whupped your ass at darts the other week, I assume you told them I was super fit and well.'

'You really must stop watching those American cop shows. Whupped my ass?'

'Actually it's about the skeleton I'm ringing. So far our North Yorkshire colleagues haven't been able to find the wife. The last trace they've mentioned to me was of her spending a lot of money at NYA in Brundall. I imagine they've asked for your assistance?'

'Yes, we've been pursuing some enquiries with NYA. Is this confidential?'

'I have you on hands-free but only Paula is here.'

'Hi Paula. I assume I can rely on your discretion? NYA has records going back pretty much to the Ark. It would seem that one Rachel Treadwell bought a Broom 50 in late autumn 2011. Interestingly, their records indicate that she moved it to a mooring just down the river in Brundall and stayed there a while. They don't have any record of where she went after that but it seems unlikely that she moved it single-handed. She could have done of course, if she was an experienced yachtswoman, but that doesn't seem probable given her background. So we're asking around to see if anyone knows anyone who might have given her a hand.'

'Jim, d'you mind if I do some asking myself? As you know, I'm in and out of lifeboats like the proverbial and some of the inshore crews might know something. Of course if I find anything I'll share it straight away.'

'Just tread carefully Ben. You know not to compromise the situation, and you also know how short-handed we are. Just ask questions, don't answer them. I don't want anything leaking to the press.'

'No worries.'

'So now we're in Australia instead of the US. You really must stop watching so much TV,' and Jim rang off.

Ben's first two shouts on Monday morning were land-based. One took him to the Parish Hall at Scratby, where a volunteer in the kitchen had spilled boiling water over their hands. The second callout was to a possible heart attack that turned out to be a probable indigestion. As the indigestion victim had been in Fleggburgh, Ben had time for a quick pie at the King's Arms and a phone call to one of his old mates from Hemsby Inshore Lifeboat. Patrick, an old Broads man, knew every in and out of the dykes, rivers and lakes that made up the northern Norfolk Broads. He tended to draw the line at Great Yarmouth, arguing that the Bure, the Ant and the Thurne with all their tributaries were enough knowledge for any man. He knew where otters could be found, where the rare bittern nested and where most of the bodies were buried. If anyone knew where the Broom 50 had gone, Patrick could probably offer some suggestions; provided of course she had stayed on the Broads. Since his shift was due to end late afternoon, Ben suggested a pint or two at the pub at Winterton. It was always good for a meal if the mood took them.

Patrick grinned when the subject was broached. He took a hearty swig from his pint of Wherry, then wiped the foam from his lip.

'The *Edith Cavell*.'

'The nurse shot in the war?'

'That's the one. The old Broom was named after that nurse.'

'How d'you know?'

'The name stuck in my head because I'd just seen a special exhibition about the Great War with a picture and information about Edith Cavell. She were a Norfolk lass you know. It weren't long after that I saw the boat. When I saw her, she was lying at Brundall, so that must've been just after she changed hands. I don't know where she went after that, but if she stayed here, the Broads Authority ought to have her registered details. Also,' he said, leaning back in his chair, 'if another Wherry refreshed my memory I might just be able to remember the name of the chap who helped her new owner move the *Edith* from Brundall.'

'Coming up.' When Ben got back with another pint for Pat he sat down again at the small round table. 'Come on then, Pat, cough up.' Patrick grinned so that his weathered features corrugated into a wholly new pattern.

'I think it might be worth asking Richard Jackson. He was working for the Norfolk Yacht Agency at the time and I know he sometimes did little jobs helping new owners shift their boats to new moorings. I don't know for sure he was the one who helped move the *Edith Cavell*, but there's a good chance that if he didn't, he'll know who did.'

After a couple more pints of Wherry (for Pat) as a thank you, and a couple of Cokes for himself, Ben dropped Patrick off at his Hemsby chalet bungalow and got on the phone to Jim Henning. 'You've probably found this out already,' he said, 'but just in case I'm ahead of you, I now know the name of the boat and a possible lead to where she may have gone.'

'*Edith Cavell*,' said Jim Henning. 'Yes, we got that far, but not much further yet. She's registered with the Broads Authority but they don't have an address for the owner and as you know they don't register a boat to a particular mooring. However, they have dug out her last safety certificate and it would appear it was issued by the boatyard Ultramarine at Womack Water, so it may be that she's nearby. In the meantime, thank you for the tip about Richard Jackson. I'll follow that up myself.'

'If it's today, can I come with you?'

'I was planning to pop over this evening. It seems likely that's the best chance of catching him at home. I'll pick you up in half an hour.'

Richard Jackson lived in a semi-detached bungalow in Brundall with his two terriers, Salt and Pepper. It was still light when Jim and Ben pulled up in the drive, and Richard was busy in the garden. Salt and Pepper were too although their digging, albeit energetic, seemed a little misguided.

'Stop,' thundered Richard when he spotted what they were doing, and the small lavender plants now lying forlornly by the path with their roots exposed.

'I'm Detective Inspector Jim Henning,' said Jim. 'We spoke briefly on the phone. This is an old colleague of mine who's been giving us some help. I hope you don't mind him sitting in?'

'Damn dogs,' Richard said to Jim, 'come on in and I'll see what I can do to help.'

In the small kitchen-diner Richard washed his hands perfunctorily and dried them on the tea towel.

'Drink?' he offered. Remembering the mantra from his nursing days, 'never accept a cup of tea unless you've inspected the kitchen', Ben suppressed a shudder and declined with thanks. The room was not precisely filthy but it was a long way from clean and the sink was piled high with stained mugs and plates. He spotted two dog bowls in the mix too, along with the dishes presumably used by Richard.

'Sorry about the mess,' he said. 'Never seem to get round to a thorough clean-up. If you won't have a drink, come through to the sitting room.'

He led the way down a narrow passage to the room at the front of the house. It was marginally better than the kitchen but not by a wide margin. The dogs instantly appropriated a chair each and had to be turned off before Jim and Ben could sit down. The plush-covered sofa and chairs had seen better days and greasy heads had marked them on the backs.

Richard sat on the chair by the electric fire and the visitors settled opposite.

'Helping the police with their enquiries eh,' said Richard. 'I hope that's not as sinister as it sounds.'

'Not this time. We're looking for a lady who bought a Broom cruiser from the marina here in 2011. We believe you may have helped her move it to its new berth.'

'I help a lot of people,' said Richard.' And seven years ago is a long time. I'll need to check my diaries for any details. Just a tick,' and he disappeared out of the room.

There was a short pause during which Jim and Ben waited in silence. After one attempt by Ben to wander round the room, which provoked a warning growl from both watching dogs, they also waited without moving a muscle.

'I hope he's not too long,' said Ben after some time had passed. 'I may need the loo soon and I'd rather use it with all my appendages intact.' There was another warning growl from Pepper, and Salt moved to guard the door.

'Cross your legs,' advised Jim. 'You should know better than to come out without going first.'

'You try getting info out of Patrick without downing a few drinks to keep him company,' hissed Ben. 'If he doesn't come soon I'm going to have to make a dash for the door anyway. Oh God,' he groaned as the dogs stood up to growl some more, but just then Richard came back with an armful of old desk diaries.

'Sorry about the delay,' he said. 'Loo!' said Ben, and dashed past him to the passageway and the hoped-for bathroom.

When he got back, the dogs gave him a cheery smile before turning round twice and settling down on the hearth rug.

'Sorry about that,' said Ben, giving the dogs a malevolent glare.

'No problem,' said Richard absently, still leafing through diaries. 'Ah, this is the one. December 2011, I took a Broom, the *Edith Cavell*, from Brundall to Womack Water. One lady owner, Rachel Treadwell. She renamed the boat,' he explained. 'It was called *Broad's Lady* before, but I remember now that she thought that sounded a bit rude. She'd just seen an exhibition about Edith Cavell and renamed the boat in her honour.'

'Do you have a note of where she was living?'

'She was living on the boat. Her and her dog. Funny name. Something like Bristle. Border collie cross. Nice dog though.'

'No home other than the boat?'

'Not as far as I know. Her mooring was one of those eleven-month ones, so provided she moved around a bit from time to time, it's perfectly legal to live on it. I remember she had a mooring with a power point, so she wouldn't exactly be roughing it. The Broom is a big boat. Lots of room for just one person and a dog.'

'Thank you, Mr Jackson,' said Jim. 'You've been very helpful.'

'So what's she done?' asked Richard.

'We don't know she's done anything yet,' replied Jim. 'But North Yorkshire Police want a word with her about one of their cases. They'll be very pleased with your information.'

Back in Yorkshire, DI Geldard was pleased with the local help.

'That's great, thank you Jim. Clearly I have good reason to come down to your neck of the woods now. Did I understand you to say you've checked she's still there?'

'Yes. I sent a DC there quietly and he did some asking around at the visitor centre in Womack Water. The *Edith Cavell* is moored in some private grounds near the public staithe and it seems the owner is someone named Rachel Treadwell. I didn't want to rush in without your say-so, as it's your case. What do you want us to do?'

'If all seems quiet, then I'd like for us to call on her ourselves, if that's okay with you. I'll come down with a colleague tomorrow. A female DC, just in case we need to take her into custody.'

'That seems likely,' agreed Jim.

'Yes. I think so. At the very least she has some difficult questions to answer. If you want to accompany us, you'd be very welcome. If we make an early start we should arrive with you around ten, then we can all go on to Womack Water.'

'Sounds like a plan. I'll see you tomorrow.'

'Yes, Good. I don't suppose there's any way to keep an eye on her in the meantime?'

'I don't have the resources to stand a watch,' said Jim, 'but I can ask the local car to call round a few times. We had a case of arson not long ago. They can use that as the excuse.'

'I owe you one,' replied Geldard. 'See you tomorrow.'

15

Return of a Nightmare

The coolness arising from Philip's reaction to Brizo's illness lasted some months. I couldn't say I was sorry. With Amy's warnings in mind I gave some serious thought to how I could break it off with Philip, but got no further than that. I didn't contact the police, but I did fit the webcam. For a few weeks I checked it almost obsessively. It was activated by movement within its 130-degree range of the upper saloon, so mostly what it showed me was an empty saloon, or occasionally the flicker of movement as a bird on the deck outside activated the camera. On the rare occasions when I did leave Brizo alone it showed me how she spent her time; quite a lot of it either asleep or watching the movements of the waterfowl, occasionally worrying at her Kong. Eventually, I almost forgot about it.

I did consider handing in my notice to Philip, but decided against it. I needed the money; the new, more professional relationship felt less threatening and all in all there did not seem to be any rush to make major changes. If I stopped working at the staithe it would both make a hole in my budget and create a coldness right on my doorstep, so I did nothing.

Round about October, Philip started joining me for coffee again, and intangibly the atmosphere grew warmer. We started seeing each other more, and I did enjoy the social contact. But Amy's warnings still rang in my head. I couldn't help but notice that I was having to earn his forgiveness for my 'ill-treatment' of him when Brizo had been ill. I seemed to be in some way on probation and I felt that only a completely blot-free copybook was going to return me to the sunlit uplands. Eventually I began to feel guilty that I had not given more thought to my other responsibilities. Perhaps it had been unreasonable of me to just let him down like that. Perhaps I could have explained more fully, and sooner, why I was not going to turn up for work. I said something of this to Amy. Her only response was to bang a saucepan down in the sink.

That Christmas I was not invited to spend time with Philip. I briefly considered inviting him to join me on the *Edith*, but didn't have to make the difficult decision. Joe at the pub contacted me to say he was going to be short-handed at Christmas and asked would I work both Christmas Day and Boxing Day. It seemed a neat answer to my quandary, except for the problem of leaving Brizo, and I agreed subject to my being able to get off early each evening to feed her and take her for a walk. I discussed the arrangements with Amy, and she also applauded my plan.

I had a great time on Christmas Day. Okay, it was hard

173

work, and I was rushed off my feet serving food and clearing up, but there was something cheering about spending time with people determined to enjoy themselves. We, the staff, got our lunch around 3pm. It was a pretty snatched meal, but very welcome for all that, and tired as we were, we still had crackers and hats. We were just laughing at the usual execrable cracker jokes when my phone made the noise that indicated my webcam was operating. 'Just a second,' I said, laughing at the last dreadful pun, and picked my phone up. The tiny screen showed Brizo going wild with rage, leaping up and down and hurling herself at the saloon door. The camera didn't show what was driving her wild. I watched for a few moments.

'I'm sorry, Joe,' I said, 'there's something wrong at my boat. I need to pop over for a few moments.' Then my phone rang.

'Rachel, this is Amy. I'm at your boat.'

'Amy,' I was amazed, 'what are you doing there? Sorry, that came out a bit wrong. Is there a problem? Brizo seems to have been upset by something.'

'I knew you were working today, so when I decided to walk off my Christmas lunch I wandered down here to check everything was okay. Rachel, I'm sorry to worry you, but when I got here there was an intruder on your boat. A man in dark clothes was doing something on the deck near the saloon door. When I shouted he jumped onto the bank and ran off through the trees. Brizo was going mad, but she's settled down now. I'm standing on the bank looking into your boat. I can't see a problem but you should perhaps come back and have a look round.'

'I'm on my way.'

I explained to Joe and pedalled off. Amy was still waiting when I got there.

'Amy, come in, you must be frozen, hanging about in this weather.'

The *Edith* was warm from the heating left on for Brizo, who greeted us both with delight then jumped onto the bank and appeared to be following a trail into the woods. I called her back and she came aboard, snuffling round the foredeck and saloon door. As far as I could see, there was no change, no sign that the door had been forced or that anyone had been up to any mischief. I said so to Amy as I made her a coffee.

'Perhaps I arrived just in time,' she said. 'How did you know Brizo was upset?'

I showed her the webcam and she grinned at me over her coffee.

'So you're not as green as you're cabbage looking,' she said. 'I'm relieved you're taking some precautions. But I'll still take a walk down here tomorrow, as you're working again.'

'Amy, I'm very grateful indeed, but do you really think I'm at risk?'

'I don't know, but I do know that the *Edith* and Brizo are very important to you, and that a walk after a heavy lunch benefits me as well as you. It's no hardship to walk down here by the water. I won't deny,' she went on, 'that the intruder did startle me. I wasn't sure what I would do if he came my way, but luckily he ran when I shouted.'

'It was definitely a man then?'

'I suppose I don't know for sure. I just assumed it was. Thinking about it now, I think it probably was. It was tall and flat for a woman, if you know what I mean. But whoever it was had covered their hair with a balaclava and was wearing dark jeans and a dark jacket. Those are pretty unisex really. Are you going to report it to the police?'

'I'll think about it.' I spoke quickly. 'But what could I say? You saw someone you can't identify and who did nothing except run off. I doubt it would be high-priority for them, and as no damage was done I don't even need a crime number for insurance.' Amy looked as though she was minded to take the point further, but I changed the subject. I didn't want the police prowling round my private little set-up.

I embarked on 2015 in a very confused state of mind. When I was with Amy I felt pressured to do something about my relationship with Philip. When I was with Philip I oscillated between enjoying his company and worrying about where we were headed. I mentioned the Christmas Day intruder to Philip and he was dismissive of what he termed a pair of women in a tizz. As I found we got on much better when I behaved as he wished, I pushed the memory to the back of my mind. Philip liked me to be pleasant, relaxed, and available when he suggested something for us to do together. When I met those expectations we had a fun time. When I didn't, he made it plain that I had fallen short.

A theme about my shortcomings, mainly based around my commitment to Brizo, became more and more evident. He made me feel stupid for making time for a dog. He made jokes down the pub, when we popped in for a drink together, about 'mad dog ladies' who turned animals into 'fur babies'. People I worked with laughed at my expense. The only person who didn't laugh was Amy, but I noticed that Philip never went near Amy if he could help it. When I commented on this, he was very short with me. He said she was a 'mad, jealous, fantasising bitch' and I shouldn't be working there at all if I valued his friendship. I dug my heels in about Amy, and it earned me several weeks' coldness and a temporary cessation of invitations to drinks or the theatre.

When warmer relations were resumed, initially to my relief, there seemed to be a lot of invitations that, for one good reason or another, got in the way of me looking after Brizo as I would wish. Even if we went for a walk, there was a good reason why she couldn't come along, whether it was transport to the start, or livestock in the fields. In vain I pointed out that Brizo was good in a car, and good on a lead. In the end I gave up. Then there were lots of invites that involved me going out straight from work, and having to ask someone else to feed Brizo and let her out for a run around. Some days I only saw her in the morning and at night. I felt guilty, but if I raised the subject with Philip he either scoffed or sulked. In the end, Amy took me on one side and told me, bluntly, 'You're neglecting that dog. Is that really what you want?'

I felt so ashamed I bailed out of a visit that Philip had arranged to the pub at Horning. I gave him plenty of notice, but even so he was furious.

'I arranged that lunch so you could meet some of my friends,' he said, 'and you let me down for no good reason. Are you seeing someone else?'

I stared at him aghast. 'Of course I'm not, although why I shouldn't I don't know! We're not in an exclusive relationship are we? And you never said anything about meeting anyone else. It was just a drink. That's what you said to me.'

'Well it wasn't. It was going to be a surprise.'

Unluckily for Philip, the words took me back to 'surprises' Matthew had arranged for me. They had all been humiliating and always ended in a row.

'I don't like surprises,' I snapped, 'I'm spending the day with Brizo.' And I marched off.

Brizo and I had a great day. We did lots of things I knew she would enjoy. After we had breakfasted together on the *Edith* we drove in my car to Caister. So early in the year, I was able to park for free near the lifeboat station and we walked for miles, first in the dunes down towards Great Yarmouth, then back on the beach. We came back to the car park around lunchtime and I left Brizo in the car for a moment while I popped into a nearby chip shop, then she and I lunched together at one of the picnic tables behind the old lifeboat station – plaice and chips for me, jumbo sausage for Brizo. Very good it was too. Just as I was putting our waste paper into a handy bin, someone in a navy blue uniform pulled up in a car. It gave me quite a start, thinking it was the police, but it was just one of the Coastwatch staff coming on duty for the afternoon shift.

'Afternoon,' he said, not knowing how he had startled me.

When we got home that evening, Brizo and I snuggled up together in the downstairs saloon. I didn't put the TV on. I wanted to do some serious thinking.

I thought about Brizo, her unwavering loyalty and her forgiveness when I let her down. The way she was always glad to see me. The way she greeted me with joy, no matter how long I had been gone or why.

I thought about Philip; about the fun we had, about friendship and how it warmed days that could be lonely even with a dog, about having the opportunity to exchange ideas, to comment on meals, plays, films. Then I thought about the jokes about mad dog ladies in front of my friends, about how he put me down for poor choices, about the sulks if I failed to put him first, about how he went out of his way to exclude poor Brizo.

Then I reflected on the unexplained happenings. The Christmas Day row that had left me lying in the road, the New Year fright, the fire, the intruder, and Brizo being doped.

'But I don't know that for sure,' I argued with myself. 'It was only the vet's idea. Nothing was proved. And perhaps I expect too much from someone who isn't a natural dog lover. Perhaps it is my fault,' and just articulating those words brought me up short. Bizarrely, both Amy and Matthew came into my mind. Amy's voice: 'you're neglecting that dog' and 'bad things seem to happen to people who upset Philip Sayer.'

And Matthew: 'I would be a lot keener on sleeping with you if you lost some weight.' 'Can't you learn to appreciate wine? Drinking lager is so lower class'; 'I really think you could try harder. I think I deserve that much at least'; 'You are always letting me down.'

My conclusion was that I needed to get away from Philip. The only problem was, I had no idea how to do it without tearing up my whole life in Ludham.

Finding a resolution to my problem was about to get a whole lot harder. The following week, Philip turned up at my mooring carrying two suitcases. It was one of my days working

179

with Amy and I wasn't due to start until ten. I gaped at Philip as he heaved the cases over the gunwale and dumped them on the foredeck.

'Sorry to take you by surprise, but I've been too busy to ring.' He bustled past me with the cases and into the saloon, where he put them down. Brizo growled and backed off. I stared at him. I still hadn't managed to articulate a single word.

'I've got a plumbing problem at the cottage. It's going to be uninhabitable for weeks. You don't mind putting me up do you? I haven't anywhere else to go.' He looked at me with an attempt at little boy lost. What could I say?

'Where should I put these?' he asked.

I found my voice.

'In your usual berth I suppose.' I followed him to the door. 'How long do you think it will be?'

'A few weeks,' he said, emptying the first case. He seemed to have brought quite a lot of clothes. 'I don't know exactly. It's not a problem is it?' He pulled a bottle of champagne out of the case and waved it at me. 'Perhaps this will make me more welcome.'

'You don't need to do that,' I said. 'It's just that this is not a big boat. Of course I can put you up for a time, but...' my voice trailed off.

'But what? You never have any other visitors and it's an enormous boat. You're not being exactly welcoming, Rachel.'

'I'm sorry. It's just a surprise. I'll see you later. I have to go to work now,' and I put the long lead on Brizo that I used when she was going to run alongside my bike. 'Make yourself at home. You know where things are, although I suppose you'll be going to work too. I'd better give you the spare key,' and I hooked it out of the jar on the shelf to give to him.

'Thank you. Surely you're not taking that dog to work with you?'

'Yes, I always take her to Amy's. Ever since she was doped.' I looked at him squarely, just to see if there was a reaction, but his face was in his case again.

'Bye,' he said.

Amy's reaction can be imagined.

'Oh, Rachel,' she said, as she sank down on the nearest chair. 'You can't let him do that.'

'I can't stop him,' I said. 'I'm helpless in the face of his confidence and his assumptions. What should I do, Amy?'

'Well if you're not willing to throw him off your boat, then at least set him a deadline. Tell him one week and then he must leave.'

'But he says the work is going to take weeks!'

'That can't be right, unless the place is literally falling around his ears. Nothing needs to take that long. Who's he got working on it?'

'I don't know. He didn't say.'

'Well see if you can find out and I'll ask around. I know most of the craftsmen around here and I'm sure I can find out something. Meantime, for God's sake give him a deadline!'

I tried to do as she said that evening, as we sat down to a reheated lasagne. Philip turned his nose up at that.

'Tesco,' he sneered. 'I thought you would have done a bit better than a Tesco ready meal.'

'I'm sorry, Philip, but you arrived without any warning. What is the problem at your cottage? Who've you got working on it?'

'Questions, questions,' he said. 'Anyone would think you didn't want me here. It's a problem with the plumbing, as I said, and I'm still trying to find a local man who can sort it. Can we have something a bit more gourmet tomorrow? I have a long day ahead of me at the staithe.'

It was clear that I would be the one expected to cook again.

'It depends what I have time for,' I said. 'How long do you think you need to stay here?'

'I said I don't know.' He was getting irritable. 'I thought I'd be welcome but apparently not.'

'Of course you are welcome,' I said, 'but it would help to have some idea of time scale.'

'Oh, a few weeks. I'll keep you abreast of progress.'

Over the next couple of weeks, I kept a careful eye on the webcam whenever I had to leave Philip and Brizo together on the boat. As far as I could tell Philip hadn't noticed it was there, sitting unobtrusively on the bookshelf in the dark corner above the TV. For the first few days, man and dog seemed to occupy the space with a sort of armed truce. Philip would sit astern, Brizo by the door awaiting my return. If Philip went to the door, Brizo would move astern, always taking whichever route was furthest from Philip. It seemed she was well aware of how he felt about her. If I felt guilty about spying on Philip without his knowing, I quieted my conscience with the reminder that I hadn't invited him. He had, in effect forced his way aboard. Over time, however, my concerns grew. Philip took to shouting at the dog, calling her names; once he even threw his newspaper at her. Brizo continued to behave as if he wasn't there. I didn't know what to do. If I let on about the webcam, its usefulness was gone. Then came the day, an unseasonably cold day, when he shut Brizo into the unheated cockpit and refused to let her into the saloon. I couldn't leave her there and, making an excuse to Joe about feeling ill, I pedalled back to the *Edith* more than an hour early. I found Brizo exactly where the webcam had suggested, and Philip in the saloon.

I burst in, absolutely furious and reckless.

'What are you doing here and why is Brizo shut out?'

'And good morning to you too, Rachel. I didn't realise I had to get permission from you now to take a day off.'

'Why have you shut her out?'

'She was making a noise and getting in my way.'

'It's a cold day. You can't just leave her on deck.'

'She's a dog. She'll survive.' He folded his paper, his tone careless. I saw red.

'She's my dog and this is my boat. She lives here and has every right to be treated with kindness.'

'Oh listen to yourself, Rachel. She's a dog. Surely I come first.'

'Not at Brizo's expense!'

'Well that's telling me. Why did you come home so early anyway?' He looked at me with narrowed eyes.

'I wasn't feeling well. But funnily enough, my headache went when I saw how you were treating my dog. Come, Brizo!'

'Where are you going now?'

'To Amy's.' I knew that would annoy him, but I didn't care.

*

Amy took us both in and gave me tea. When I had calmed down, she sat with me.

'I've been making some enquiries. I've asked around all the local plumbers. Philip hasn't approached any of them to get any work done. And as far as they know he hasn't approached anyone for miles around. I think he's having you on, Rachel. You should ask him to leave. And if he won't, get the police involved.'

'I'll think about it, Amy. I really will.'

I did think about it. I thought very hard. The similarities to Matthew were now getting through even to me. That night, my old nightmare returned.

16

Plans and Precautions

The next few weeks were difficult. They would have been impossible but for the secret place in my head. Every time Philip got difficult, every time he put me down, ridiculed me, got sulky and complained that I did not care about his feelings, I retreated to my secret place. To Amy I seemed to have given up. Philip carried on living on the *Edith*, his so-called plumbing problems continued to be unaddressed, and I just kept calm and carried on. In view of the way my mind kept returning to the disposal pit and the weeks after Matthew died, the old wartime slogan seemed very appropriate. No, in this secret place let me be honest with myself if with no one else – the weeks after I *killed* Matthew, concealed his body, and got away with it.

I found myself wishing I had a handy waste disposal pit; then stopped in my tracks, I had shocked myself so much. Brizo got to the end of her lead and then stopped too, and looked at me. I had never meant to kill Matthew. I had never planned it, I had never meant it to happen. It would never have happened if I hadn't been pushed to the limit, but it had certainly solved a problem. If the only way to stop Philip hurting Brizo was to do the same thing again, might I react in the same way? A little voice added, 'and if the only way to get rid of Philip is to kill him, and I had the opportunity, would I take it?'

I shook my head and strode on. But the little voice was not silenced. Admit it or not, the possibility of a radical solution to my problem had been considered and not dismissed. It was a small step from idea to plan. Not that I intended to do anything, you must understand that. But if I was pushed into a corner again, perhaps it wasn't such a bad idea to have a way out. I need never use it. But it would be there. A small comfort in my mind.

The real problem I had to resolve was how to dispose of a body. The ideal, it seemed to me, was a place like our old disposal pit, which concealed a body so effectively it was not found. Unfortunately, I no longer had that facility to hand. I started to think about what I did have, which basically came down to the *Edith*, and the water on which she floated. Then, my webcam revealed something that suggested I might have a bigger problem than I'd thought.

One afternoon, while I was working for Amy and Brizo was safe in her back room, I checked the webcam footage just out of curiosity to see what Philip got up to when neither I nor Brizo were about. I watched on and off for most of the morning, and very boring it was. But then, about an hour before I was due to go home, he put his paper down and went to my bookshelves. I tensed, afraid he would find the webcam, but he went straight to the plain-covered little book I use to list my access details and passwords for various accounts including my savings accounts. It looked as though he'd found it on some previous occasion and knew where to look. I watched as he flicked through the book, then put it back in its place. After that I kept an eye on the webcam with almost paranoid persistence, but saw nothing of any great note. That afternoon when I logged in to one of my savings accounts I noticed the line at the top of the page that gave the date of my last log-in. It was only a week previously, and I knew it hadn't been me. I checked the balance on the account with my heart in my mouth, but no money had been removed. I changed the password, and then logged in to my other accounts and changed the passwords on those too. When I got home, I waited until Philip went out, then I got the book out and changed the passwords listed in the book – but not to the ones I was now using. Then, feeling melodramatic, I closed the book on a hair pulled from my head and put it back on the shelf.

Over the next few days I served coffees, sold paperbacks, cleaned up after cream teas and pulled pints in all my different jobs but with my mind on a completely different problem. What did Philip have in mind for me? Was he just nosy, or was he planning to steal from me? If the latter, how did he think he could get away with it once I noticed the losses? Did he think he could brow-beat me into letting him get away with it? Or, and the thought caused my hands to pause while pulling a pint for so long that I spilled the beer and had to apologise to Joe, was he planning to first steal from me, and then get rid of me?

If that was the case, I thought, then I needed to accelerate my plan. I needed to get rid of Philip before he got rid of me. The option of involving the police passed briefly through my head and out again. No, I still couldn't take that route. Either they'd not believe me, dismiss me as a fantasist, a silly woman, or they'd take too much interest. I couldn't risk that.

By this time it was the end of May, and Philip still hadn't sorted out his plumbing problem. Amy sat me down and gave me a serious talking-to. I decided I couldn't leave her with the impression that I was finding my visitor a problem, so I told her we were getting on fine, and that we were planning a little holiday. She rolled her eyes, but gave up on me.

The more I thought about it, the more I decided that the problem was not the deed but the body. With hindsight, I was fooling myself. In truth, I couldn't bring myself to contemplate the deed, but I could consider how to tidy up afterward.

Without a tractor and a handy disposal pit, what would I do with the body? The obvious solution was the Broads, but with most of them only a few feet deep and, what's more, heaving with tourists in paddle steamers, cruisers, yachts, dinghies and canoes, to say nothing of the paddle boarders and wild swimmers, it was hard to think of anywhere accessible to the *Edith* that would provide sufficient secrecy. If I could wait until winter, then the Broads would be quieter, but could I wait so long? Philip might have plans of his own, not least because the excuse of his plumbing was wearing increasingly thin.

One evening when Philip was out, I sat down with a map of the Broads and the connecting rivers. This was moving away from fantasy now, as I began to feel more and more trapped in what had been my refuge. This was me planning to kill Philip. I faced the fact. It was not comfortable, but what I had got away with once, I could again. Turning my attention to the map, I ruled out all the Broads on grounds of shallow water. It would be impossible for even a weighted body to be hidden there for long, and most were busy with visitors. Those that were quieter were mainly in places where the *Edith* could not penetrate. Focusing my attention on the rivers took me downstream to Great Yarmouth. That gave me the germ of an idea. I knew the river flowed very quickly through the bridges in Great Yarmouth to the sea, and it was not far from the areas open to cruisers. Suppose a body went into the water at the turn of the tide? It would surely make its way down to the sea and would soon be unrecognisable.

I sighed, and tossed the map onto the shelf. There was a problem. A body floating down that stretch of water would surely be seen. There were several bridges between the yacht station and the sea, and a good few ships entering and leaving the port. It would be spotted. Before I went to work I checked the little book. My hair had gone. My intentions were reinforced.

Philip came home that evening in time for supper, and for once he wasn't complaining. He was in a good mood and keen to keep topping up my glass. I was less keen, but it was hard to keep saying no without destroying the good mood, so I had rather more than I would have liked. I went to bed rather fuddled and slept very heavily. In consequence I didn't notice when Brizo slipped in with me and curled up by my bed.

I woke with a start to find someone on my bed with me. I was still woozy and struggling to make sense of this person being there and pulling at my nightclothes when Brizo let loose a bloodcurdling growl and threw herself onto the bed. The person I realised, even in my confusion, had to be Philip. There was a lot of muffled cursing, and he rolled off the bed, taking most of my bedclothes with him. The door slammed with Brizo just this side of it, all tangled up in the duvet.

By the time I had sorted out my bed again, I was beginning to wake up if not sober up. I was fuddled and confused, my memory even of the most recent events hazy. I got back into bed with a glass of water and, anticipating a hangover, took an ibuprofen. Then I wrapped my arms around my legs and did some hard thinking, trying to make sense out of what had just happened. I could have dreamed it, and got the bedclothes in a state as I thrashed around in a nightmare. It was unlikely, but not impossible. It could have been an intruder again, but again, unlikely, and if so how had they got aboard without any of us noticing? As soon as the weight of a person came aboard the boat would rock. Even if I was too far gone to notice, Philip or Brizo would have. And come to that, why hadn't Brizo reacted until the person was on my bed? I was forced to the conclusion that it was either a nightmare or Philip, and I didn't think it was a nightmare. For that matter, if it *was* a nightmare and I had made a racket by thrashing around, why hadn't Philip come to ask what was the matter?

Because, I thought, he is nursing a bite or two from Brizo. I decided to lay low until morning, then ask Philip if he had heard anything in the night. I could also see if Brizo had left any marks.

Even though I still felt woozy, my ravelled sleeves looked like staying unknitted. I propped myself up on my pillows with Brizo beside me, and was just reconciling myself to a sleepless night when a bright idea struck me. The river from Yarmouth seawards was fairly deep. It had to be, given the size of shipping that came up it. If a body could be persuaded to float just under the surface, it could make its way to the sea unobserved. With the fuzziness in my head slowly clearing, I reached for my iPad and did some googling on diving sites. It seemed roughly 10 per cent of body weight would provide enough negative buoyancy to make a body float under the surface, but not plunge to the bottom. I couldn't know how much difference it would make if the body was dead, rather than alive and breathing, but I seemed to remember that bodies already dead when they entered the water did not end up with water in the lungs. So, I reasoned, it shouldn't make too much difference.

I went on to Amazon and looked up diver's weights, but then realised that if a non-diver was found with a weighted belt around them, in the event a body *was* found, it would cease to look like an accident. I needed some way to weight the body so that, if my luck was out and the corpse turned up, it would still look accidental. I went to sleep on the problem, and woke up in the morning still propped up in bed, my iPad on the duvet beside me, and a solution in my mind. I also had a hangover.

By the time I got into the kitchen, Philip had left for work. I looked in his bedroom, but it looked as always. I returned to the kitchen and got out some cans and my scales. I guessed that Philip weighed around fourteen stone, or a bit under ninety kilos. That meant, according to Google, I needed around eight to nine kilos in weights. That would be about sixteen standard-sized cans of food. They would fit into a smallish rucksack, which could be secured onto a body in such a way that it wouldn't fall off but wouldn't look too unnatural. If I could slip Philip over the side at the yacht station in Great Yarmouth, there was a good chance that, so weighted, he would make the journey out to sea without ever popping to the surface.

As to the deed itself, suddenly it didn't seem so unthinkable. The last night had provided the impetus I needed. I was now backed into that corner with no way out. This man was threatening everything I had. There was no one but me to deal with it. I looked at my Le Creuset frying pan and smiled to myself. It hadn't been so hard the last time around. How hard could it be this time? All I now needed to do was check the tide tables and plan my trip with Philip as guest – one way at least.

I went in to work at the staithe a little late, a little hungover and a little grumpy. The last was not wholly acting. The lack of sleep and the headache were getting to me. Philip was grumpy too, and favouring his right arm. When I asked him if there was anything the matter he snapped at me, and I was very tempted to snap back, but bearing my master plan in mind, I kept quiet. Later in the day, when we both seemed in a better temper, I broached the subject of a little trip.

'Perhaps next week,' I suggested. 'If we could get someone to cover, we could take two or three days. Maybe go down to Yarmouth, stay there overnight and then have a day or two in the southern Broads.' He seemed quite keen, and I made a note to make sure that the convenient dates were also convenient in tide terms.

Then Amy showed me something in a national paper that changed everything.

'This story from Yorkshire is quite spooky isn't it?' She flapped her paper at me, then put it down on a table and pointed at some columns at the bottom of the front page. 'Imagine the shock for the poor blokes who found the skeleton. One minute they're exploring some old war-time hideaway, the next they're tripping over a human skull. It doesn't bear thinking about.'

I approached the paper hesitantly, my fingers going cold and stiff with anticipation. Luckily a customer came in at that moment and Amy bustled away. I looked where she had pointed. The story was sensational, but clear as to detail. They had found Matthew. Our old pit turned out to be a World War II hideaway; archaeologists had gone down into it and found the skeleton. It surely couldn't be long before they worked out whose it was. I knew vaguely that teeth could be used to identify someone, and Matthew had been an assiduous visitor of the dentist. Then I remembered with some relief that his dentist was in Cambridge, not Yorkshire. Hopefully it might be sometime before a newspaper article named the victim. Then I laughed, as I folded the paper onto a less significant page. Who was I kidding? The police were bound to assume the skeleton was the missing Matthew and they would soon come looking for me.

*

I dithered all through that day. At times I almost snatched up my bag and Brizo and dashed for my car. Then I thought again and stayed put. Poor Amy had to put up with a lot of inattention and mistakes, even though we weren't terribly busy for the time of year. An unseasonable drizzle had set in and it seemed to have depressed custom as well as me. Only Brizo was unaffected by the general gloom, and set off back to the *Edith* at the end of our shift with a jaunty swing to her tail.

On our way back, with a vague notion of keeping my options open, I stocked up on some essentials such as bread, pasta and dog food, and with a last-minute remembrance of ancient sailing problems such as scurvy, also bought some fresh fruit.

I realised at that point that I was subconsciously planning an escape on the *Edith*. True, she was slow compared to a car, but she had the inestimable advantage of being capable of going to sea. In the *Edith*, I could sail down the Yare and head for France or Belgium. The fact that I seriously contemplated doing that with no seagoing experience, no chart and no radio perhaps gives some indication of my state of mind.

My second, and possibly more realistic, idea, was to up sticks and move the *Edith* to another quiet location on the Broads. I could change my name again. I could last quite a time on my savings and stocks, and could just lay low for a while until everyone lost interest and my story became chip wrappings. It would also have the advantage of solving my Philip problem. I realise now this was never a very realistic option, but it had some very seductive advantages.

That evening Philip was out until late and I went to bed

early. It didn't help much as I tossed and turned all night, but by daylight I had made my mind up. I would try Plan A, and lay low in the southern Broads somewhere. And I would set off that morning; no hesitation, no goodbyes.

Philip went off as usual around 7.30 to open up at the staithe, and I made swift preparations for departure. It didn't take me long and after a quick toilet walk in the woods for Brizo, we were ready to leave. I couldn't bring myself to think about Amy in particular, but I thought she might assume I was fleeing Philip. I hoped she wouldn't think too badly of me.

I had cast off the *Edith* and was pulling away into the dyke when to my horror I heard Philip's voice and felt the boat rock as he jumped aboard.

'Going somewhere, Rachel?' he said, and sat down beside me in the cockpit.

I didn't look at him and carried on into the dyke.

'You've picked a bad time to jump aboard, Philip.' I tried to keep my voice light. 'I've got itchy feet. I'm going on a little trip.'

'Suits me. I've been getting a bit bored too. A little boat trip is just what I need. Where are we going?'

'I'll be gone a few days,' I stressed. 'What about your businesses? I'll drop you at the staithe,' and I started to turn the *Edith*.

'No need. I've got cover on call. A phone call or two will sort it.' He put a firm hand on the wheel and steered her out into the main channel again. 'Come on, Rachel. Don't be so unwelcoming. I'll make us some coffee.'

He bustled down to the kitchen and I heard him filling the kettle.

'Lucky I filled the tank recently,' I thought. Then I settled down to my twin tasks: steering the boat and working out how to get rid of Philip.

We made good time down the Thurne and saw little traffic until we reached the Bure. At Thurne Mouth I turned south towards Acle and Philip pulled a face.

'This stretch of the river is so dull,' he complained. 'Why don't we go the other way towards Horning?'

'I thought we'd go across Breydon Water and up the Yare towards Norwich,' I said. 'That would make a nice change.'

I was trying to work out whether I could put my 'getting rid of Philip' plan into operation at the Yarmouth Yacht Station. It was possible. We arrived at the Yacht Station around midday and I suggested to Philip we could be tourists for an hour or two.

'We could visit the model village,' I suggested. He didn't look keen so I added hurriedly, 'or the Nelson Museum? Then a meal in town before heading back to the boat. We could walk over to the Imperial Hotel. They have a good restaurant.'

He brightened and picked up his phone. 'I'll see if they've got a table.'

They had, and we booked for 7.30. That gave us a few hours at the museum or sightseeing, then time for me to walk Brizo by the river and us to change for dinner.

It was a still evening and the walk through town would have been pleasant, except for the crowds of drunk teenagers in the market place. Once we had navigated that obstacle, the streets nearer the sea front were quieter and we got a friendly greeting at the hotel. I had eaten there a couple of times before and the seafood was, as ever, excellent. But I wouldn't say it was the most convivial dinner I had ever experienced. We each probably exchanged more words with the waiters than with each other. I wasn't sure what Philip's problem was, but I found myself preoccupied by my plans for the night. With that in mind, I was assiduous in refilling Philip's glass and was very careful how much I drank myself. When we eventually stepped out into cool sea air around 10.30, I was stone cold sober and Philip just a little tipsy. Not enough to stagger as he walked, but enough to make him move with exaggerated care. 'Just enough,' I thought to myself, still focused on my plans. The focus lasted until we returned to the *Edith*. I lifted Brizo onto the bank for a run about, then got back on board. 'Nightcap, Philip?' I asked. 'Shall I pour you a glass of brandy? Or port?'

'That would be very pleasant, Rachel. Brandy please.'

We were in the galley, and therefore pretty close together. I picked up the brandy: 'The glasses are in the cupboard behind you, Philip. On the bottom shelf.' As he turned and bent I thought 'this is my chance' and reached up for the frying pan on its hook near the stove. I had my hand on it. I was lifting it from the hook... then realised that I couldn't do it. Not just like that. Not even to Philip. I left the pan where it was and as Philip turned round I poured brandy into one of the glasses he was holding. 'I'm suddenly tired,' I said. 'I think I'll go to bed after all.' And I left him there in the galley, one glass of brandy in hand, one unused frying pan swinging slightly on its hook.

And that was that. I was out of ideas. I decided I would just have to head towards Norwich and find an opportunity to dump Philip somewhere along the Yare, then double back and go down the Waveney towards Beccles. Surely he would want to go ashore for a pub meal somewhere tomorrow. And surely I could find an opportunity to escape back to the *Edith* and off on my solo travels. 'Reedham,' I thought. 'I'll head that way and we can moor at Reedham for a pub meal. I can make an excuse about needing the ladies', and then dash back to the *Edith* and away. No need to further complicate my life with another death. Just a run for it.'

We started late the following morning, partly because we had to wait for the tide to slacken, partly because Philip was unsurprisingly hungover from the night before. If I was unsympathetic, it was because I couldn't help thinking he was lucky not to have a much worse headache. I didn't regret my decision, if anything it was a relief, but I still had a problem to solve. We had a makeshift lunch, then set off under the Yarmouth bridges at slack water. I let Philip take the wheel for a while and put Brizo's life jacket on. If we were going to cross Breydon Water I was taking precautions.

'I notice the dog gets a life jacket and I don't,' Philip remarked.

'I assume you have the good sense not to jump overboard.' I was quite tart with him. 'Brizo might not have!' Then we were in Breydon Water and Philip dropped his bombshell.

'When were you planning to tell me about Matthew, Rachel?' he asked.

For a moment I didn't take in what he had said. We continued up the marked channel. 'I don't understand.'

'Oh come on, Rachel. Don't take me for a fool. One day the *EDP* has an article about a Rachel Wade and her dead husband, found in a hole in the ground on a Yorkshire farm. The next day my Rachel, mystery woman with no family, no background, no past but lots of cash, decides to make a run for it on her boat.'

'You're fantasising,' I said. 'It's madness. Just because I'm named Rachel and don't choose to gossip to all and sundry about my past, I'm suddenly a murderer fleeing justice. Is that what you really think of me, Philip?'

'So I'm all and sundry, am I?' said Philip, focusing on what was apparently the most important element of my speech. 'Well, it doesn't matter now. And who or what you were doesn't matter either.' He leaned over and cut the power. The *Edith* slowed and started to drift to a halt.

'What do you mean, it doesn't matter?'

'I mean, Rachel my dear, that I am tired of dancing to your tune. You are plainly unstable, whether murderer or not, and no one will be surprised about a terrible accident on the Broads. To be completely clear, because I wouldn't like you to be under any illusion, there is about to be an accident that involves you falling into the Yare and drowning. Perhaps you fell in trying to rescue that damned dog. Yes, that's a good idea, then I can get rid of the dog too. I will of course, be heartbroken at my failure to save you. I'm good at that. I've had practice. And your little savings pot will provide some comfort.'

To say I was gobsmacked is an understatement. I froze to my seat. My jaw dropped. I stayed frozen, until Philip took me by the throat.

He could have done exactly as he said and I doubt I would have been able to stop him, except for Brizo. He already had me half over the side when Brizo leapt at him and, judging by the yell, sank her sharp teeth into Philip's buttock. He let go of me and turned on Brizo while I scrambled back into the cockpit. I'm not clear exactly what happened next, it's all confused in my head. I think he went for Brizo and I grabbed him from behind. He pulled out of my hold easily and went for me again, but I was ready for him this time and Brizo had him by the leg. Somehow, it was Philip who went over the side.

He was splashing around in the water, cursing horribly, while I frantically tried to start the *Edith*. The first three times she wouldn't start, and then I realised it was because she was still in gear. I sorted that, but by this time Philip had a grip on a stanchion and was trying to pull himself back on board. To my enormous relief, the engine caught and I flung the *Edith* into gear and wrenched the throttle back. We took off like a bat out of hell and I had to swing her round sharply to avoid ending up on a sandbank. The swing was my salvation as it threw Philip off his hold and I turned downriver. We were going so fast at the start that we were planing, and steering was tricky to say the least. Once we were well clear of Philip I slowed down a little and we passed a Broads Authority boat going the other way as I headed back towards Great Yarmouth and Plan B.

17

From Yorkshire to Norfolk

As arranged, Fiona picked DI Geldard up in York. It was the first time she had been to his home and she was impressed by the ultra-modern block of flats by the river. She found a space for the car in Marlborough Close and buzzed the entry phone.

'Come up, Fiona. I'll be with you in a tick.'

She took the stairs to the third floor, where the door was already open. Walking in, she was blown away by the huge open-plan space and the view from the balcony of the river beyond.

'Like it?' Geldard was just shrugging into his jacket, a piece of toast in one hand.

'Love it.'

The colours were all neutrals and wide windows lit the generous space. A Shaker-style kitchen occupied the shorter arm of the L-shaped room, and a pale oak dining table divided the cooking area from the living room. Well-worn leather sofas surrounded the fireplace and a large flat-screen TV occupied one wall, with a music centre in the corner.

'It suits us. It wouldn't do for a family, not least that the spare bedroom is part music room, part office, but it's great for Isabelle and me. I'm sorry I can't introduce you. She's still away on her tour in the US. Right, I'm ready, let's go.'

The drive to Norfolk was uncommonly tedious. The A1 southbound was busy and the A17 was, as is notoriously the case, clogged with lorries heading in both directions. Stuck at a boring 55mph behind an unusually smart lorry advertising fresh veg all over its rear and sides, Geldard pulled out some paperwork and got stuck in.

'Mind if I have the radio on, Sir?'

'Not at all, provided it doesn't blow my hair off.'

Fiona selected Radio 4, then after a few moments of boredom switched to Classic FM. The 3rd Brandenburg filled the car, and was followed by a Mozart clarinet concerto. Peace reigned for an hour or so, then Geldard put his papers back in the briefcase.

'Fiona, what do you think we'll find when we catch up with Rachel Wade? What sort of picture have you got of her?'

'Honestly, Sir, I'm not expecting a master criminal. From what everyone has said, I think Rachel may have been abused by her husband, in which case what we have here is a woman who lost it under pressure.'

'What specifically gives you that impression?' Fiona glanced from the road ahead to her boss and Geldard added, 'I'm not trying to catch you out. I'm interested in your perspective. And it would be useful to review what we think we know about her before we interview her.'

'Well, some of her farming neighbours think she was bullied and that it may have been physical. Her brother says she changed when she married, became cut off from friends and family, stopped doing things she enjoyed and was good at, lost weight and lost confidence. The village variously describes her as stuck up, distant, always busy – indeed the hardest-working partner in the marriage – but also says they hardly saw her except when Matthew wanted her to attend events in his shadow. Her grandfather is widely known to have insisted on the farm staying in her name alone, which suggests he knew something that led him to believe Rachel needed protection. Oh, and Sharon Dyble thinks Matthew was having an affair, but no one saw him with anyone. I tend to discount most of what Sharon Dyble said,' she added, 'a fair bit seems to be fantasy and all of it is malicious.'

'So, plenty of motive, but why not just divorce?'

'How many abused women divorce their abusers?' she countered.

'Fair point. Most seem to blame themselves. Some even seem to love the swine regardless. You're thinking it was manslaughter on impulse? A loss of control. But in that case, why not call an ambulance? Why hide the body and why the elaborate trail laid in London, if it is a trail.'

'You said yourself Sir, the pattern of expenditure on the card is exactly what you would expect if it had been stolen. Perhaps it was stolen earlier, and has nothing to do with the case?'

'Perhaps, but it's a bit serendipitous if so.'

As they passed Norwich on the A47, already behind schedule, Geldard rang Jim Henning. 'Sorry, Jim, we're late thanks to traffic, would it make sense to meet in Ludham?'

'Ok by me. When do you expect to arrive?'

Geldard checked the map. 'I would say around ten thirty. Where do you suggest we meet?'

'There's a car park at Ludham Staithe. We could meet there and then go to the mooring to find the lady. According to the conversations my DC's had in the village, she works in one or two of the village hostelries, so if she's not on the boat she shouldn't be far.'

Geldard's phone rang just as they made it down the narrow lane and pulled into the car park.

'Jim, just arriving now. I should see you any moment.'

'Sorry Greg. Bad news I'm afraid. According to the locals, Rachel should have been at work in the tea shop today, but the boat has gone. I've checked the mooring and the *Edith* is not there. The *EDP* ran a copy of the item saying we were looking for Rachel Wade yesterday, and it's probable she saw it. Anyway, this doesn't seem to be a planned trip on her part. I think we should assume the worst and hope for the best. Either way, I guess you would like to find her.'

'How far can she get in a boat?'

'This one is capable of putting to sea. If she has fuel, she could potentially leave the river system and cross the Channel.'

'Hell. How do we put out an APB on a river?'

'My DC is already on the radio requesting patrol cars to keep an eye out at obvious public moorings, particularly those on her likely route. Now,' and he started tapping numbers into his phone, 'I'll ask the Broads Authority to help us with one of their boats. They're probably nearest. Do you think this justifies a police helicopter search?'

Geldard thought quickly. 'Yes, I do. Apart from the risk of losing her, I think there's also a risk she might do something stupid.'

'In that case, I'll radio Wymondham and we'll see what we can do.'

The Broads Authority were delighted to help. Some quick phone calls later, Geldard and Fiona were back in their car and Jim with them to give directions.

'There's no point the Broads boat picking us up here,' he explained. 'It would take hours for us to follow her down the river by boat, but we can get ahead in a matter of minutes if we go by car to the Yarmouth Yacht Station.'

'And if she's gone the other way?'

'Then it's a dead end as far as the boat is concerned. In a boat that size she can only go as far as Potter Heigham in one direction, and Wroxham or Ludham Bridge in the other. The Broads Authority have asked their contacts at all those places, plus Horning, to keep an eye out and let me know if they see the *Edith*; but if she's on the run, the logical route to take is downriver to Yarmouth. From there she can go out to sea, up the Yare to Norwich, or even down the Waveney to Lowestoft.'

As Jim had promised, the route to Great Yarmouth from Ludham was fairly swift for a county with no motorways, and only twenty minutes had elapsed before they were piling out of the car and onto the wharf at the Yacht Station. A rather smart boat flying the Broads Authority flag was waiting, floating well below them, the pilot's face below their feet.

'Mind your step,' he said. 'The river is low and the tide is just on the turn.'

Fiona blessed her decision to wear trousers and scrambled down the ladder to the boat below, followed by Geldard and Jim Henning, who dropped into the boat and pushed her off from the side with the ease of long practice.

'I'm Andy,' said the pilot, offering a hand and steering the boat into the centre of the river. 'With the tide on the turn we're pretty much at slack water, so the run under the bridges should be easy. But put the life belts on just in case.'

They were the swanky slimline versions that inflated when, or as Geldard devoutly hoped, *if* you hit the water.

'None of my contacts have seen the *Edith* upriver and she hasn't gone past me, so she's probably somewhere in the Yare. She's definitely not between here and Acle, because I've come down that stretch this morning and there aren't many places you can hide a boat the size of the *Edith*.'

He swung the boat under the first bridge then took a right-hand turn into the River Yare.

'I checked with the harbourmaster while I was waiting for you and no cruisers have come through the harbour in the past few hours, so she's likely somewhere in the upper reaches of the Yare or Waveney.'

'The harbourmaster controls the last couple of miles of the Yare between here and the sea,' explained Jim. 'No one is supposed to sail down that stretch without seeking permission, so any strange boat wandering through will definitely be challenged.'

They followed the river between rather dilapidated industrial banks, then under a big road bridge.

'That bridge can open for large ships,' pointed out Andy, 'but the *Edith* will have no problem here provided she keeps to the marked channel.'

Their view suddenly opened out into a wide vista of water, mudflats and sandbanks, the latter exposed at this point of the tide. Andy handed out a couple of pairs of binoculars.

'You might find these useful if we spot them,' he said. 'In the meantime, there are some great populations of wading birds in this area.'

He looked at Geldard's face and laughed. 'I know. That's not what we're here for.' All the same, Fiona did take a surreptitious look round under the guise of adjusting the binoculars, but was interrupted by a crackle on the radio.

'Police Call-sign Romeo/Delta to Broads Authority, are you receiving me. Romeo/Delta to Broads Authority, are you receiving me, over.'

With a nod from Andy, Jim took the radio mouthpiece. 'Broads Authority to Romeo Delta, receiving you. This is DI Henning. Over.'

'That's the helicopter,' he said in an aside to Fiona and Geldard. 'She should be over the river by now.'

'Broads Authority to Romeo/Delta, what is your location? Over.'

'Romeo/Delta to Broads Authority. I am hovering over What3Words *needed/sofa/distinct*. Repeat, *needed/sofa/distinct*. There are three cruisers below me that might fit your description. Do you wish me to go lower to check? Over.'

As he repeated the location, Andy referred to an app on his iPad. 'What3Words provides a geolocation to within three metres,' he explained. 'We've only had it for a few months but it's invaluable, especially on the Broads. That code places him over the Yare where she runs though the Berney Arms reach. Ask him where those three boats are.'

Jim passed on the request and the reply came back.

'Two in the Yare, heading towards Reedham, one more or less stationary at the junction of the Yare and Waveney where Breydon Water narrows into the two rivers.'

Geldard checked the chart beside Andy and looked at Jim.

'We're not far from the third boat, and the others are now safely upriver in the Yare. Can he keep an eye on those moving while we check out the third? Andy, can this boat go faster?'

'We can here in Breydon Water, but there's a speed limit in the river,' and he pushed forward on the throttle. The boat surged away and as they swung round the bend in the river they spotted the long, low outline of a large white cruiser ahead of them. As the helicopter had reported, she seemed to be more or less stationary in the water, just drifting gently on the tide. Fiona focused her binoculars on the boat.

'She's definitely not under power,' remarked Andy, turning towards Fiona as she refocused the glasses.

'I can see two people on board. On the top. No wait, they seem to be struggling! God!' she exclaimed. 'One's gone overboard!'

'What?' Geldard was struggling to focus his own binoculars, but as they watched, the white boat swung round and headed at speed back down the river towards them. The navigable channel was narrow just there and they could all clearly see a woman at the wheel as she shot past within a stone's throw of the Broads Authority boat. They also saw the boat's name clearly marked on the stern, 'The *Edith Cavell*'.

'After her, or retrieve the person in the water?' asked Andy calmly.

Grinding his teeth, Geldard said, 'We'd better get them out of the water first. Can't just let them drown.'

'I've still got the binoculars on them,' said Fiona, said glasses clamped to her face. 'They're doing a lot of splashing but the head's above water.'

'Good girl,' said Andy. 'Keep them in sight and let me know if they go under.'

In a matter of moments, they were alongside a spluttering and highly indignant Philip Sayer.

18

The Chase

A flurry of radio messages followed as the helicopter was tasked to follow the *Edith* downriver and the Broads Authority boat tried to catch up.

Fiona attended to the soggy and furious article they had, with some difficulty, pulled from the river. She handed him a blanket and they inspected their catch. It was an exceedingly muddy man of middle age and medium height, almost dancing with rage.

'Get after that murderous bitch,' he spluttered. 'Don't hang about for God's sake. Get a bloody move on.'

He plunged towards Andy as though planning to seize the controls. Jim and Greg pushed him back forcibly.

'Just a moment,' said Jim. 'We're police officers. Take a seat back there and we'll come and have a word. We have a bit of a situation here.'

'A situation,' the man shouted. 'That's a bloody laugh.

That lunatic tries to kill me and you have a situation! If you're police, then bloody well do something. Get after her and arrest her!'

'We have that in hand, Sir. Sit down and please keep out of our way. We'll interview you in a moment. Just for the record, who is on the *Edith Cavell* and who are you?'

'Philip Sayer. I mean, I'm Philip Sayer, obviously. The woman on the *Edith Cavell* calls herself Rachel Treadwell, but I think she's Rachel Wade.' He looked at the police with triumph in his eyes. 'So I suggest you get a move on and arrest her. She just tried to kill me.'

Jim looked at Greg and he nodded to Fiona.

'Keep an eye on him will you please, DC McCrae? He can wait for the moment.'

The white cruiser was now out of sight from river level, and the helicopter informed them that Rachel had followed the Yare southward and appeared to be making for the sea at some speed. 'Judging from my speed following her and the wake she is throwing up, I estimate she is doing between twelve and fifteen knots.'

'She's breaking the speed limit then,' remarked Andy. 'There's a seven-knot speed limit in the harbour, and you're encouraged to keep below that anyway because of ships manoeuvring.'

'What's that in miles per hour?' asked Fiona.

'The speed limit is around eight miles per hour. She's doing nearly eighteen miles per hour, and she's putting herself and other harbour users at risk. I'm not following her at that pace.'

Geldard exclaimed in frustration, but whatever he was going to say was drowned in a stern intervention from the radio.

'Harbourmaster to the *Edith Cavell*, harbourmaster to the *Edith Cavell*, come in please, over.'

'Harbourmaster to the *Edith Cavell*, you have made an unauthorised entry to the harbour and are exceeding the speed limit. Please slow down immediately and turn back.'

'Harbourmaster to the *Edith Cavell*, you are exceeding the speed limit and are approaching ships that are manoeuvring. SLOW DOWN IMMEDIATELY and turn back or I will be forced to take action.'

The messages were repeated several times.

'I don't think she's got a radio,' Andy said. 'And if she has she's not listening.'

'There is no radio,' contributed the man at the back.

Andy got on to the radio himself.

'Broads Authority boat BA 101 to harbourmaster, are you receiving me? Over.'

'Harbourmaster receiving. Can you cast any light on this lunatic? Over.'

'Broads Authority to harbourmaster. We are in pursuit of the *Edith Cavell*, with police officers on board. Request permission to enter the harbour. Over.'

'Permission granted, but unless she slows down or hits something, and hitting something is currently looking very likely, you are not going to catch her in that boat before she reaches the sea.'

'Do you have eyes on the *Edith Cavell*?'

'No, but she has AIS.'

'Good God,' exclaimed Andy. 'That's a stroke of luck.'

He turned to Geldard and explained, 'AIS is the automatic tracking system that operates from a transponder on ships. Most small cruisers don't have one, but some of the bigger ones do. Obviously the *Edith* does, and obviously she's forgotten to turn it off. Look for the Shipfinder app on my laptop, and we can track her.'

It didn't take long for them to locate the *Edith* on the computer screen, and also to see that she was still approaching the mouth of the river at some speed. In the background the radio continued its barrage of increasingly urgent instructions for the *Edith* to slow down and turn back.

On the screen, Geldard and Fiona could see the cause of the urgency. In the river near Southtown, a ship was turning to head downstream, while near the river mouth a second was heading upstream. Others were waiting offshore to enter the river or the outer harbour, but further movements had been put on hold pending resolution of the crisis being brewed by the rogue cruiser. As they watched, the *Edith* swung round the turning ship, and they could only imagine the consternation she was causing.

'We need to get someone to intercept her at sea,' said Jim. 'We're unlikely to catch her in the river, even if it was safe to do so. And we're not equipped for boarding! Where's the Border Force ship? That might be our best bet.'

Andy pointed to the Shipfinder display.

'Unfortunately she's between Felixstowe and Orford Ness. Too far away. I think we should ask the coastguard to launch the Gorleston lifeboat.'

'Except the lifeboat seems to be down near Lowestoft as well,' said Fiona, pointing.

'Damn. Pity, because the lifeboat station is near the mouth of the river. In that case what we need is the Caister lifeboat. It's not far away and they have what they claim is the fastest lifeboat on the east coast.'

He got on the radio to the coastguard and explained the situation, while Andy slowed the boat and pulled over to the side.

'It's out of our hands now. Let's see what the Caister lifeboat can do.' He tied up on the North Quay and the police turned to their passenger.

'Back to the station, I think,' said Jim, 'and a chat with Mr Sayer here. We can monitor the chase from there.'

To Rachel on the *Edith*, the last few minutes seemed the shortest in her entire life. She had turned the *Edith* and run away from Philip entirely on autopilot. Once she slowed to a manageable pace, she checked that Brizo was okay and looked about her. The boat behind seemed to be trying to recover Philip, and she could well imagine the story he would tell. The police couldn't be far away and she could see no way out, other than to head for the sea and to cross the Channel. How hard could it be just to go across the Channel in a straight line? Once she got to the French coast she could find another small boat to follow into a harbour. Or she could lose herself among the canals of the Netherlands. The lack of a chart was a bit of a bugger, but she could google one surely, as soon as she had some signal.

Anyway, the immediate problem was to get out to sea and keep heading east before she was stopped.

She picked up speed again; not so fast as when she

began her flight, but as fast as she felt she could manage. The instruments said fourteen knots. She remembered that there was no speed limit on Breydon Water, and she felt comfortable with that. She turned under the road bridge, noting the sign that said 'no hire boats past this point', and kept going. Brizo jumped on to the passenger seat next to her, and the movement distracted her enough that she failed to notice the speed limit sign on the river bank.

The first stretch of the river downstream was fairly empty of traffic, although there were some sizeable ships tied up alongside the wharves. Some chaps on board an old herring drifter waved at her vigorously and she waved back. She was surprised to hear some cursing as she went by what she saw was named the *Lydia Eva*, but pressed on. A quick glance behind showed her an empty river, so it seemed there was no one following. Over the sound of the *Edith*'s engine she thought she heard something, and looked up. There was a helicopter hovering not far away and she froze. Was it after her? She kept an intermittent eye on it as it hovered above and some way behind her, then looked ahead to see, to her horror, that a ship was turning in the river ahead of her. There were several men running around on her deck and shouting, then the ship's siren sounded and drowned everything else. She had no time to think and no time to stop. It seemed only seconds before the steep orange side of the ship hung over her like a cliff. She swung the wheel wildly and, with feet to spare, ran alongside the ship. There was a rapidly narrowing gap at the stern of the ship as she used the full width of the river to turn. Rachel headed for the gap without stopping to calculate, pushed the throttle forward and by some miracle slipped through at speed and into the river beyond. The ship was still making a hideous racket with her siren as Rachel slowed down a little to her steady fourteen knots. It was a salutary reminder that her attention needed to be on the river ahead, not what was behind.

She spared a glance for her passenger, but Brizo seemed unperturbed by both the speed and the noise. The sudden manoeuvring, well, that was another matter as the sharp swing had precipitated her from her perch on the co-pilot's seat to the floor. She climbed back up with a reproachful look that Rachel missed as she was now, lesson learned, looking ahead.

This stretch of the river ran straight between banks lined with bulk storage silos and warehouses. There were no ships moored here and she had a clear view to where the river appeared to take a sharp turn to the left. In front of her, another ship was coming upriver. There was more sounding of sirens, which Rachel ignored, not knowing whether this was normal or a reaction to her presence. To her eye, there was plenty of room between the vessel and the bank. She ran down its side, ignoring the shouts from the deck, and continued down the river and round the left-hand bend. She could see a lot of tall derricks and cranes, which she assumed to be the much publicised outer harbour, and in front of her was open water. The sea at last. She was tempted to open up the throttle still further, but caution about rate of fuel use came to her mind, and she left it where it was. Once clear of the outer harbour she looked at the *Edith*'s little compass and headed east.

*

Back in Great Yarmouth, still on the Broads boat, top priority was to contact the coastguard and get a lifeboat launched. Against a background of rising grumbles from Sayer about being cold and wet, Jim rang to ask for assistance. After a few moments' conversation, Jim turned to Sayer.

'Just shut up a moment, man, and answer a question. Has Rachel got a weapon on board? A firearm or anything like that?'

'Never saw one.'

Jim turned to his phone again and said, 'No, not according to the only witness we have. But they should proceed with caution. At the very least she may be a risk to herself—'

Sayer interrupted, 'She has got a dog on board. A mad rabid brute. You'll need to watch out for that. It bit me. Come to that,' he added, 'I want a doctor.'

'In good time,' replied Jim, then to the phone, 'you heard that, did you? I think you can take rabid with a pinch of salt. What breed is it?' he asked Sayer with a grin. 'Chihuahua?'

'Collie cross,' he snapped and then shut up.

'Collie,' Jim said to the coastguard, then 'I think that's a very good suggestion.'

Putting the phone down, he said to Greg and Fiona, 'They've contacted Caister lifeboat and they'll launch within ten minutes. There's a first responder in the area and he'll go with them, to help out if needed. I know the chap and he has been both policeman and nurse, so he's ideal.'

'Not Ben Asheton?'

'Yes, of course, you've met him. I worked with him in the force, he'll be a good help. Right. Let's go to the station and we can keep in touch with the lifeboat by radio. I've sent the helicopter home. No need to waste his expensive time when the *Edith* is kindly signalling her location by GPS.'

Greg, Fiona and the damp bundle that was Philip Sayer were picked up by an area car and taken to the police station in Howard Street. From the outside it looked a boring six-ties-style office block, but inside both Greg and Fiona were more interested in getting warm and interviewing their 'person of interest' than reviewing architecture. The unexpected and (relatively) high-speed travel on the river had left them chilled even on a summer's day. Jim took them to his office and took orders for coffees while Philip was taken away for dry clothes and then to an interview room.

'Whatever happened on the river was on your territory,' said Greg to Jim over their steaming mugs. 'I don't want to tread on your toes, but obviously I am interested in anything I can learn about Rachel Wade/Treadwell. And how do we keep abreast of what is happening with the lifeboat?'

'I have a chap on the radio. He'll give us a shout as soon as they get within sight of the *Edith*. In the meantime, I suggest you and I have a quick chat with Philip Sayer. Fiona can watch from the next room if that's okay.'

'Good plan.'

Dressed in paper coveralls while his clothes dried, Philip Sayer was, if anything, even more sulky.

'Have you caught Rachel?' he demanded, before they had even sat down.

'Shall we take things in the right order,' said Jim, switching on the recorder. 'Introductions first. I am Detective Inspector Jim Henning of Norfolk Police. This is Detective Inspector Greg Geldard of North Yorkshire Police. Can you please introduce yourself for the benefit of the tape?'

'Philip Sayer. Do I need a lawyer?'

'That is entirely up to you Mr Sayer, but we only want to ask you some questions about Rachel and what went on aboard the *Edith Cavell* today. You will note that I have not accused you of anything or cautioned you. We are just looking for some help.'

'Oh. Okay. What do you want to know?'

'How long have you known Rachel?'

'For the last three or four years or so. Ever since she came to Ludham.'

'And how did you meet?'

'On the staithe. She was looking for part-time work and started to work for me. I run a shop and some other businesses on the staithe,' he explained. 'Our relationship grew from there?'

'Is there a Mrs Sayer?'

'No. I am a widower.'

'So, what exactly is your relationship with Rachel?'

'Good friends and before you ask, just good friends.'

'But I understand you've been living on her boat for some weeks,' Greg chipped in.

'Yes, but we were still just good friends.'

'Where do you normally live?'

'Ludham, but I had a plumbing problem in my cottage and Rachel was putting me up.'

'I see. So what happened today? What changed?'

'I don't know. We decided to take the boat trip on the spur of the moment. At least, Rachel decided and I went along with it. She chose the route. We spent last night moored in Yarmouth and had dinner at the Imperial. Then this morning we set off for Norwich and when we got to Breydon Water she seemed to flip. She started shouting, making wild accusations about me forcing myself on her, and then went to hit me. With hindsight, I'm guessing her behaviour had to do with the news items in the *EDP*. If she killed her husband, perhaps I had a lucky escape.'

Jim ignored the sidetrack and asked, 'Had you tried to force yourself on her?'

'Absolutely not. It was all in her mind. Anyway, when she went to hit me, I caught her by the arm, we struggled and then that damn dog bit me. In the struggle I went over the side, and she sailed off. Then you lot turned up. End of story. Ask your medic if you don't believe me. He's just treated me for dog bites on my arse.'

There was a knock on the door and a head came round it. Jim nodded and stopped the tape.

'Thank you Mr Sayer. We'll be in touch. You'll be given your clothes back and we'll ring for a taxi.'

'Don't I get a lift home?' he exclaimed.

'We don't have spare cars for that. You'll be fine in a taxi.'

'And Rachel?'

'We'll be in touch. Please don't leave Norfolk without letting us know, Mr Sayer. We may need to talk to you again. Particularly if we lay charges against Rachel.'

'Oh. Oh I see. Yes. Thank you.'

Jim and Greg joined Fiona in the corridor.

'This way,' said Jim. 'The lifeboat has got the *Edith* in their sights. We can keep track of events in the radio room. What did you think of Sayer?' he asked Fiona.

'Wouldn't trust him an inch. Some conversations in Ludham might be helpful. But of course,' she realised, 'that's not really our case, sorry.'

'No problem. As it happens I agree with you. The radio is in here.'

19

Rachel – The Remembrance of Things Past

It had all begun so well. I was deliriously happy. In fact, I could hardly believe that I had been so lucky. Here I was, 1990, thirty years old, married to a man who fitted so many of my dreams: intelligent, educated, good-looking, popular, sophisticated even. The plain-ish girl from school, who didn't have a boyfriend until she was fifteen and was never in the gang of really dashing sophisticates that ran the upper sixth, had landed the Greek god of her dreams. With the 20:20 vision of hindsight I should perhaps have spotted the warning signs, should have realised that I was taking Matthew on his own assessment, should have remembered that 'sophisticated' can also mean 'contaminated'. But my foresight was as myopic as my hindsight is clear.

The first incident that should have raised the hairs on the back of my neck was during our first holiday together. The explosion of rage in the Italian car park when a small

Fiat bulging with children pinched the spot that Matthew reckoned was his. When he pounded his fist on the roof of the tiny car the outraged reaction from the child-loving crowd around can be imagined. The only reason there wasn't an all-out fight was the intervention of the Carabinieri. For some reason an exceptional amount of leeway was granted the non-Italian-speaking tourists and we were allowed to continue on our way unmolested.

The second was the motorbike that was pushed over when the rider came, in Matthew's view, dangerously close to him as he was crossing the road. As I say, a wiser woman would have taken note of these sudden explosions of ungovernable rage, but I didn't. It never occurred to me that I might one day be the focus – no, let's be plain – the victim of such events.

My beloved grandfather was a wise old chap and must have seen what I didn't. He didn't try to dissuade me from marrying Matthew, although, to be fair, he was not very enthusiastic. But then, he never tried to dissuade me from doing something foolish. He just waited for me to learn from experience. The time when, aged six, I built a raft to sail the village pond comes to mind. He didn't try to stop me. He didn't even put barriers in my way. But he was there the day I launched my trans-pond expedition, ready and equipped to fish me out. A multitude of similar experiences come to mind and make up the fabric of my memories of Grandfather. His approach to Matthew was similar. He showed up on the wedding day, he gave me away (my father having died some years earlier) and he presented me with the most valuable wedding present you can imagine: a home of our own and the land around it to enable us to make a living. The fact that we live what, from the outside, looks like an affluent county life is thanks to my grandfather. And the fact that I'm protected from some of the practical vicissitudes of life is down to his caution in placing the deeds in my name. He never explicitly warned me off Matthew, but he made me promise I wouldn't add his name to the deeds. After the first time, on our honeymoon, Matthew never raised the subject of the deeds again for as long as Grandfather was alive.

The farmhouse is fairly large and comfortable. On the face of it we lead a very comfortable existence. What you might call 'well found'. In practice, it is a sham. A charade. All my tidiness and obsessive order are just the skin. Or perhaps, they are my attempt to impose some order on a fundamentally disordered and uncontrolled environment. I walk on eggshells on our bland and well-hoovered carpets. I arrange our collections neatly because nothing else is neat in my life. The books are sorted into alphabetical order because they are the only things I can sort. I certainly can't sort my life.

I am trapped in this hidden existence with a man who can smile one moment and lash out the next. Who can be voluble, even garrulous one week, and then fail to address one single word to me for the whole of Christmas Day. Who will spend money on antique glasses, then smash the lot in one sudden and unprovoked rage because I have changed their layout on the shelf. Who banged so hard on the keys of the piano that they fell off, because he could hear me hoovering in the next room. I hide the bruises under my immaculately ironed blouses and hide the dogs in the garden shed when his violence threatens them as well as me. On good days, the days when the eggshells are still in one piece under my feet, I move with caution and watch every word, afraid of provoking an outburst. It's exhausting. On the worst days, when I can't get away physically, I have learned to retreat to the secret place in my head. The one where I am safe – or at least where I don't have to care any more.

I really don't know how all the hopes and dreams ended up like this. I suppose it crept up on me. The episodes of rage became more frequent, or perhaps just less hidden. Then I became the target rather than the witness. After a while, it wasn't even the violence that caused me the most distress. It was the subtle and insidious limitations on my personal freedom. First I was eating the wrong things, then my choice of drinks was uncouth. Lager, after all, was drunk by louts not ladies! What I ate and drank was only the beginning. Next it was what I was wearing, the time I took to do my hair, the friends I met after work at the hospital, and even the promotions I sought. The money I brought in from my HR job was welcome enough, but the time I spent off the farm was not. He never actually banned me from seeking promotion, but it was years before I realised that some on-farm crisis invariably meant that I arrived at an interview either late or stressed or both. Gradually, meeting with friends became something that I rarely did. Invitations to after-work events dwindled and then stopped because I was never available. Village events always seemed to clash with some work that needed doing on the farm. Except, of course, the times when I was called upon to play Lady of the Manor to Matthew's

Squire. I was very good at that by then. I was well aware that the village thought me stuck up and remote when compared with Matthew's bonhomie. Ironic, when you think that I was the one born only a village or two away and Matthew was the incomer. I often reflected that my grandfather would have been heartbroken but not in the least surprised.

What *really* trapped me, of course, was that with all this I still loved Matthew. Even through the fear and the exhaustion, I clung to the hope of the odd days when things went right. I was still the girl who couldn't quite believe she had caught the glamorous star of local society. And you may find it hard to believe (sometimes I find it faintly surreal too) but I still cared about Matthew. You see, *I* knew the hidden Matthew. The one who always felt just that little bit inadequate. Not quite quite. His parents had an army background (no taint of trade there) and he had a degree in PPE from Cambridge. He had a strong belief in his abilities as a deep thinker, mainly based on feedback from his mother. But the degree was only lower second class honours, and although he always got a lot of praise from his mother, it was usually only in passing.

'Marvellous, darling,' she'd say, as she sailed past in an elegant dress ready for an afternoon tea party or a game of bridge. According to his cousin, in his younger days Matthew would often throw a tantrum about the lack of attention.

'You never look at me,' he would rage. 'You never actually look at *me*!'

As he grew older the rage seemed to became more internalised, and he learned to accept the little he got. In his teens, 'Marvellous darling' had become the theme tune of his existence and since he got it whatever he did, that possibly accounted in some measure for the lower second.

But Matthew, I well knew, thought he was entitled to better than a provincial HR officer and a small farm. Indeed, his main disappointment about Cambridge was not the degree, but the failure to land a titled heiress. He did, after all, possess both classic good looks and a quick wit. He played both tennis and croquet competently and was a really good shot. All these qualities should have made him very acceptable to that section of Cambridge society that was just a little more aristocratic and a lot richer than he. Unfortunately for Matthew, the titled heiresses at Cambridge were not just well connected and rich but also smart. Behaviour they were happy to tolerate in a partner for a dance or a party was not what they wanted in a life companion. And they were sufficiently acute to detect the inadequacies and anger that Matthew thought were so well hidden. It was my tragedy that I was not so smart. Or perhaps, that I had a softer heart and thought that the 'real' Matthew could be reclaimed.

So, if he was upset, I hurt for him. If he felt slighted or disregarded by society, I smarted for him. I defended him to anyone who dared to criticise. Mostly they didn't. I defended him to myself too. It was, after all, my fault he lost his temper. I drove him to it with my stupidity and ineptitude. If only I didn't make so many mistakes, if only I was more sophisticated in my tastes, he would be a happier man and we could both be a happy couple.

It was only later, with the clarity that time can give to a foggy view, that I saw how my feelings of inadequacy were his creation, and that our unhappiness came from something deep in him, not in me, and that I would never be able to fill the gap. At the time, I occasionally noted that other couples seemed to have more fun. Other families had in-jokes that did not stab. Other husbands cherished rather than punished. But I never linked these effects with the obvious cause. You don't do you? You keep on from day to day, doing your best and keeping your head down.

Lambing was always the worst time of the year. Lack of sleep made me stupid and Matthew even angrier than usual. The combination was infelicitous. The 2007 lambing was sheer hell. The foot and mouth outbreak in 2001 had been bad enough. Notwithstanding our location quite near the origin of the outbreak, we had been spared both direct infection and the effects of the contiguous cull, but the knock-on effects on regulatory controls and prices were still rumbling on. Matthew's reaction to all stress, to start spending money, had not helped. I was well aware that we had financial difficulties but didn't appreciate the size of the mountain of debt until Matthew was off the scene. He had started to talk about raising a mortgage on the farm and I had avoided all discussion. I knew he couldn't do it without me and I lay awake many nights wondering how I would summon up the courage to say no. Lying awake worrying on the nights it was my turn to sleep didn't make me any more efficient when it was my turn on duty in the lambing shed. Before long I was in trouble for making inaccurate returns in the lambing book or overfeeding newly lambed ewes. I had been on the receiving end of the usual impatient shoves and had collected a few bruises. I was by now used to the fact that bruises always occurred on my body or arms below the neck and above the wrists. Never anything that anyone else would see. It didn't occur to me that this suggested more control over his temper then I credited him with.

In any event, the final trigger was not a blow to me but a blow to a ewe. As it happened, the worm only turned when it was animal welfare that was threatened, not my own. The sheep in question was one of a number who proved to be uncooperative when being persuaded to foster a lamb not her own. Hardly unusual; in fact, a day-to-day experience for every shepherd in the country, but it was not one that Matthew was able to take calmly. On this occasion he gave the ewe a vicious punch behind her ear and she dropped like a stone. I thought he'd cracked her skull or broken her neck and for the first time I saw red too. The fostered lambs were in a pen near the feed bin so that we could readily keep an eye on them. On top of the feed bin was the mallet that we used when setting up the pens. I don't remember picking it up. I don't even remember hitting Matthew with it. But I do remember looking down and seeing the dent in his head. I remember standing there with the hammer drooping in my hand, listening to Matthew's stertorous breathing. I remember waiting until the sounds stopped and I remember checking for the pulse in his neck. It wasn't there.

I also remember my next actions with second-by-second clarity. It was coming up to 5 o'clock and feeding time, so that was what I did. I left Matthew where he was and fed the ewes. I mixed the milk for the pet lambs and tipped it into the feeding buckets with the teats. I supervised their feed, making sure the big bullies didn't get more than their fair share. I noticed, with what pleasure I could still feel, that the ewe Matthew had punched had got to her feet. I took away the foster lamb and put him back with the pets. It seemed to me she'd earned some peace and quiet with her own single lamb. When all the feeding and watering was done I fetched the old Leyland with the fore-end loader to the back door of the lambing shed – the one away from the road.

I stripped Matthew of his clothes. It wasn't easy, trying to get them off the body that was all that was left of Matthew, so I used the dagging shears and simply cut them off. I remembered to remove his watch and his wedding ring. After that, he was just another naked body to be disposed of and the solution was obvious. I put Matthew and the couple of lambs that had died the day before into the bucket on the fore-end loader. One lamb was partly rotten already, as it had died in utero and been delivered dead. The other was a big, well-grown Suffolk cross whose mother had suffocated it by sitting on its head. I remembered how cross Matthew had been when he'd found it. I drove across the field in the gloaming, the tractor headlights lighting up the ground before me, the loader bouncing as we jolted over the ruts. I could see lamb legs and one of Matthew's arms waggling up and down.

At the hatchway, I strained to haul the plywood lid to one side, then manoeuvred the loader bucket over the gaping void and pulled the lever. The body flopped and slithered as it fell into the shaft head first, landing with a thud and an audible snap on the animal remains below. I took one quick last look at what had been my husband, lying face up with limbs twisted and neck at a strange angle, then I tipped the dead lambs after him. I remember they landed to one side.

The plywood back in its place, weighted down by two breeze blocks, I drove back to the farmyard, checked around the ewes, and went in to the house. I celebrated with a bacon butty. Behind me, nothing stirred except the grazing ewes with their lambs at foot.

20

All at Sea

Ben had often liaised with lifeboat crews, on and off their boats, so the call to join Caister lifeboat for a rescue mission was not particularly out of the ordinary. It was lucky too that he had just completed a shout in West Caister, so he was close by and could easily meet the crew's deadline for a quick launch. By the time he got to the lifeboat station the fast offshore boat was already on the beach. He joined the crew on board, the big caterpillar tractor backed them into the sea and they took off at speed.

'Where are we headed?' he shouted into the wind of their passing. 'All I know is that a boat is headed to sea with a lone sailor, specifically an inexperienced and possibly unstable woman, at the helm.'

'We don't have much more. She's a Broom cruiser, the *Edith Cavell*, and the woman on board is believed to be a suspect in a murder case—'

'Don't tell me,' interrupted Ben. 'Rachel Wade.'

'That's right. You've been reading the papers then.'

'More than that. A friend of mine owns the farm where the skeleton was found and I was talking to Rachel's brother only the other day.'

'We need to tell the coxswain that. If we have to talk our way on board, some family knowledge might be handy. Hi, Bob. You need to hear what Ben's got to say.'

The coxswain put his head out of the cockpit.

'We've got the *Edith* on the AIS. She's just off the outer harbour at present and appears to be heading due east. She's going to run aground on the banks if she doesn't watch out. Either way we should come up with her pretty soon.' He listened in silence to what Ben had to say, then said, 'Let's see how we get on. It's not going to be a case of boarding through the smoke. We're not the Border Force nor HMS *Surprise*. If she doesn't welcome our rescue we'll need to talk our way on board. I may come to you for some help, Ben.'

For all it was a fine July day, Ben was glad of his waterproofs. As the coxswain opened up the *Bernard Mathews II* to her top speed of thirty-seven knots, she flew through the water and an awful lot of spray flew at them. The engine noise and wind both made talking on deck difficult, and Ben contented himself with checking he had everything he might need to hand. It was only ten minutes since the call out by the coastguard to the launch of the *Bernard Matthews II* and within another ten minutes they sighted the *Edith* heading out to sea at a fair pace. It was clear her departure had been hurried as her fenders were still hanging over the side, banging and bouncing in the waves, rather than neatly stowed on deck.

Several of the crew were studying her through binoculars.

'Only one crew visible,' they reported. 'And a dog.'

'Oh shit, not another dog,' said one particularly burly crewman, and everyone else laughed.

'A lab bit Jack last week,' someone said.

'Yes, and just as I was rescuing the damn thing,' said Jack. 'Next time I'll bloody well leave it to swim.'

The lifeboat slowed as she approached the *Edith*, then circled her at some distance, taking careful note of what they could see and who was on board. Just the one woman visible.

To Rachel, the boat appeared out of nowhere. One moment she was beginning to enjoy a peaceful sail across an empty sea, next moment she was being circled by a large, orange and extremely fast lifeboat apparently stuffed full of very large men. The lifeboat pulled alongside some feet away and hailed: 'Ahoy *Edith Cavell*. Can we come aboard?'

'No!' shouted Rachel, and reinforced the message with a wild swing towards the lifeboat. The much faster boat pulled clear without difficulty, and they continued to follow, a respectful distance from the *Edith*. They attempted dialogue several times, but either the noise and the distances were too great or they were being ignored, and the *Edith* continued on her way.

On the radio to the police the lifeboat operator asked, 'Do we know when she last refuelled?'

'As far as we know, at Ludham Staithe but we don't know when. It may have been recently, or weeks ago.'

'And since then she has come down the river?'

'With a short diversion through Breydon Water as far as the Berney Arms.'

'And how long has she been doing more than fourteen knots?'

'All the way from Breydon Water.'

As they were speaking, the waves were getting up, along with the wind, and it was noticeable that the *Edith* was getting knocked off course. As they watched, she slowed a little and the lifeboat slowed with her.

'She's heading east,' noted the coxswain, 'but she's not allowing for the current. Typical rookie mistake. And at her current rate of drift she going to go aground on the banks. Can't she see—'

He was interrupted by a shout on deck, and the sight of the *Edith* coming to a sudden halt. There was a flurry of water at her stern, then a pause and another flurry. Then nothing. The *Edith* was firmly aground on the sandbank hidden just beneath the waves, listing a little to port. The figure at the helm seemed to put her head in her hands.

Rachel was completely taken by surprise by the shuddering halt as the boat hit the hidden bank. She had noticed the low green island to the left, barely above the waves, and had steered what she assumed to be a safe course to the south of it. The first indication she got that her calculations had been flawed was the change in motion beneath her as the *Edith* nosed onto the soft sand and then stopped abruptly. Only her grip on the wheel stopped her flying forward and Brizo was again precipitated to the deck. She pushed the throttle forward in an attempt to drive over the obstruction, then, realising her mistake, threw it back into reverse. Too late. The *Edith* was firmly stuck and didn't look like going anywhere until either the tide changed or she was hauled off. She realised she couldn't even remember whether the tide was coming in or going out, and sank her head into her hands. Her great escape was over before it started.

It was over, but the risks had not diminished. The coxswain kept the lifeboat circling at a safe distance from the banks and checked the weather. The wind was continuing to pick up and conditions were only going to deteriorate.

'We can take off the passengers easily enough, provided they are willing; and we can probably haul the *Edith* off the bank provided we do it sooner rather than later. It all depends on how cooperative she is going to be.'

'Launch the inflatable,' the coxswain decided.

'Can I go with them?' asked Ben.

'Yes. Thank you.'

The inflatable was launched with the efficiency of long practice and Ben joined the three crewmen on board. They bounced over the waves to the *Edith*, approaching in the lee, and hooked onto the side of the cruiser. The water there was so shallow the inflatable itself was barely afloat.

'Can I come aboard?' Ben called.

He didn't get a response and looked at his fellow crew. He tried again, but still no response, and after a nod from the others he cautiously climbed onto the *Edith*'s swimming deck and up to the cockpit.

'I'm Ben, Ben Asheton,' he said to the woman at the now useless wheel. 'I'm a first responder. A sort of paramedic,' he went on, as he continued to get no response. 'Are you hurt?'

He went towards her and at last got a reaction.

'Don't come too close.'

'Sorry.' He stopped. 'Are you hurt?'

'No.'

'You're not even wearing a life jacket, although I see the dog is,' he said. 'Have you got one you can put on?'

'Yes. No. I don't know. It doesn't matter.'

'It matters to me,' said Ben. 'We can't get you safely into the lifeboat without you wearing a life jacket.'

'I'm not going to the lifeboat. I'm not going anywhere.'

'Well this boat certainly isn't. She's well aground. Look, it's going to get cold and dark out here soon. Let me get you both to the lifeboat. We can make you warm and safe and take you ashore. We may even be able to haul the *Edith* off the sandbank.'

For the first time she turned her head and looked at him. He saw an exhausted woman with huge black circles under her eyes and no hope in them. She saw a slim man in his fifties with greying hair retreating at the temples and a kind look about him.

'Let's not pretend,' she said tiredly. 'You know who I am. You know what I'm accused of. You know what I'm facing if I go back. There's no point any more. Take Brizo and go. There's no reason she has to stay with me now. Ask Dogs Trust to rehome her again.' She knelt by the dog and hugged her close, with tears running down her face. The dog licked them off.

'Bye, Brizo. Thank you for everything. Now just take her,' she said again to Ben.

'And do what? Just leave you here? What're you planning

to do then? Sit on this boat until she breaks up, or jump over the side? You must have heard of the Caister lifeboat motto,' he said.

'No. What?'

'Caister men never turn back. That means that lifeboat,' and he pointed, 'is not going anywhere without you. She'll stay here until she can make you safe. She'll probably be joined by the Gorleston lifeboat as well. More lives at risk. Come on, Rachel,' he said. 'Drowning is a horrible death. What's the worst that can happen if you come back with us? A court case and possibly prison, but possibly not. From what I've heard, your husband was a bully and an abuser. You may have had good reason for what happened.'

'What do you know about it?'

'Not much. Just what your neighbours have said, and your brother Edgar. You need to come back and tell your story, Rachel. Your story.'

She hesitated, still holding Brizo close. 'You've seen Edgar?'

'Yes. He's very worried about you. He made me promise to tell him if I found you.'

'He's better off not knowing. If I come with you I'll still lose Brizo won't I?'

'Possibly, Rachel. I won't lie to you. But my way, you may be able to see her. You may be able to get her back. Your way, it's the end of everything and you never get to tell your story.'

There was a shout from the inflatable and Ben looked round. 'We're running out of time, Rachel. Come with me. Please. For Brizo's sake. And Edgar's.'

Rachel stood up decisively and for a moment Ben wasn't sure what the decision had been. But he was reassured when she reached for her life jacket behind the pilot's chair.

'Come on then,' she said. 'I just need a few papers from the saloon.'

Ben kept a careful eye on her, standing in the doorway so she couldn't shut herself below, but all she took was a folder of papers in a shoulder bag, and then she walked steadily up a deck and to the bulwark.

Jack, in the inflatable, was *really* chuffed when he spotted Brizo, but to his relief she allowed herself to be lifted aboard by her lifejacket harness without complaint. Rachel dropped into the inflatable, then looked back at the *Edith*.

'What will happen to her?' she asked as they bounced over the waves to the lifeboat.

'Ask the coxswain, but he did say something about retrieving her,' said Ben.

Rachel asked as soon as she was aboard the lifeboat, but the coxswain, his eye on the sea state, was keen to get everyone safely back to land.

'She's firmly aground and the tide's dropping. She should be fine where she is overnight and she's not likely to become a hazard to other ships either. We can organise a tow tomorrow at high tide if that's what you want.'

'Yes please,' said Rachel, but Ben remarked, 'We may need to clear that with the police. They may regard the *Edith* as a crime scene.'

'A crime scene, why?' asked a mystified Rachel.

'Well they've just told us that your passenger of a few hours ago is accusing you of assault and attempted murder.'

'Philip is accusing me!' For the first time Rachel had some colour in her cheeks. 'Me! He attacked me. If it hadn't been for Brizo I would have been the one overboard. And it wasn't the first time.' Her fury mounted. 'He's tried to dope me before now. And Brizo too. And *he's* accusing *me!*'

'Time we got back,' said the coxswain, and turned the *Bernard Matthews II* for the harbour entrance. 'The police can sort this little lot out!'

21

Questions and Answers

The lifeboat was met at the Great Yarmouth North Quay by a couple of police cars. Geldard and Fiona had been waiting for some time, along with Jim Henning and a few Norfolk uniformed constables. The media was gathering too, having listened to the radio exchanges from the lifeboat, but had been fended off for the moment with the promise of a statement later. As the lifeboat moored, Geldard stepped forward, his priority agreed with his Norfolk colleagues.

'Rachel Wade, I am arresting you for the murder of your husband Matthew Wade. You do not have to say anything, but it may harm your defence if you do not mention, when questioned, something which you later rely on in court. Anything you do say may be given in evidence.'

The press, kept back by the constables, started to surge forward and at a nod from Geldard Fiona stepped forward to usher Rachel to the car. Brizo, held on a lead by Ben, jumped forward and tried to follow.

'Don't worry, Rachel,' said Ben. 'I will personally ensure that Brizo is looked after. I promise.' Rachel nodded through the car window, tears streaming down her face, but couldn't bring herself to look at the dog.

Geldard turned to Jim.

'As we discussed, I realise you have a complaint to deal with too.'

'Yes, I plan some enquiries around Ludham to establish whether there is a realistic prospect of taking a case to court. But for now, I suggest you get out of this before we lose control of the ladies and gentlemen of the press. I'll deal with this lot and see you back at the station. Unless you want to stay and answer questions for *Look East*,' Jim said with a grin.

'No thanks. Just get the message across that this has been an exemplary case of cross-force cooperation and I'll be happy. Thank you for your help. Let me know if we can return the favour.'

The two men shook hands as cameras flashed, then Geldard got into the driving seat and set off. Fiona sat in the back with Rachel, who seemed completely subdued.

'We're calling at the station first, for a short stop to refresh ourselves, then we'll be going on to York. We'll get their doctor to look you over too.'

'No need,' said Rachel, rousing herself. 'I'm fine. What will happen to the *Edith*?'

'She'll be recovered from the sandbank and moored in a safe location under the supervision of Norfolk Police. Depending on how they want to progress the complaint from Philip Sayer, she may be a crime scene.'

'What about my complaint against Philip? He attacked me, you know. And it wasn't the first time. You can ask my vet and Amy at the tea shop in Ludham.'

Geldard exchanged a look with Fiona through the rear-view mirror. 'If you wish to make a statement, we can do that at the station. I'll have a word with Detective Inspector Henning about it.'

In fact, Jim Henning had just been informed about the counter-accusation by Ben, and was already on his way back to the Great Yarmouth station. By the time Rachel's statement about Philip had been taken, the evening was well advanced and it was decided that the Yorkshire contingent would stay overnight and set off in the early morning. Rachel spent the night in the cells.

'I'll share whatever we turn up in Ludham,' said Jim, as they were setting off the following morning. 'Keep me posted.'

The drive back to Yorkshire continued in silence. Rachel broke it only once to ask after Brizo, and Fiona undertook to find out what was happening when they got to Malton. On arrival Rachel was escorted to an interview room, while Geldard and Fiona were congratulated by the rest of the team.

'Thank you thank you,' said Geldard with a mock bow, 'but save the celebrations until we have a conviction. Finding Rachel is just the beginning. All our evidence so far is circumstantial. We have nothing that ties her directly to the murder of her husband. We have some way to go yet.'

'There's a solicitor waiting for Rachel, organised by her brother Edgar Treadwell,' said Peter. 'It seems he was told we had Rachel in custody and leapt into action. He's also hired a barrister. It's Leah Isaacs.'

'Oh lord. Right. Well this is going to be interesting. She's one powerful advocate. And something of a specialist on abuse cases. That gives us a clear steer where the defence will be going.'

Rachel's conversations with her legal team were difficult. While her solicitor's initial preference was that she should keep quiet, Rachel was tired of running.

'It's no good, Michael. I'm too tired to make up a load of lies. I did hit Matthew with the mallet. I did strip him and put his body in the pit with the dead lambs. But I didn't plan any of it. I acted on impulse, and then I just did what…' she hesitated, 'I did what seemed natural at the time. I had three dead animals waiting for disposal and I did with them what we always did.'

When it came to the interview with Geldard she said the same. He was relieved and elated that he had an admission on record and under caution.

'To be clear and for the tape,' he said, 'you are stating that you struck Matthew on the head with a mallet that was lying around, stripped his body and disposed of it in the pit along with the bodies of a couple of dead lambs.'

'Yes. I've just said that. He punched the ewe and I saw red. I thought he'd killed her. The mallet was there on the top of the feed bin. I picked it up and hit him with it, to make him stop.'

'How many blows?'

'Just one.'

'What did you do with the mallet then?'

'Dropped it on the straw.'

'Then how do you explain the broken neck?'

'I didn't know he had a broken neck. I hit him just once, on the side of his head nearest me.'

'But the forensic evidence is that he had a broken neck too. How did that happen?'

'I don't know.'

Michael intervened.

'I don't think you can ask my client to speculate. She's told you twice she doesn't know.' Geldard moved on.

'What did you do with the clothes he was wearing.'

'I burned them. By the time I had cut them off they were just rags.'

'And his other clothes? Your brother says that when he arrived to help out, most of Matthew's belongings had gone.'

'I don't know.'

'How can you not know? By this time Matthew was dead in the pit. You must have done something with his clothes.'

'No. I don't know.'

'I suggest, Rachel, that you had planned how you were going to kill Matthew, how you were going to dispose of his body, and what you were going to do with his clothes. There never was a blow to a sheep. You planned the whole thing and you got away with it for over seven years.' Rachel was silent.

'What did you do with the clothes, Rachel?'

'I don't know. I don't know anything about the clothes.'

'Did you burn them? What about his shoes? They would

245

have been harder to burn.' No comment again from Rachel.

'Well, let's try something else then. What happened to Matthew's credit cards? How did they end up in London?'

'I don't know.'

'We have evidence they were used in London in April. You know that. You had the bank statements too. By that time Edgar was on the farm with you. Who was using the cards in London?

No answer. Geldard looked at Fiona and tried again. 'How did the cards get to London, Rachel?'

Rachel was silent again and Geldard, looking at her, felt a dawning concern. Her eyes were staring, not at him, but at nothing. He continued to ask questions and she continued silent, the eyes still staring, staring. He glanced at the solicitor, who was also watching his client with some worry.

'I think perhaps my client needs a break,' he said. His voice was quiet, as though he feared waking someone up. Geldard agreed, shuffling his papers together.

'Interview suspended at 14.50. I'll send the doctor in,' he said to the solicitor.

'I think that would be best,' Michael replied.

The doctor diagnosed exhaustion and suggested that interviews be suspended until the following day. Rachel was returned to her cell, and Michael went to consult with Leah Isaacs.

'It was weird,' he said, after explaining that Rachel had admitted striking the blow but insisted it was on the spur of the moment. 'When Geldard went on asking questions she just sort of went away. As though she wasn't there. She was sitting next to me, but her mind wasn't there. Her eyes were empty.'

'And what happened after?'

'She stayed completely silent until after the doctor's visit. She didn't respond to his questions either, but after he left she sort of gradually returned to the room. He got so little out of her, I'm not surprised he went for an obvious explanation, but I'm not convinced it was the right one. I think we should seek a specialist opinion. I'll have a word with Edgar Treadwell about it.'

'In your opinion, do you think the police will go with a charge of manslaughter?'

'No. I don't think so. If she had called them at the time, then no question. But the problem is that they think she covered up so well, it must have been planned.'

'Then it's down to us to convince a jury otherwise. We have two possible lines of defence, that this was a spur-of-the-moment action, undertaken at a moment of severe stress and following a long period of abuse. And/or, the balance of her mind was disturbed. We need some facts about Rachel's life with Matthew. And I agree, we need a specialist opinion.'

'And the issue of what happened to Matthew's clothes? And cards?'

'We can't speculate. I can think of several explanations. Matthew may indeed have been planning to leave and had a little trip to London earlier in the year. He may have removed the clothes himself. Or Rachel destroyed them somehow, and either doesn't remember or doesn't want to say. I don't think exploring these lines helps our case. Finding out more about Matthew's abuse and Rachel's mental state does. Can you talk to Edgar Treadwell again? I think he has some insight into how Matthew Wade treated Rachel, and he may be willing to do some investigating. In the meantime, I think another chat with Rachel is in order.'

Waiting in the interview room at Askham Grange women's prison, Leah shuffled her papers as she marshalled her arguments. Rachel was pale and looked tired, but otherwise composed. Leah regarded her in silence for a moment, then said, 'Tell me about your life with Matthew.'

'There's not much to tell.'

'Well what about the routines on the farm?'

'We got by. It was hard work, but we got by.'

'According to your neighbours, you did more of it than Matthew.'

'That's not fair. I was just more used to it than Matthew. Except when he'd stayed with friends on their estates he didn't have much hands-on experience. I did.

'Poor Matthew, his problem was that he was designed by nature to be a land *owner*, he was no way designed to be a land *worker*. The day-to-day work of the farm bored him stiff. He hated the exhaustion and general muck that followed lambing. He was bored rigid by sitting on a tractor. He had a little joke. He would describe jobs such as turning silage, mowing grass and topping pastures as "a simple repetitive task suitable for a woman".'

'That was a joke was it?' asked Leah, with more than a little acid in her tone.

'Oh yes. Although...' Rachel hesitated, 'sometimes I did

248

think it was how he felt about farming. Sometimes. But there were things he liked.'

'Such as?'

'He liked markets and sales. He liked to stand on the edge of the farmyard and look down over his acres towards the Vale of York.' Rachel grinned suddenly. 'He never abandoned acres for hectares. I was never sure whether that was tradition, or because our area sounded better in acres. Bigger. He took a lot of pleasure in contemplating land that he felt to be rightly his. He used to say he felt like Julius Caesar, kneeling and seizing the sand of his landing in his possessive grasp. Most fine evenings he would stand by the post and rail fence on the edge of the farmyard and just gaze down the hill, watching the peewits and swallows performing low-level bombing runs around the sheep.

'He liked taking his grandfather's shotgun out too. He'd wander by the hedgerows, shooting pests and prey. Mainly rabbits and pigeons, but sometimes the odd hare or a game bird that'd strayed over from next door. I hated seeing the dead hares. It seemed so sad. Actually I hated all the dead things, but I had to deal with them when he brought them home.'

'But it wasn't his land, was it, Rachel?' said Leah softly. 'It was yours. It was never his land. It was never in his name.'

Rachel flushed angrily. 'You don't understand! Matthew had a lot to put up with. Lots of my habits drove him nuts. He didn't like how I ate, said it made me fat. And the music I liked was very ordinary. He thought I spent too much time in choirs and pubs too. In fact, he didn't like a lot of what I did. I wasn't posh enough when it came down to it. I didn't measure up. And in the end, when my little foibles stopped being amusing, I bored him.' Rachel looked down at the table between them, and picked at her finger ends. She had nibbled the skin round her nails and they looked sore. Her voice dropped still lower, so that Leah struggled to hear. 'I bored him in lots of ways,' she said sadly. 'That's why I wouldn't have been surprised if he had taken a mistress. Someone more suitable for his lifestyle. Someone who wasn't so mean with cash. He hated it when I tried to rein in our spending.'

'To sum up then,' said Leah in a deliberately crisp tone, 'he enjoyed all the fun bits of being a landowner while dodging all the hard work; he bigged up "his" estate to anyone who would listen, even though it was yours not his; he stopped you doing all sorts of things you enjoyed and put you down at every opportunity, while spending money you couldn't afford on himself. Do you recognise a pattern here, Rachel?'

Rachel remained focused on the table. 'That's not fair,' she muttered. 'He spent time down the pub and shooting or playing golf in order to make useful contacts. It was part of marketing our stock. And he had to maintain his position.'

'That sounds like a quote, Rachel. Are you quoting Matthew?' Met only with a stubborn silence, Leah sighed. 'Let's try another tack. Tell me about what happened before Matthew died. Tell me how that day started.'

'It wasn't a good day. It was one of those depressing days you get with sheep sometimes. It'd been Matthew's turn to get up in the night to the lambing ewes and he'd been really unlucky. He told me when I got up that he'd found chaos in the lambing shed when he went in at 2am. One heavily pregnant old girl had laid claim to at least six lambs, none of which were hers. It happens sometimes. Usually the lambs have been polished to within an inch of their lives but are getting pretty cross about no drink at the milk bar. It always causes mayhem. The old ewe has her hormones on overdrive and snatches every lamb as it appears. All the other mums are rushing about wondering where their lambs have gone. It takes hours to sort out a mess like that, trying to match up the right lambs to the right mothers. And if you get it wrong, some of the lambs are rejected later, causing more work. It always means a sleepless night. No wonder Matthew was ready to hand over to me in the morning.

'It didn't help that I'd made a bit of a muddle in the lambing book. He found a ewe, which according to the book had apparently given birth to twin girls, with a ram lamb; and another ewe that I'd logged as having had twins only had a giant single. I'd been so tired the day before, but he was pretty cross about my mistakes. After that I went to Malton for some shopping, but when I got back he'd found another case of mastitis so he was cross again. I tried to be careful not to wind him up any more, but it was always difficult when he was in one of those moods. You could walk on eggshells, but eventually something would set him off. I managed to keep out of his way, but the young ewe didn't. I felt so sorry for her. She hadn't done anything wrong. I can't stand cruelty.' Rachel fell silent and Leah looked up from her notes.

'When something "set him off" what would usually happen, Rachel? Did he strike you? Had he been physically abusive to you?'

Rachel did not answer and Leah sighed again. 'Change of subject. Tell me about Philip Sayer?'

'I don't want to talk about Philip. I want to go back to my cell.'

'But when you were brought to York, you told the officers that Philip had tried to attack you. Was it all happening again, Rachel?'

'I want to go back to my cell,' repeated Rachel, and looked at Leah with blank eyes. Leah and Michael exchanged glances, then Leah tried putting the question again. There was no response from Rachel, and now no indication she was taking anything in. After another silent exchange between barrister and solicitor, Leah knocked on the door for the warder. Rachel was taken away and her legal team left in contemplative silence.

The planned phone call to Edgar was followed, very swiftly, by a phone call from Edgar to Ben Asheton.

'I wanted to thank you for letting me know about Rachel. It was really helpful. It gave me chance to organise a legal team for her.'

'No problem, Edgar. I promised to let you know, so I did. I've some news for her about Brizo too. It might come better from you than me.'

'That's the dog?'

'Yes. A friend of Rachel's at Ludham got in touch with me. She has offered to foster Brizo for as long as necessary. It's not that character Philip Sayer,' Ben added. Ben had not been impressed by what he had seen and heard about Philip Sayer. 'It's a lady who runs a tea shop. It seems she's a good friend of Rachel's and knows the dog well. As I say, she has offered to foster Brizo until Rachel can have her back. Could you ask Rachel whether she would like to give permission for that to happen?'

'Yes of course. It sounds a great solution. Although,' he added gloomily, 'it may be she is signing up for a long stint. Rachel has admitted striking Matthew and concealing the body. Unless we can argue that she was abused, and quite possibly not entirely in her right mind when she struck the blow, she's going to be convicted of murder. And Rachel isn't helping herself. That's why I rang you. It's a lot to ask I know, but you're already familiar with the case and you have all the right skills and experience. Would you help me dig around up here and see what we can find out? I'll happily pay you,' he added.

Ben hesitated. In his heart, he had to admit he was horribly tempted. He hated leaving the story halfway through. Even these last few days of relying on media reports, what few there were, had been frustrating after being at the heart of it. And what he had heard about Philip Sayer from Amy had left him with a strong sympathy for a woman who seemed to be particularly vulnerable to manipulative bullies. He made his mind up.

'My wife is going to kill me for this,' he said, oblivious to the inappropriate metaphor. 'I can only spend a limited amount of time in Yorkshire, although I may be able to negotiate some more leave. The best use of my time would be for us to talk over the phone, and for you to let me have copies of any relevant documents. Then I can focus my efforts when I do come up. I'll also make some enquiries down here. It seems Philip Sayer was another Matthew in the making. There may be a pattern emerging of Rachel being particularly susceptible to attractive, plausible bullies.

'And you don't need to pay me, other than my expenses if that's okay. I can stay with Tristan when I come up.'

'Thank you so much. I'll always be in your debt,' said Edgar. 'I'll send you what I have and I'll set down in writing anything I can think of that's material. We can take it from there.'

A couple of days' perusal of Edgar's excellently clear notes, and Ben rang him up.

'Edgar, I'm coming up at the weekend and I think there are a couple of points worth pursuing. One is the issue of Matthew's impact on Rachel's mental state. Do you have evidence of how much she changed after she married? For example, could you list the things she stopped doing, and the organisations she stopped attending; like the choirs. Can we find from their records precisely when she stopped? How did her attendance at family events change? Can we evidence that? And can the barrister lay hands on a psychiatric expert who might be called upon to give evidence as an expert witness?'

'I'm sure she can, although in my limited criminal experience; I mean as a solicitor,' Edgar added, 'when one side produces an expert witness to say one thing, the other side can generally find one to say the opposite.'

'That brings me to my next point. You mention at one point in your excellent notes that Rachel had an injury to her face that you had your suspicions about. Can you enlarge on that?'

'It was a couple of years before Matthew died. On one of the rare occasions when I did see her, she had a swollen eye and cheek on her left side. I asked some pointed questions at the time, but she said she had been to the doctor and there was no need for treatment. She claimed to have been butted by a sheep but it looked like a blow to me.'

'The important point is: *did* she see a doctor?'

'I believe so.'

'Then let's try and find the doctor and talk to them. With luck, they may be a witness of fact, and in the right circumstances that can trump an expert witness speaking hypothetically.'

'The other problem is that Rachel may not cooperate with this approach. She still seems inclined to defend Matthew.'

'Then you need to persuade her. If she wants to get out of prison before Brizo dies of old age, she needs to get real.'

Edgar tried that line when he succeeded in seeing Rachel to get her permission for Brizo's fostering. She was delighted with that solution and full of gratitude to Amy, but turned sullen when the subject of Matthew's behaviour came up.

'Look, Edgar, I'm not going to turn on Matthew now. He's dead and can't defend himself. I'm not saying he was perfect, he did have a temper, but since I knew that I should have taken more care not to annoy him. I know I often did. I let him down.'

Edgar finally lost his temper. 'Matthew has the entirety of North Yorkshire Police and the Crown Prosecution Service to defend him! For God's sake don't let him influence what you do now. It was bad enough what he did when he was alive! And have you listened to yourself? You should have taken care not to annoy him! You let *him* down! Rachel, you're talking like a victim, and I've never seen my sister as a victim before.' He stormed out, convinced that he had failed.

The next day, he was surprised to get a phone call from Rachel.

'I don't have long,' she said, 'but I need to tell you that I have been awake all night thinking about what you said.'

'Which bit?'

'The victim bit. And what you said about Brizo,' she added, with the suspicion of a smile coming down the phone line. 'No, really, Edgar, what you said about me behaving like a victim: that struck home. Anyway, I think you're right and I will cooperate. That time I saw a doctor for the broken cheekbone; I told him it was a farming accident and I know he didn't believe me. He said it was the sort of injury he saw after a Saturday-night fight, and he looked at me very straight. He was a young man so he may still be around at the Norton practice.'

That Sunday evening, Edgar and Michael met Ben at Coombe Farm and settled round Tristan's dining table for a council of war. Tristan murmured an excuse and prepared to leave them in private but Edgar stopped her.

'No, stay, Tristan. You are as involved as anyone, given where Matthew's body was found. Please stay.'

'So what have we got?' asked Michael.

'Well, first and most importantly, Rachel is now willing to cooperate with an honest picture of their marriage and how Matthew treated her. I am sure you and Leah will have lots of questions for her on that. Second, over to Ben for what he has found out.'

'I have managed to turn up a couple of witnesses in the village who are willing to state that they saw Matthew bullying Rachel, and one who says she saw bruising on Rachel's arms. It's not a lot, but it adds to a consistent picture. More importantly, I have spoken to the GP who treated her at the time of the injury to her face. He also acts as an emergency doctor at the Minor Injuries Unit in Malton, so he has a lot of experience of that sort of injury. His notes record that she had a slightly depressed fracture of her cheekbone, only his notes say zygomatic arch. He recommended having it seen by the specialist at York, but she rang the following day to say that she was okay and didn't need further treatment. His notes, *his contemporaneous notes*, also record that he thought the explanation given for the injury was inaccurate and that it was exactly the injury he had seen so often after Saturday-evening brawls. His opinion, expressed to me after checking what he wrote at the time, was that the injury had been caused by a blow from an open hand, like a hard slap. He said that a blow with a fist would have produced more bruising. He thought the explanation of a butt from a sheep would also have produced more bruising. He is willing to say the same in court.'

'Finally,' said Edgar, 'I also have lots of detail about when Rachel left the operatic group, the choir and the AmDram society. They were all within the first six months of her marriage to Matthew.'

'The prosecution will argue that was just a young bride focusing on her new husband,' objected Michael.

'Yes, I agree it's not conclusive. But it is relevant context, taken together with the fact that Matthew, at the same time, joined the golf club, the Inner-Wheel and the Masons. The goose and the gander appear to have been operating to different rules. Also, several of her old friends from these clubs said she seemed depressed and subdued, and that she left because "Matthew didn't like me being out so much".

There was a pause, which Tristan interrupted. 'Look, I am hesitant to butt in, but I am the only one of us here who knows what it's like to cope with a full-scale lambing on her own. While you are planning a defence involving assessments of Rachel's state of mind, can I suggest you brief counsel to ask about the impact of exhaustion and sleep deprivation on thought processes. I'm happy to outline the issues if that would help. There are also some good sources on the issue of mental health among farmers.'

'That's a brilliant thought, Tristan. Thank you. Even though I saw the state she was in when I came to help, I hadn't considered that angle. I'll certainly talk to Leah Isaacs about that and get back to you,' said Edgar.

'I hesitate to add to the complexities,' said Ben, 'but we need to consider the complication from Norfolk. As you know, the chap who was on board the *Edith* with Rachel when the police caught up with her has alleged that she tried to throw him overboard. Rachel, on the other hand, says that *he* attacked *her* and that he had been behaving oddly before. He forced his way on board the *Edith* and stayed there as a sort of squatter, she suspects him of doping Brizo and says he used her laptop to access her savings accounts. Don't worry, she changed the passwords,' he added to Edgar.

'How on earth did he get them in the first place?'

'She'd written them down in a notebook.'

'I don't believe it!' Edgar was outraged.

'Well, she had the sense to write down spoof ones after that, but that's not really the point. I think even the accusation could damage Rachel in the eyes of a jury. If we're not careful, she is going to look like a potential serial killer.'

Edgar went very quiet, and Ben added hurriedly, 'It's not all lost Edgar. From just a brief conversation with the lady who is fostering Brizo, I think that Philip Sayer is worth looking into. If it's okay with you, I'll do that when I get back to Norfolk.'

Conversations in Ludham village very quickly elicited two important facts. Rachel had been well regarded and liked; a welcome addition to their community. Philip Sayer was not. Rachel's riparian landlord had only good things to say about her and greatly regretted the loss of his model tenant. He asked Ben to pass on to Rachel that, if all went well, she was welcome to bring the *Edith* back to his mooring. By comparison, on the subject of Philip he was subtly disparaging. With careful diplomacy he managed to convey a clear impression of a man who was successful with some ladies, while provoking a clear desire among menfolk to give him a good kicking. He also, like a number of others, pointed Ben firmly in the direction of Amy-at-the-tea-shop.

Ben called at the end of the afternoon when things were beginning to quiet down. As by then there was little choice of cakes left, he settled for a cup of tea and a bun. Amy joined him with a sigh of relief as she took the weight off her feet.

'Brizo is just in the back garden,' she told Ben. 'I'll get her in a moment so you can get a message to Rachel saying how she looked to you. She's settled in very well, although I think she misses Rachel and the boat. When I get a day off, I thought I might take her on the river in a hire boat, for a bit of a treat.' She took a gulp of her tea and then placed the cup precisely in its saucer.

'But I don't think you came to talk about Brizo,' and she looked at Ben squarely.

'Only partly,' he admitted. 'You probably know Philip Sayer has made accusations about Rachel.'

'I had heard. What do you want to know from me?'

'Several people in the village have suggested I talk to you. They seem to think you know Sayer better than most.'

'Better than I'd like, that's true. Before Rachel arrived here, I was the target of his attentions. Until, that is, he found I had no intention of lending him money or investing in his business. Things got quite unpleasant between us, until Rachel arrived and he redirected his attentions.'

'What do you mean by "quite unpleasant"?'

'Oh, a lot of things that could be put down to bad luck if you were of a credulous turn of mind. Power cuts that turned out to be problems with my fuse box, cancelled orders that I didn't cancel, things like that.'

'And you suspected Philip.'

'I did yes. And my suspicions were reawakened when the same sort of thing happened to Rachel. Brizo doped, the fire at her mooring that nearly burned down the *Edith*, the intruder who nearly frightened her to death on New Year's Eve; and all after she turned Philip's request for a loan down. I've told all this to the Norfolk Police, and I got the impression they were following up at the vets. They already have Rachel's laptop, so they'll be able to see how her accounts were accessed on a day when she was working here.'

'You know about that then.'

'Rachel told me at the time. I had been trying to persuade her to give Philip the old heave ho for months, but latterly she seemed to be falling under his spell again.'

'I'll tell you one other thing,' Amy went on, 'and I have no proof of this so, while I'll be happy to be a witness or make a statement about everything else I've told you, this stays unofficial. I think the police should take a look at Mr Sayer and what happened to his wife. Rumour has it that she shuffled off her mortal coil remarkably conveniently for her husband's finances.'

Ben's subsequent approach to Jim Henning was circumspect.

'Jim, you need to know that Rachel Wade's brother asked me to help him explore some of the angles to this case, so don't tell me anything you shouldn't. I'll let you know what I've been up to.'

'Go on then,' said Jim with some caution, and when Ben had talked him through what was known, suspected and rumoured in Ludham he said, 'Most of that's old news I'm relieved to say, and we have looked up Sayer's wife's death. There were some suspicious aspects, but nothing we could pin on him at the time. As for his relationships with Amy and with Rachel, a lot of it falls into the category of one word against another. Having said that, there does seem to be a pattern emerging.'

'What about the intel from Rachel's laptop?'

'I thought you weren't going to ask me anything! No, it's okay,' he said over Ben's apology, 'it'll be disclosed to the defence anyway if this ever comes to trial. We found exactly what Rachel claimed: a log-in from her laptop to her building society accounts at a time when she was working in the tea shop.'

'You said *if* it comes to trial?'

'It's not looking very likely at the present. Shortly after we started asking questions in Ludham, Mr Sayer became notable for his absence. The last I heard, he had closed up his shop on the staithe as well as his cottage. Unless we turn up something in relation to the death of his wife, or Rachel wants to press charges, I think this is likely to go quiet.'

'One thing that was interesting on her laptop,' he added just before he rang off. 'She seemed to have been thinking of taking up scuba diving. At any rate she had been looking up information on dive websites. Either that, or Philip was using her laptop again.'

22

Clouds of Justice

Asked afterwards about her experience of prison, Rachel was always vague.

'It was okay,' she would say, and change the subject. In truth, she did find the confinement broadly bearable. She missed Brizo desperately, constantly catching herself looking round for the familiar shadow at her feet, the familiar smiling face and lolling tongue waiting at her knee when she finished a meal, the joyful welcome of every new day. On the other hand, the actual loss of liberty itself was less of a problem than she had feared and she found a way to get on with most of her fellow inmates, particularly when they discovered she was willing to help with writing letters or filling in forms. If she could have had Brizo with her, it would have been tolerable. As it was, if anything got too much, she retreated to her secret place. Her room-mate learned to leave her alone when she went silent.

The run-up to the trial was complicated for Rachel by an argument with her counsel and with Edgar about what she would wear. Counsel was making a fuss about presenting the right look for the jury. Rachel couldn't care less, provided she didn't smell, and found the whole subject both tedious and faintly ridiculous.

'Surely a trial for murder is not going to be influenced by whether I appear in the dock dressed as a navvy or a tart.' When she voiced this view, Leah cast her eyes to heaven and Edgar, for only the second time in Rachel's memory, lost his temper.

'Unless you want to be mistaken for a member of the press, you'll tidy your hair and wear what I bring you,' he growled. So it was she found herself sitting in the dock dressed in a smart navy suit and white shirt bought by her brother. Looking sideways at the press gallery, she acknowledged the truth of Edgar's comment.

Rachel found afterward that she remembered only intermittent snippets of the two-week trial, as though clouds had repeatedly passed between her and illumination. Oddly, one of her clearest memories was the swearing-in of the jury. Although no doubt routine to the presiding judge, he invested in the proceedings all the due solemnity of their role in determining justice. The shadow of Magna Carta hung over the court and Rachel found herself remembering the story of the seventeenth-century jury that, having delivered a verdict the judge did not like, were imprisoned without food, water, heat or light yet still refused to give way. She hoped hers would be as principled.

Other memories centred around voices. The clear passionless voice of her counsel as she cross-examined witnesses; the hoarse and virus-laden voice of the prosecution, the resonant and dispassionate tones of the judge, and the distinctly Yorkshire-accented words of the clerk to the court.

But for most of the trial she retreated again into her secret place, and as a result missed a good deal of the case presented by the prosecution. She was vaguely aware of a procession of witnesses: the two archaeologists who had been unlucky enough to find Matthew's skeleton, the new owner of Coombe Farm who had bought considerably more than she bargained for, and to her surprise a couple of villagers who seemed to have been more aware of what happened between her and Matthew than she had imagined.

She listened with some indignation to the examination of the expert witness called by her defence team.

'Dr Longston, perhaps you could explain to the court what you mean by dissociation?'

'Dissociation can involve a wide spectrum of symptoms from mild detachment from immediate surroundings to more severe detachment from physical and emotional experiences. The major characteristic of all dissociative phenomena involves a detachment from reality. In mild cases it can be a coping mechanism or defence mechanism. It can be used to minimise or tolerate stress. It can also involve amnesia.'

'What causes it?'

'It is commonly caused by trauma, which can be a single traumatic event, or a series of events such as sustained abuse.'

'Such as the sustained domestic abuse inflicted by a controlling husband?'

'Yes, that can be a cause.'

'And have you detected signs of dissociative behaviour in the defendant, Rachel Wade?'

'I have, yes. Under circumstances of stress, such as that imposed in an interrogation, she withdraws from contact with her surroundings. I have seen this behaviour myself, and it is reported in the police transcripts of her interviews. The prison authorities have also reported times, during her detention, when she has become withdrawn and unresponsive.'

'And what is the impact of these periods of dissociation?'

'In the first instance, she ceases to experience the trigger events in any meaningful way, thus removing herself from the trauma. It also means that she has little recollection of what happens while she is in this state.'

'Is this process under Rachel's control?'

'Not in my judgement, no. She has described herself as having a secret place in her head to which she can retreat. This fits with the use of dissociation as a coping mechanism. However, I think that the mechanism has now become so embedded that it has become a reflex, outside of her control. Trigger events are followed by a period of dissociation without conscious volition.'

'Could this be an explanation of what happened at the time of her husband's death?'

Dr Longston hesitated. 'I must be clear that since so much time has passed I cannot state definitively what Rachel was experiencing at the time. However, the default into a dissociative state by an individual who is already prone to this coping mechanism as a result of abuse is highly likely in the circumstances that have been described.'

'And this could explain both Rachel's decision-making following the impulsive act that killed her husband, and her failure to remember any details of what happened after she disposed of his body?'

'Yes. The separation from reality could explain both the poor decisions and the amnesia.'

'No further questions, your honour.'

'Mr Fielding, do you wish to cross-examine this witness?'

'Yes indeed, your honour. Dr Longston, could Rachel Wade be faking the symptoms you have described?'

'Yes, of course she could. But it is unlikely in this instance and I don't think she is.'

'Why is that? Because you are too clever to be fooled by her?'

'By no means. I am basing my view on consistency of behaviour under a range of trigger situations. There is evidence in her interviews with me, with the police and in the conditions pertaining in the prison that she consistently reacts in the same way to stress. By which I mean she removes herself psychologically from the unacceptable reality.'

'But you cannot say that, without a doubt, Rachel Wade is suffering from dissociative episodes and that such an episode was the cause of her behaviour at the time she killed her husband and subsequently.'

'No I cannot say that without a doubt.' Dr Longston would have continued but was interrupted by prosecuting counsel.

'Thank you, Dr Longston.'

'Do you wish to re-examine, Ms Isaacs?' enquired the judge.

'Yes please, your honour.'

'Dr Longston, you have, in reply to learned counsel for the prosecution, stated what you cannot say. What can you say?'

'That in my expert opinion, Mrs Wade does suffer from repeated dissociative episodes and that in all the circumstances of the case it is highly likely that such an episode would have been triggered when she struck the blow that killed her husband.'

The voice of the GP from Norton was also an unwelcome reminder of an unhappy time, and again her counsel pursued a line of questioning that Rachel found uncomfortable.

'Dr Shah, you have stated that, according to the records made at the time, Rachel Wade attended your surgery on 24 October 2006 for an injury to her face. Page 21 of the bundle, your honour,' she said to the judge, who nodded his thanks.

'What was the injury?'

'A depressed fracture to the left zygomatic arch.'

'What treatment did you recommend?'

'That she attend a clinic at York General Hospital for assessment, because I thought surgery would be necessary to correct the depression.'

'Did Rachel Wade take up the further treatment?'

'No. I was told that she telephoned to cancel the appointment, saying that she was too busy, and that the injury was not so bad.'

'What explanation was given for the injury?'

'That she had been kicked in the face by a sheep.'

'And what was your view of the explanation?'

'I thought it was a lie. As I said at the time in my contemporaneous note, I would have expected such a kick to produce more bruising or even a cut or graze, given the cloven-hoofed nature of a sheep's foot. It was, on the other hand, exactly the type of injury I see on a Saturday night, resulting from a hard, open-handed slap. A slap from a right-handed assailant.'

'Did you challenge Mrs Wade about her explanation?'

'I did, as I wished to give her an opportunity to open up if she was being abused. She said she had nothing to add...'

Fragments of her own appearance on the stand also remained with her.

'Mrs Wade, why was the mallet so conveniently to hand?'

'We used it to set up the lambing pens – that is individual pens in which we put a ewe with her newborn lambs for a day or two before turning them out.'

'And where did you put it after striking your husband?'

'I don't know for sure. I think I dropped it on the straw.'

'And after that?'

'I don't know. I suppose that at the end of lambing I would have put it away in the tool shed.'

'How did you remove the clothes your husband was wearing?'

'I cut them off with the dagging shears.'

'Which are?' enquired the judge.

'Shears used to trim dirty wool away from the ewe's hindquarters,' explained Rachel.

'And these were also conveniently to hand?'

'Yes of course. Ask any shepherd. We use them all the time at lambing. To trim off soiled wool and to make it easier for the lambs to suckle.'

'How did you transport your husband's body across two fields to the disposal pit?'

'The same way we always transported bodies to the pit. In the bucket on the front of the tractor.'

'But this wasn't any old body was it, Mrs Wade. This was your husband.'

Rachel was silent.

'Well?' asked prosecuting counsel.

'Sorry. I didn't think that was a question.'

Leah frowned at Rachel, who got the message. 'Don't get smart. The jury don't like it…'

'Of course, the thousand-dollar question, Mrs Wade, is why on earth didn't you dial 999 and ring for an ambulance? For all you knew, your husband may have still been alive. How did you know he was dead? Lots of people survive head injuries.'

'He wasn't breathing. There was no pulse. I knew he was dead.'

'But you might have been wrong. Wasn't the natural thing to do to ring 999?'

'I don't know.'

'Isn't the reason you didn't ring because you had always planned to kill your husband and you already knew how you would hide his body?'

'No. I told you. It was when he struck the ewe. I acted on impulse.'

'But the disposal of the body wasn't an impulse was it? It proved very effective for over seven years.'

'No. I don't know. I just did what we always did with dead bodies.'

More witnesses were paraded through court, forensic anthro-pologists, psychiatrists and the police, official and measured as they explained the route of their investigation. She only emerged from the shadows when Leah Isaacs took up the cudgels in her final speech to the jury.

'I want to begin by acknowledging those facts which are not in dispute. Rachel Wade has told you that she took up the mallet, most unfortunately to hand, and struck the blow that killed her husband. She has explained to you how she concealed the body in what she knew as a waste disposal pit and which has subsequently been revealed as a historically important relic of the Second World War. These facts are not in dispute.

'The prosecution would have you believe that these actions justify a conviction of murder. I say to you that they have not provided evidence, beyond reasonable doubt, that Rachel Wade undertook these actions with forethought and planning. They have not demonstrated any degree of premeditation...

'On the day that Rachel Wade struck her husband that single blow, she had been awake for more than twenty hours out of the previous twenty-four; and this pattern of sleep deprivation had been repeated and repeated over the previous four weeks. We have heard from experts, psychiatric and agricultural, about what this level of sleep deprivation does to the human capacity to take decisions, to the short-term memory, and to impulse control...

'The prosecution would have you believe that this evidence need not be taken seriously because "if so, every shepherd's family in the country would be at risk". In fact, as the witness from the NFU was able to explain, there *is* considerable evidence that the agricultural sector, with its stress-laden and isolated jobs, does indeed have a disproportionately high level of suicides and mental health problems...

'But in this case, Rachel Wade was suffering not just from the effects of sleep deprivation, but from years of psychological abuse by a bullying and controlling husband. We have heard, mostly from other witnesses rather than from Rachel herself, because this woman still feels loyalty to her abusive husband, we have heard of the social activities forgone, the bruises hidden, the broken cheekbone ascribed to other causes to avoid the shame of admitting that her husband was the cause, the misery of never, ever, being able to come up to his exacting and arbitrary standards...

'We have also heard from a respected expert witness that, almost certainly as a result of this abuse, Rachel suffers from repeated episodes of a dissociative disorder. The expert, Dr Longston, has characterised this disorder as a coping mechanism involving a detachment from reality and sometimes amnesia. We have heard evidence that she has experienced such episodes while in police custody and while on remand. We cannot demonstrate for certain that Rachel suffered such an episode following the trigger that resulted in the death of her husband, but Dr Longston has expressed the view that such an episode would be highly likely.

'Is it so surprising therefore, that in that moment when she saw her husband cruelly harming an innocent animal, this abused and stressed woman took action on the spur of the moment to stop the cruelty. And that following that single impulsive action, operating on the autopilot of sleep deprivation, exacerbated by a dissociative episode, she disposed of her husband's body along with those of the dead lambs, and went back to work…

'The prosecution has made much of the fact that Rachel is unable to explain what happened to her husband's bank card, why it was used in London after his death. Given how much of his life outside the home was a mystery to her, why is this so surprising…'

Finally, the judge took the jury through the arguments for and against, explaining where the evidence was strong, and where it was weak. Laying the threads of the case neatly before them like an unravelled jumper, he dismissed them to consider their verdict.

It seemed an age until the court official came to tell Rachel the jury was returning; although in fact the speed of their deliberations had taken at least the prosecuting barrister by surprise. He rushed into court, slightly breathless and with his collar askew.

The slight young woman with the blue-streaked hair and the formidable expression rose when asked.

'Foreman of the jury, have you reached a verdict on which you are all agreed?'

'Yes, your honour.'

'On the first count of the murder of Matthew Wade, do you find the defendant guilty or not guilty?'

'Not guilty.'

There was a susurration that caused the judge to look severely around the court.

'On the second count of the manslaughter of Matthew Wade, do you find the defendant guilty or not guilty?'

'Guilty.'

'Sentencing next week,' said the judge.

Postlude

Yorkshire, 2007

It was dark, cold and silent. He did not wake, but nor was he now asleep. Slowly he became more aware, first of the cold, which made it hard to tell where his body ended and anything else began. The dark was total. Were his eyes open or closed? He tried opening his eyes, but could still see nothing, not even vague shapes. Time went by and it became clearer where the strange flesh he was lying on ended, and his body began. Where there was pain, there he was.

He tried to move, but couldn't. His arms and legs didn't seem to be working, even though everything was hurting. Then sound began to sneak back; small sounds that he didn't recognise but yet filled him with horror. Slithering sounds, and a high-pitched squeaking. Small clawed feet ran across his chest, and on to his face. He opened his mouth to scream. No sound came out, but something tore a piece out of his lip; then took advantage of his open mouth to tear at his tongue.

He managed a bubbling scream just as more of them found his sightless but not insentient eyes. Matthew died slowly and alone, except of course for the rats.

Among other topics, this book explores the issue of abuse and control within close relationships. It makes the point that this can happen to anyone, anywhere.

If this strikes a chord with a reader, I strongly recommend a chat with one of the following:

Citizens Advice
03444 111 444   www.citizensadvice.org.uk

National Domestic Abuse Helpline
0808 2000 247   www.nationaldahelpline.org.uk

Leeway
0300 561 0077   www.leewaysupport.org